LURING

(THE MAKING OF RILEY PAIGE—BOOK 3)

BLAKE PIERCE

D1596279

BOOKS BY BLAKE PIERCE

A JESSIE HUNT PSYCHOLOGICAL SUSPENSE SERIES
THE PERFECT WIFE (Book #1)
THE PERFECT BLOCK (Book #2)
THE PERFECT HOUSE (Book #3)
THE PERFECT SMILE (Book #4)

CHLOE FINE PSYCHOLOGICAL SUSPENSE SERIES
NEXT DOOR (Book #1)
A NEIGHBOR'S LIE (Book #2)
CUL DE SAC (Book #3)
SILENT NEIGHBOR (Book #4)

KATE WISE MYSTERY SERIES
IF SHE KNEW (Book #1)
IF SHE SAW (Book #2)
IF SHE RAN (Book #3)
IF SHE HID (Book #4)
IF SHE FLED (Book #5)

THE MAKING OF RILEY PAIGE SERIES
WATCHING (Book #1)
WAITING (Book #2)
LURING (Book #3)
TAKING (Book #4)

RILEY PAIGE MYSTERY SERIES
ONCE GONE (Book #1)
ONCE TAKEN (Book #2)
ONCE CRAVED (Book #3)
ONCE LURED (Book #4)
ONCE HUNTED (Book #5)
ONCE PINED (Book #6)
ONCE FORSAKEN (Book #7)
ONCE COLD (Book #8)
ONCE STALKED (Book #9)
ONCE LOST (Book #10)
ONCE BURIED (Book #11)
ONCE BOUND (Book #12)
ONCE TRAPPED (Book #13)

ONCE DORMANT (Book #14)
ONCE SHUNNED (Book #15)

MACKENZIE WHITE MYSTERY SERIES
BEFORE HE KILLS (Book #1)
BEFORE HE SEES (Book #2)
BEFORE HE COVETS (Book #3)
BEFORE HE TAKES (Book #4)
BEFORE HE NEEDS (Book #5)
BEFORE HE FEELS (Book #6)
BEFORE HE SINS (Book #7)
BEFORE HE HUNTS (Book #8)
BEFORE HE PREYS (Book #9)
BEFORE HE LONGS (Book #10)
BEFORE HE LAPSES (Book #11)
BEFORE HE ENVIES (Book #12)

AVERY BLACK MYSTERY SERIES
CAUSE TO KILL (Book #1)
CAUSE TO RUN (Book #2)
CAUSE TO HIDE (Book #3)
CAUSE TO FEAR (Book #4)
CAUSE TO SAVE (Book #5)
CAUSE TO DREAD (Book #6)

KERI LOCKE MYSTERY SERIES
A TRACE OF DEATH (Book #1)
A TRACE OF MUDER (Book #2)
A TRACE OF VICE (Book #3)
A TRACE OF CRIME (Book #4)
A TRACE OF HOPE (Book #5)

PROLOGUE

Hope Nelson took a last look around the store as she got ready to close up for the night. She was tired, and it had been a long, slow business day. It was after midnight, and she'd been here since early that morning.

She was alone now, because she'd sent the last of her grumbling employees home a little early. None of them liked to work late on Saturday nights. On weekdays, the store always closed at 5:00, which was more to everybody's liking.

Not that she had much sympathy with the help.

Owning this place with her husband, Mason, meant putting in longer hours than anybody else—getting here first and leaving here last on most days. It was no secret to Hope that local people resented her and Mason for being the richest folks in the dinky little town of Dighton.

And she resented them right back.

Her personal motto was ...

Money is responsibility.

She took her many duties seriously, and so did Mason, who served as the town mayor. They weren't ones for vacationing or even taking the occasional day off. Sometimes Hope felt as though she and Mason were the only people around who gave much of a damn about anything.

As she looked at the well-ordered merchandise—the hardware and power equipment, the feeds, seeds, and fertilizers—she thought as she often did ...

Dighton wouldn't last a day without us.

In fact, she figured the same might be true of the whole county.

Sometimes she dreamed of the two of them packing up and leaving, just to prove it.

It would serve everybody right.

She turned off the lights with a dismayed sigh. Then, as she reached to activate the alarm system before leaving, she saw a figure through the glass door. It was a man standing on the sidewalk under the streetlight, some 30 feet away.

He seemed to be staring right at her.

She was shocked to see that his face was badly scarred and

1

pitted—whether from birth or from some terrible accident, she had no idea. He was wearing a t-shirt, so she could see that he was similarly disfigured on his hands and arms.

It must be hard for him, going through life like that, she thought.

But what was he doing standing out there so late on a Saturday night? Had he come into the store earlier? If so, one of her employees must have helped him. She certainly didn't expect to see him or anyone else out here after closing.

But there he was, staring at her and smiling.

What did he want?

Whatever it was, it meant that Hope was going to have to talk to him personally. That bothered her. It was going to be a strain to pretend not to notice his face.

Feeling distinctly uneasy, Hope punched in the alarm code, stepped outside, and locked the front door. The warm night air felt good after being shut up in the store all day long with unsavory smells, most notably of fertilizer.

As she started to walk toward the man, she forced a smile and and called out …

"Sorry, we're closed."

He shrugged and kept smiling and murmured something inaudible.

Hope stifled a sigh. She wanted to ask him to speak louder. But she found it to say anything to him that resembled a command or even a polite request. She was irrationally afraid of hurting his feelings.

His smile broadened as she walked toward him. Again, he said something she couldn't hear. She stopped just a couple of feet in front of him.

"Excuse me, but we're closed for the night," she said.

He mumbled something inaudible. She shook her head to indicate that she couldn't hear him.

He spoke just a little louder, and this time she could make out the words …

"I've got a little problem with something."

Hope asked, "What is it?"

He murmured something else that was inaudible.

Maybe he wants to return something he bought today, she thought.

The last thing she wanted right now was to unlock the door and

2

deactivate the alarm system just so she could take back the merchandise and return his money.

Hope said, "If you want to return anything, I'm afraid you'll have to come back tomorrow."

The disfigured man mumbled …

"No, but …"

Then he shrugged at her silently, still smiling. Hope found it hard to maintain eye contact with him. Looking directly at his face was difficult. And somehow, she sensed that he knew that.

Judging from his smile, maybe he even enjoyed it.

She suppressed a shudder at the thought that he might take pleasure in the discomfort he provoked in people.

Then he said a bit more loudly and clearly …

"Come look."

He pointed toward his old pickup truck, which was parked next to the curb just a short distance away. Then he turned and started to walk toward the truck. Hope just stood there for a moment. She didn't want to follow him, and she wasn't sure why she should bother …

Whatever it is, surely it can wait to tomorrow.

But she couldn't bring herself to turn around and walk away.

Again, she was afraid of seeming rude to him.

She walked behind him to the back of the truck. He pulled open the cover on the truck bed and she saw a mass of barbed wire, unbundled and loose and in tangles all over the bed of the pickup truck.

Suddenly he seized her from behind and slapped a wet rag over her mouth and nose.

Hope kicked and tried to pull herself away, but he was taller and stronger than she was.

She couldn't even get free of the rag to scream. It was soaked through with a thick liquid that smelled and tasted sickeningly sweet.

Then a strange sensation began to come over her.

It was giddiness and elation, as if she had taken some kind of drug.

For a few seconds, that euphoria made it hard for Hope to grasp that she was in terrible danger. Then she tried to struggle again, but found that her limbs were weaker and seemed almost rubbery.

Whatever it was the man was trying to do to her, she couldn't fight against it.

Feeling almost outside of her own body, she was aware of him picking her up and dumping her in the back of his truck amid the tangle of barbed wire. All the while he held the rag tight to her face, and she couldn't help but breathe the thick fumes.

Hope Nelson was just vaguely aware of little stabbing pains all over her body as she fell limp and slowly lost consciousness.

CHAPTER ONE

As she prepared two ribeye steaks for broiling, Riley Sweeney thought again …

I want tonight to be special.

She and her fiancé, Ryan Paige, had been too busy to enjoy much of anything lately. Riley's grueling schedule in the FBI Honors Internship Program and Ryan's new job as an entry-level attorney had absorbed all their time and energy. Ryan even had to work long hours today—a Saturday.

Riley's 22nd birthday had passed almost two weeks ago, and there simply hadn't been time to celebrate. Ryan had bought her a pretty necklace, and that was about all there had been to it—no party, no dinner, no cake. She hoped that tonight's special dinner might help make up for that.

Besides, it was pretty much now or never as far as a nice dinner together was concerned. Just yesterday Riley had successfully completed her internship, and tomorrow she'd be heading off to the FBI Academy at Quantico, Va. Ryan would be staying here in Washington D.C. Although the distance between them was only about an hour by car or train, they were both going to be working very hard. She wasn't sure when she and Ryan would have any time together again.

Following a detailed recipe, Riley finished flavoring the steaks with salt, pepper, onion powder, ground mustard, and dried oregano and thyme. Then she stood looking around the kitchen at her handiwork. She'd made a lovely tossed salad, she had sliced mushrooms ready to broil with the steak, and two potatoes were already baking in the oven. In the refrigerator, a store-bought cheesecake was ready for dessert.

The small kitchen table was neatly set, including a vase full of flowers she'd picked up when she'd bought groceries. A bottle of inexpensive but very pleasant red wine was waiting there to be opened.

Riley looked at her watch. Ryan had said he should be home about now, and she hoped he wouldn't be much later. She didn't want to sear and broil the steaks before he arrived.

Meanwhile, she could think of nothing else that needed to be done right now. She'd spent whole day washing laundry, cleaning their tiny apartment, shopping, and preparing the food—domestic tasks that she'd seldom had time for since she and Ryan had moved in together at the beginning of the summer. She'd found it to be a nice change from her studies.

Even so, she couldn't help but wonder …

Is this what married life is going to be like?

If she achieved her goal of becoming an FBI agent, would she really spend long days making everything perfect for when Ryan came from work? It didn't seem likely.

But right now Riley had a hard time visualizing that future—or any specific future.

She plopped herself down on the couch.

She closed her eyes and realized she was very tired.

What we both need is a vacation, she thought.

But a vacation wasn't in the cards for the near future.

She felt a little drowsy and had almost dozed off when a memory forced its way into her mind …

She was bound hand and foot by a madman wearing a clown costume and makeup.

He held a mirror to her face and said …

"All done now. Have a look!"

She saw that he had smeared makeup all over her face so that she, too, looked like a clown.

Then he held a syringe in front of her. She knew that if he injected her with its deadly contents, she'd die from sheer terror …

Riley's eyes snapped open and she shivered all over.

It had only been a couple of months since she'd barely escaped death at the hands of the notorious so-called "Clown Killer." She was still having painful flashbacks of her ordeal.

As she tried to shake off her memory, she heard someone coming down the apartment building steps to the basement hallway.

Ryan! He's home!

She jumped up from the couch and checked the oven to make sure it was at its highest temperature. Then she turned off the apartment lights and lit the candles she'd set on the table. Finally she dashed toward the door and met Ryan just as he came inside.

She threw her arms around him and gave him a kiss. But he didn't kiss her back, and she felt his body sag from exhaustion. He

6

looked into the candlelit apartment and blurted …

"Riley—what the hell's going on?"

Riley's heart sank.

She said, "I'm fixing something nice for dinner."

Ryan came inside and set down his briefcase and collapsed onto the couch.

"You shouldn't bother," he said. "It's been a hell of a day. And I'm not very hungry."

Riley sat down beside him and rubbed his shoulders.

She said, "But everything's practically ready. Aren't you hungry enough for ribeye steaks?"

"Ribeyes?" Ryan said with surprise. "Can we afford it?"

Fighting down a surge of irritation, Riley didn't reply. She handled the household finances, and she felt like she knew pretty well what they could afford and not afford.

Apparently sensing Riley's dismay, Ryan said …

"Ribeyes sound nice. Give me a few minutes to wash up."

Ryan got up and headed for the bathroom. Riley hurried back into the kitchen, took the potatoes out of the oven, and seared the steaks and broiled them so that they'd both be medium rare.

Ryan was seated at the table by the time she put their meals on the table. He'd poured glasses of wine for both of them.

"Thanks," Ryan said, smiling weakly. "This is nice."

As he cut into his steak he added, "I'm afraid I've brought some work home. I'll have to get to it after we eat."

Riley suppressed a sigh of deep disappointment. She'd hoped their dinner would end more romantically.

She and Ryan ate in silence for a few moments. Then Ryan started to complain about his day …

"This entry level work—it's practically slave labor. We've got to do all the heavy lifting for the partners—research, writing briefs, making sure everything's ready for the courtroom. And we put in longer hours than the partners by far. It feels like some kind of fraternity hazing, it except never stops."

"It'll get better," Riley said.

Then she forced a laugh and added …

"Someday you'll be a partner yourself. And you'll have a team of entry level guys who'll go home and complain about you."

Ryan didn't laugh, and Riley couldn't blame him. It seemed like a lame joke now that she'd said it.

Ryan kept grumbling during dinner, and Riley didn't know

whether she felt more hurt or angry. Didn't he appreciate the effort she'd gone to make everything as perfect as she could tonight?

And didn't he understand how much their lives were about to change?

When Ryan fell quiet for a few moments, Riley said …

"You know, we're having a get-together tomorrow at the FBI building to celebrate the end of the internship. You'll be able to come, won't you?"

"I'm afraid not, Riley. This is going to be a seven-day week."

Riley almost gasped.

"But tomorrow's Sunday," she said.

Ryan shrugged and said, "Yeah, well, it's like I said—slave labor."

Riley said, "Look, it's not going to take all day. There'll be a couple of speeches—the assistant director and our training supervisor will want to say a few words. And then there will be some snacks and—"

Ryan interrupted, "Riley, I'm sorry."

"But I'm leaving for Quantico tomorrow, right afterwards. I'm taking my suitcase with me. I thought you'd be driving me to the bus station."

"I can't," Ryan said a bit sharply. "You'll have to get there some other way."

They ate in silence for a few moments.

Riley struggled to understand what was happening. Why couldn't Ryan come with her tomorrow? It would only take a couple of hours out of his day. Then something began to dawn on her.

She said, "You still don't want me to go to Quantico."

Ryan let out a groan of annoyance.

"Riley, let's not get started on this," he said.

Riley felt her face redden with anger.

She said, "Well, it's now or never, isn't it?"

Ryan said, "You've made your decision. I took it to be final."

Riley's eyes widened.

"My decision?" she said. "I thought it was *our* decision."

Ryan sighed. "We're not going to have this conversation," he said. "Let's just finish eating, OK?"

Riley sat there and stared at him as he continued to pick at his meal.

She found herself wondering …

8

Is Ryan right?

Did I just railroad us both into this?

She thought back to their conversations, trying to remember, trying to sort it out. She remembered how proud Ryan had been of her when she'd stopped the Clown Killer …

"You saved at least one woman's life. By solving the case, you may have saved other lives as well. It's crazy. I think maybe you're crazy. But you're also a hero."

At the time, she'd thought that was what he wanted—for her to pursue a career with the FBI, to keep right on being a hero.

But now that she thought about it, Riley couldn't remember him saying those precise words. Ryan had never told her …

"I want you to go to the academy. I want you to follow your dream."

Riley took some long, slow breaths.

We need to discuss this calmly, she thought.

Finally she said …

"Ryan, what do *you* want? For us, I mean?"

Ryan tilted his head as he looked at her.

"Do you really want to know?" he asked.

Riley's throat tightened sharply.

"I want to know," she said. "Tell me what you want."

A pained look crossed Ryan's face. Riley found herself dreading what he was going to say next.

Finally he said, "I just want a family."

Then he shrugged and ate another bite of steak.

Feeling a glimmer of relief, Riley said, "I want that too."

"Do you?" Ryan asked.

"Of course I do. You know I do."

Ryan shook his head and said, "I'm not sure even *you* know what you really want."

Riley felt as though she'd been punched in the stomach. For a moment she simply didn't know what to say.

Then she said, "Don't you think I can have a career *and* a family?"

"Sure I do," Ryan said. "Women do it all the time these days. It's called 'having it all,' I hear. It's tough and it takes planning and sacrifices, but it can be done. And I'd love to help you do all that. But …"

His voice faded.

"But what?" Riley asked.

9

He breathed deeply, then said, "Maybe it would be different if you wanted to become a lawyer, like me. Or a doctor or a shrink. Or go into real estate. Or start your own business. Or become a college professor. I could relate to any of those things. I could deal with them. But this whole thing with going to the Academy—you're going to be in Quantico for 18 weeks! How much are we going to see each other during that whole time? Do you thin any relationship can survive so much time apart? And besides ..."

He held Riley's gaze for a moment.

Then he said, "Riley, you've almost been killed twice since I've known you."

Riley gulped hard.

He was right, of course. Her most recent brush with death had been at the hands of the Clown Killer. Before that, during their last semester in college, she'd almost been killed by a sociopathic psychology professor who still awaited trial for murdering two other coeds. Riley had known both of those girls. One had been her best friend and roommate.

Riley's help in solving that awful murder case was how she'd gotten into the summer intern program, and it was one of the main reasons she was thinking about becoming an FBI agent.

In a choked voice, Riley said, "Do you want me to quit? Do you want me to not go to Quantico tomorrow?"

Ryan said, "It doesn't matter what I want."

Riley was struggling not to cry now.

"Yes, it does, Ryan," she said. "It matters a lot."

Ryan locked gazes with her for what seemed like a long time.

Then he said, "I guess I do. Want you to quit, I mean. I know you've found it exciting. It's been a great adventure for you. But it's time for us both to settle down. It's time for us to get on with our *real* lives."

Riley suddenly felt as though this had to be a bad dream, but she couldn't wake up.

Our real lives! she thought.

What did that mean?

And what did it say about her that she didn't know what it meant?

She only knew one thing for certain ...

He doesn't want me to go to Quantico.

Then Ryan said, "Look, you can work at all kinds of jobs right here in DC. And you've got lots of time to think about what you want to do in the long run. Meanwhile, it doesn't matter if you make a lot of money. We're not rich on what I'm making at the firm, but we're getting by, and I'll eventually be doing really well."

Ryan started eating again, looking oddly relieved, as if they'd just settled everything.

But had they settled anything at all? Riley had spent all summer dreaming about the FBI Academy. She couldn't imagine giving it up right here and now.

No, she thought. *I just can't do that.*

Now she felt anger swelling up inside her.

In a tense voice she said, "I'm sorry you feel that way. I'm not changing my mind. I'm going to Quantico tomorrow."

Ryan stared at her like he couldn't believe his ears.

Riley got up from the table and said, "Enjoy the rest of your meal. There's some cheesecake in the refrigerator. I'm tired. I'm going to take a shower and go to bed."

Before Ryan could reply, Riley hurried into the bathroom. She cried for a few minutes, then took a long, hot shower. When she put on her slippers and bathrobe and came back out of the bathroom, she saw Ryan sitting in the kitchen. He'd cleared the table and was working at his computer. He didn't look up.

Riley went into the bedroom and climbed into bed and started crying again.

As she wiped her eyes and blew her nose, she wondered …

Why am so angry?

Is Ryan wrong?

Is any of this his fault?

Her thoughts were such a jumble, she couldn't think things through. And a terrible memory started to creep up on her—of waking up in this bed with a sharp pain, then seeing that she was soaked in blood …

My miscarriage.

She found herself wondering—was that one of the reasons Ryan didn't want her to go into the FBI? She'd been badly stressed by the Clown Killer case when it had happened. But the doctor in the hospital had assured her that stress had nothing to do with her miscarriage.

Instead, she'd said that it had been caused by "chromosomal abnormalities."

Now that Riley thought about it again, that word disturbed her …

11

Abnormalities.

She wondered—was she somehow abnormal, deep down inside where it really mattered?

Was she incapable of having a lasting relationship, let alone a family?

As she drifted off to sleep, she felt as though she knew only one thing for sure …

I'm going to Quantico tomorrow.

She was asleep before she could think about what might happen after that.

CHAPTER TWO

The man was pleased to hear the woman's soft moan. He knew she must be regaining consciousness. Yes, he could see that her eyes had opened a little.

She was lying on her side on a rough-hewn wooden table in the small room that had a dirt floor, cinderblock walls, and low timbered ceiling. She was bound up tightly in a curled up position, taped fast with duct tape. Her legs were sharply bent and tightly bound to her chest, and her hands were wrapped around her shins. Her head lay sideways on top of her knees.

She reminded him of pictures he'd seen of human fetuses—and also of embryos he sometimes found when he cracked a fresh egg from one of the chickens he kept. She looked so mild and innocent, it was somehow a rather touching sight.

Mostly, of course, she reminded him of the other woman— Alice had been her name, he believed. He'd once thought that Alice would be the only one he'd treat this way, but then he'd enjoyed it … and there were so few pleasures in his life … how could he stop?

"It hurts," the woman murmured, as if out of a dream. "Why does it hurt?"

He knew that it was because she lay in a thick tangled bed of barbed wire. Blood was already trickling onto the table top, and it was going add to the stains in the unfinished wood. Not that it mattered. The table was older than he was, and he was the only person who ever saw it anyway.

He was hurting and bleeding some as well. He'd cut himself while getting her into the truck with the barbed wire. It was harder to do than he'd expected because she'd fought back more forcefully than the other one.

She had writhed and twisted while the homemade chloroform was starting to kick in. But her struggles had weakened and he'd finally subdued her completely.

Even so, he wasn't much bothered to be hurt by the sharp barbs. He knew from hard experience that such cuts healed up pretty quickly, even if they did leave ghastly scars.

He stooped down and looked closely into her face.

Her eyes were opened almost impossibly wide now. Her irises

13

twitched around as she looked back at him.

Still trying to avoid looking at me, he realized.

Everybody acted that way toward him, wherever he went. He didn't blame people for trying to pretend he was invisible, or that he didn't exist at all. Sometimes he'd look in the mirror and pretend that he could make himself disappear.

Then the woman murmured again …

"It hurts."

In addition to the cuts, he was sure that her head ached badly from the heavy dose of homemade chloroform. When he'd first mixed up the stuff right here, he'd almost passed out himself, and he'd suffered from a splitting headache for days afterward. But the preparation worked very well, so he would continue using it.

Now he was well prepared for what he was about to do next. He was wearing thick work gloves now and a thickly padded jacket. He wasn't going to hurt himself any more while getting the thing done.

He went to work on the mass of barbed wire with a pair of wire cutters. Then he pulled a length of it tightly around the woman's body and twisted the ends into makeshift knots to hold the wire in place.

The woman let out a sharp whimper and tried to twist loose from the duct tape as the barbs tore through her skin and clothing.

As he kept working, he said …

"You don't have to be quiet. You can scream if you want—if it helps."

He certainly wasn't worried about anybody hearing her.

She whimpered louder, and she seemed to try to scream, but her voice was weak.

He chuckled quietly. He knew that she couldn't get enough air in her lungs to properly scream—not with her legs bound up against her chest like that.

He pulled another length of barbed wire around her and stretched it tight, watching as blood dripped from where each barb pierced her flesh beneath her clothes, soaking through the fabric, spreading and making spots much wider than the wound itself.

He kept right on pulling strand after strand around her until she was all bound up like some kind of enormous wire cocoon, not looking human at all. The bundle was making all kinds strange low sounds—sighs, gasps, whimpers, and groans. Blood trickled here and spurted a little there until the whole tabletop was bathed in red.

Then he stepped back and admired his handiwork.

He turned off the overhead light and walked out into the night, closing the heavy wooden door behind him.

The sky was clear and starry, and he couldn't hear anything now except the dense rumble of crickets.

He took a long, slow breath of the clean, fresh air.

The night seemed especially sweet just now.

CHAPTER THREE

As Riley lined up with the rest of the interns for their final formal photograph, she heard the door to the reception room open.

Her heart leapt, and she turned around expectantly to see who had arrived.

But it was only Hoke Gilmer, the program's training supervisor, returning after having stepped out for a few minutes.

Riley suppressed a sigh. She already knew that Agent Crivaro wouldn't be here today. Yesterday he'd congratulated her on completing the course and said he wanted to get back to Quantico. It was obvious that he simply had no taste for ceremonies or receptions.

Her secret hope was that Ryan might show up out of the blue to help her celebrate the completion of the summer program.

Of course she knew better than to seriously expect that to happen.

Even so, she couldn't help but fantasize that somehow he'd change his mind and he'd arrive at the last minute and apologize for his cold behavior last night and finally say those words she longed for him to say …

"I want you to go to the academy. I want you to follow your dream."

But of course, that wasn't going to happen …

And the sooner I get that through my head, the better.

The 20 interns formed three rows for the photograph—one row seated at a long table, with two rows standing behind them. Since the interns were arranged in alphabetical order, Riley found herself in the back row between other two other students whose last names began with S—Naomi Strong and Rhys Seely.

She hadn't gotten to know Naomi or Rhys very well.

But then, that was true for almost all the other interns. She'd felt out of place among them ever since the first day of the program 10 weeks ago. The only student she'd gotten close to during that whole time was John Welch, who was standing a few students to her left.

On that first day, John had explained why the others were giving her odd looks and whispering to each other about her …

16

"Pretty much everybody here knows who you are. I guess you could say that your reputation precedes you."

She was, after all, the only intern who already had what everybody called "field experience" under her belt.

Riley fought down another sigh at the thought of those words …

"Field experience."

She found it weird to think of what had happened back at Lanton University as "field experience." A nightmare seemed more like it. She'd never be able to shake off those memories of finding her two close friends with their throats cut in their blood-drenched dorm rooms.

Back then, the last thing she'd had in mind was training with the FBI. She'd gotten caught up in the case through no choice of her own—and she'd helped solve it, which was why pretty much everybody here had known who she was from the very first day.

And then when the program got underway, and all the other students had started learning about computers and forensics and other less thrilling matters, Riley had tracked down the deadly Clown Killer. Both of those cases had been traumatic and life-threatening.

Getting a "head start" on "field experience" had hardly made her popular with the other interns. In fact, their unspoken resentment had been palpable all along.

And now at least some of them envied her for moving on to the Academy.

If only they knew what I've been through, she thought.

She doubted that they'd envy her then.

She felt horror and guilt at the memory of her two friends being murdered at Lanton, and she wished she could turn back time and stop it from happening. Not only would her friends still be alive, but her own life would be completely different right now. She'd have a psychology degree and some kind of run-of-the-mill job and a whole lot of uncertainty about what she was going to do with the rest of her life …

And Ryan would be perfectly happy with me.

But she doubted that she would be happy. She hadn't felt passionate about pursuing any career until the possibility of being an FBI agent came up—even if she did feel like this career had chosen her, not the other way around.

When the three rows of interns were properly posed, Hoke

Gilmer told a joke to make everybody laugh while the photographer snapped their picture. Riley didn't feel in a humorous mood, so the joke didn't strike her as funny. She was sure that her own smile looked forced and insincere.

She also felt insecure about her own pantsuit, which she'd bought months ago at a thrift shop. Most of the other interns were better off financially than she was, and markedly better dressed. She didn't look forward to seeing the photo that was being taken.

Then the group broke up to enjoy the snacks and refreshments arranged on another table in the middle of the room. Everybody clustered into groups of friends, and as usual, Riley felt isolated.

She noticed that Natalie Embry was clinging to Rollin Sloan, an intern who was headed straight for a high-paying job as a data analyst in a big Midwestern field office.

Riley heard a voice at her side …

"Well, Natalie sure got what she came here for, didn't she?"

Riley turned and saw John Welch standing beside her.

She smiled and said, "Come on, John. Aren't you being a bit cynical?"

John shrugged and said, "Are you telling me I'm wrong?"

Riley looked again at Natalie, who was flashing her new engagement ring at someone.

"No, I guess not," Riley said to John.

Natalie had been showing off that ring to everybody ever since Rollin had put it on her finger a couple of days ago. It had been a real whirlwind romance—she and Rollin hadn't even met before entering the summer program.

John let out a sigh of mock sympathy.

"Poor Rollin," he said. "There but for the grace of God go I."

Riley laughed aloud. She knew exactly what John meant. Starting on the very first day of the program, Natalie had been on the lookout for a prospective fiancée. She'd even targeted John until he'd made it clear that he really didn't like her.

Riley wondered—had Natalie ever been interested in the program at all? After all, she'd been smart enough and accomplished enough to be accepted into the honors internship.

Probably not, she figured.

Natalie seemed to have joined the program for the same reason that some of Riley's friends had gone to college—to catch herself a successful husband.

Riley tried to imagine how it would feel to go through life with

Natalie's priorities. Things would surely seem simpler, at least, when decisions could be so clear-cut...

Finding a man, moving into a nice house, having a few babies
...

Riley couldn't help envy Natalie's security, at least.

Even so, Riley felt sure she'd be bored to death by such a life—which was exactly why things were bad between her and Ryan right now.

Then John said, "I assume you're heading straight to Quantico when this is over."

Riley replied, "Yeah. I guess you are too, right?"

John nodded. Riley found it exciting to think that she and John were among the small handful of interns who were continuing on to the FBI Academy.

Most of the rest of them looked forward to other possibilities. Some would be going to graduate school in fields that had caught their interest this summer. Others would be starting new jobs in labs or offices right here in the Hoover Building or at Agency headquarters in other cities. They could begin FBI careers as computer scientists, data analysts, technicians—jobs that offered regular hours and didn't lead to life-threatening situations.

Jobs that Ryan would approve of, Riley thought wistfully.

Riley almost asked John how he was going to get to Quantico today. But of course she knew—he was going to drive there in his expensive car. Riley briefly considered asking him for a ride. After all, it would save her money for both a taxi and a train ticket.

But she couldn't bring herself to do that. She didn't want to admit to him that Ryan wasn't even going to drive her to the train station. John was a sharp guy, and he'd surely sense that things weren't right between her and Ryan. She'd rather he not know about that—at least not right now.

As she and John continued chatting, Riley couldn't help notice yet again how attractive he was—rugged and athletic, with short curly hair and pleasant smile.

He was well-off and wore an expensive suit, but Riley didn't hold his wealth and privilege against him. His parents were both prominent DC lawyers who were heavily involved in politics, and Riley admired John's choice of a humbler life of dedicated service to law enforcement.

He was a good guy, a true idealist, and she liked him very much. They'd actually worked together to crack the Clown Killer case, covertly communicating with the riddling killer to draw him out of hiding.

Standing close to him and enjoying his smile and their conversation, Riley found herself wondering how their friendship might grow at the Academy.

They were definitely going to be spending a lot of time together …

And I'm going to be far away from Ryan …

She cautioned herself not to let her imagination run away with her. For one thing, the problems she was having with Ryan were probably only temporary. Maybe all they needed was some time apart to remind them of why they'd fallen in love in the first place.

Finally the interns finished eating and started to leave. John waved to Riley on his way out, and she smiled and waved back. Still clinging to Rollin, Natalie kept flashing her ring around all the way through the door.

Riley said goodbye to Hoke Gilmer, the training supervisor, and Assistant Director Marion Connor, both of whom had given short congratulatory speeches to the whole group a little while ago. Then she left the reception room and went to the locker room to get her suitcase.

She found herself alone in the big, empty locker room. She looked around wistfully. The room was where all the interns had gathered for meetings during the summer. She doubted that she'd ever be here again.

Would she miss the program? She wasn't sure. She'd learned a lot here, and she'd enjoyed much of her intern experience. But she knew it was definitely time for her to move on.

So why do I feel sad? she wondered.

She quickly realized it was because of how she'd left things with Ryan. She remembered her own sharp words to him last night before she'd gone to bed …

"Enjoy the rest of your meal. There's some cheesecake in the refrigerator. I'm tired. I'm going to take a shower and go to bed."

They hadn't spoken since that moment. Ryan had gotten up and left for work before Riley had even awoken this morning.

She wished she hadn't spoken to him like that. But what choice had he given her? He hadn't shown a lot of sensitivity to her feelings—to her hopes and dreams.

The weight of her engagement ring felt strange on her finger. She held her hand in front of her face and looked at it. As the modest but lovely gem sparkled under the fluorescent ceiling light, she remembered the sweet moment when Ryan had knelt shyly to propose to her.

That seemed like a long time ago now.

And after their ugly parting, Riley wondered—were they even really engaged anymore? Was their relationship over? Had they broken up without actually saying so? Was it time for her to move on from Ryan, just like she was moving on from everything else? And was Ryan ready to move on from her?

For a moment, she toyed with the idea of not catching that cab and that train to Quantico—at least not right now. Maybe it wouldn't hurt for her to be a day late for classes. Maybe she could talk to Ryan again when he got home from work. Maybe they could put things right.

But she quickly realized …

If I go back to the apartment now, maybe I'll never go to Quantico.

She shuddered at the idea.

Somehow, she knew that her destiny awaited her in Quantico, and she didn't dare miss it.

It's now or never, she thought.

She got her suitcase and headed on out of the building, then caught a cab to the train station.

CHAPTER FOUR

Guy Dafoe didn't particularly like getting up so early in the morning. But at least these days he was working hard to take care of his own cattle rather than the herds he'd handled for other owners. Early morning chores seemed well worth the effort now.

The sun was rising, and he knew it was going to be a beautiful day. He loved the smell of the fields and the sounds of the cattle.

He'd spent years working bigger ranches and bigger herds. But this was his own land, his own animals. And he was feeding these animals right, not raising them artificially on grain and hormones. That was a waste of resources, and production-line cattle lived miserable lives. He felt good about what he was doing.

He'd plunged all his savings into buying this farm and a few cattle to start out with. He knew it was a big risk, but he had faith that there was a real future in sales of grass-fed beef. It was a growing market.

The yearling calves were clustered up around the barn, where he'd penned them up last night in order to check on their health and development. They watched him and mooed softly, as if waiting for him.

He was proud of his small herd of Black Angus, and sometimes he had to resist the temptation to become fond of them, as if they were pets. These were food animals, after all. It would be a bad idea to get very attached to any of them individually.

Today he wanted to turn the yearling calves into the roadside pasture. The field they were in now was eaten down short, and the good legume and grass pasture down by the road was ready for grazing.

Just as he swung wide gate open, he noticed something odd on the far side of the pasture. It looked like some kind of tangle or bundle over near the road.

He grumbled aloud …

"Whatever it is, it probably isn't good."

He slipped through the opening and pushed the gate shut again, leaving the yearlings where they were. He didn't want to turn his stock into this field until he found out what that strange object was.

As he strode across the field, he grew more puzzled. It looked

22

like a huge wad of barbed wire hanging from a fence post. Had a roll of the stuff bounced off of someone's truck and wound up there somehow?

But as he walked closer to it, he saw that it wasn't a new roll. It was a tangle of old wire, wrapped in all directions.

It didn't make any sense.

When he reached the bundle and stared into it, he realized that something was inside.

He leaned toward it, peered closely, and felt a sudden cold chill of terror.

"Holy hell!" he yelled, jumping backward.

But maybe he was only imagining things. He forced himself to look again.

There it was—a woman's face, pale and wounded, contorted in agony.

He grabbed the wire to pull it off her, but quickly stopped himself.

It's no use, he realized. *She's dead.*

He staggered over to next fencepost, leaned on it, and retched violently.

Pull yourself together, he told himself.

He had to call the police—right now.

He staggered away and broke into a run toward his house.

CHAPTER FIVE

Special Agent Jake Crivaro sat bolt upright when his office phone rang.

Things had been too quiet at Quantico since he got back yesterday.

Now his gut told him instantly …

It's a new case.

Sure enough, as soon as he picked up the phone, he heard the sonorous voice of Special Agent in Charge Erik Lehl …

"Crivaro, I need you in my office right now."

"Right away, sir," Crivaro said.

He hung up the phone and grabbed his go bag, which he always kept at the ready. Agent Lehl was being even more laconic than usual, which surely meant urgent business. Crivaro was sure that he would be traveling somewhere soon—probably within the hour.

He felt his heart pumping just a little faster as he hurried down the hall. It was a good feeling. After a 10-week stint serving as a mentor for the FBI's Honors Internship Program, this was a welcome return to normality.

During the first few days of the summer program he'd been pulled away by a murder case—the notorious "Clown Killer." After that he'd settled in to the more mundane work of mentoring just one of the interns—a talented but exasperating kid named Riley Sweeney, who had shown startling brilliance helping him on the case.

Even so, the program had passed too slowly for his taste. He wasn't used to spending such a long period out of the field.

When Jake walked into Lehl's office, the lanky man rose up from his chair to greet him. Erik Lehl was so tall that he barely seemed to fit into any space he occupied. Other agents said that he looked like he was wearing stilts. He looked more to Jake as though he were *made* out of stilts—an awkwardly assembled assortment of lengths of lumber that somehow never seemed to be perfectly coordinated in their movements. But the man had been a crack agent and had earned his position at the FBI's Behavioral Analysis Unit.

"Don't make yourself comfortable, Crivaro," Lehl said.

24

"You're leaving right away."

Jake obediently stayed on his feet.

Lehl looked at a manila folder that he was holding and heaved a grim sigh. Jake had long since observed Lehl's tendency to take every case extremely seriously—even personally, as if he felt directly insulted by any sort of monstrous criminality.

Not surprisingly, Jake couldn't remember ever finding Lehl in a cheerful mood.

After all …

Monsters are our business.

And Jake knew that Lehl wouldn't be assigning him to this particular case if it weren't unusually heinous. Jake was something of a specialist in cases that defied human imagination.

Lehl handed the manila folder to Jake and said, "We've got a really ugly situation in West Virginia. Have a look."

Jake opened the folder and saw a black-and-white photo of a weird bundle held together by duct tape and barbed wire. The bundle was dangling against a fence post. It took a moment for Jake to realize that the bundle had a face and hands—that it was in fact a human being and obviously dead.

Jake inhaled sharply.

Even for him, this was a uniquely grisly sight.

Lehl explained, "The photo was taken about a month ago. The body of a beauty parlor worker named Alice Gibson was found bound up with barbed wire and hanging from a fence post on a rural road near Hyland, West Virginia."

"Pretty nasty stuff," Jake said. "How are the local cops handling it?"

"They have a suspect in custody," Lehl said.

Jake's eyes widened with surprise.

He asked, "So what makes this an FBI case?"

Lehl said, "We just got a call from the chief of police in Dighton, a town near Hyland. Another bundled-up body like this was found just this morning, hanging from a fence post on a road outside of town."

Jake was starting to understand. Being in a jail cell at the time of the second murder gave the suspect a pretty good alibi. And now things looked like a serial killer was just getting started.

Lehl continued, "I've given orders that the current crime scene not be disturbed. So you need to get there ASAP. It would be a four-hour drive across the mountains, so I've got a helicopter waiting for you on the airstrip."

Jake was just turning to leave the office when Lehl added …

"Do you want me to assign you a partner?"

Jake turned and looked at Lehl. Somehow, he hadn't expected the question.

"I don't need a partner," Jake said. "But I'll need a forensics team. The cops in rural West Virginia aren't going to know how to get a good reading on the scene."

Lehl nodded and said, "I'll get the team together right now. They'll fly out with you."

Just as Jake was stepping out the door, Lehl said …

"Agent Crivaro, sooner or later you're going to need another regular partner."

Jake shrugged awkwardly and said, "If you say so, sir."

With a hint of a growl in his voice, Lehl said. "I do say so. It's about time for you to learn to play nice with others."

Jake stared at him with surprise. It was rare for the taciturn Erik Lehl to say anything the least bit snide.

I guess he really means it, Jake realized.

Without another word, Jake left the office and headed through the building. As he walked briskly along, he thought about what Lehl had said about him getting a new partner. Jake was well-known for being tough to work with in the field. But he really didn't think he gave anybody a hard time unless they deserved it.

His last regular partner, Gus Bollinger, had certainly deserved it. He'd gotten fired for smearing the fingerprints on a piece of vital evidence in the so-called "Matchbook Killer" case. As a consequence, the case had gone cold—and there was little that Jake hated more than cold cases.

On the Clown Killer case, Jake had worked with a DC agent named Mark McCune. McCune hadn't been as bad as Bollinger, but he'd made stupid mistakes and thought too highly of himself for Jake's taste. Jake was glad that their partnership had been only for that one case and that McCune remained in DC.

As he stepped onto the tarmac where the helicopter waited, he thought about someone else he'd worked with recently …

Riley Sweeney.

He'd been impressed with her ever since she'd been a psych student who had helped him solve a serial case at Lanton University. When she'd graduated, he'd pulled strings and stirred up the ire of some his colleagues to get her into the Honors

Internship Program. Perhaps against his own better judgment, he'd enlisted her help on the Clown Killer case.

She'd done some really brilliant work. She'd also made some really outrageous mistakes. And she was a long way from learning how to obey orders, but he'd only known a handful of even seasoned agents with such powerful intuitions.

One of those was himself.

As Jake stooped below the spinning propeller blades and climbed up into the helicopter, he saw the four-man forensic team trotting across the tarmac. Then the forensics guys climbed into the chopper, which took to the air.

It seemed silly to be thinking of Riley Sweeney right now. Quantico was a huge base, and even though she was at the FBI Academy, their paths weren't likely to cross again.

Jake opened the folder to read over the police report.

*

After the helicopter cleared the Appalachian mountain ranges, it passed over rolling meadows dotted with Black Angus cattle. As the chopper descended, Jake could see where police vehicles had blocked off a stretch of gravel road to keep onlookers away from the crime scene.

The helicopter set down in grassy pasture. Jake and the forensics team climbed out of the vehicle and headed over toward a small group of uniformed people and several official vehicles.

The cops and the medical examiner's team were standing on both sides of a barbed wire fence that ran along the road at the edge of the pasture. Jake could see what looked like a snarled bundle of wire hanging from a fencepost.

A short, sturdy-looking man of about Jake's height and build stepped forward to greet him.

"I'm Graham Messenger, the chief of police here in Dighton," he said, shaking hands with Jake. "We've had ourselves a couple of pretty awful incidents, at least for these parts. Let me show you."

The chief led the way to a fence post and, sure enough, a weird bundle was hanging from the post, all held together with duct tape and barbed wire. Again Jake was able spot a face and hands indicating that the bundle was actually a human being.

Messenger said, "I guess you already know about Alice Gibson, the earlier victim over near Hyland. This looks like the

27

same damn thing all over again. The victim this time is Hope Nelson."

Crivaro said, "Was she reported missing before the body was found?"

"Yeah, I'm afraid so," Messenger said, pointing pointed toward a stunned-looking middle-aged man standing near one of the vehicles. "Hope was married to Mason Nelson over there—the town mayor. She was working in their local farm supply store last night, but she didn't come home when Mason expected. He called me in the middle of the night about it, sounding pretty alarmed."

The police chief shrugged guiltily.

"Well, I'm kind of used to folks going missing for a spell, then turning up again. I told Mason I'd look into in today if she didn't turn up. I had no idea …"

Messenger's voice trailed off. Then he sighed and shook his head and added …

"The Nelsons own a lot of property in Dighton. They've always been good, respectable folks. Poor Hope didn't deserve this. But then, I don't reckon anybody does."

Another man stepped toward them. He had a long, aged face, white hair, and a bushy old-fashioned mustache. Chief Messenger introduced him as Hamish Cross, the county's chief medical examiner. Chewing on a weed, Cross seemed relaxed and mildly curious about what was going on.

He asked Jake, "Ever seen anything like this before?"

Jake didn't reply. The answer, of course, was no.

Jake stooped down beside the bundle and examined it closely.

He said to Cross, "I assume you worked on the earlier murder."

Cross nodded and stooped down beside Jake and twirled the weed in his mouth.

"That I did," Cross said. "And this one's pretty near identical. She didn't die here, that much is certain. She was abducted, bound up first with duct tape and then with barbed wire, and bled slowly to death. Either that or she suffocated first. Bound up tight like that, she'd hardly have been able to breathe at all. All that happened somewhere else—there's no sign of bleeding here."

Jake could see that the face and hands were almost as white as paper, and they glistened in the late morning sunlight like pieces of china. The woman simply didn't look real to Jake, but more like some kind of sick, grotesque sculpture.

A few flies had gathered around the body. They kept landing, roaming around, then flying away again. They looked like they didn't know what to do with this mysterious object.

Jake rose to his feet and asked Chief Messenger, "Who found the body?"

As if in reply, Jake heard a man's voice calling out …

"What the hell's going on here? How much longer is this going to take?"

Jake turned and saw a longhaired man with a scraggly beard coming toward them. He looked wild-eyed with anger, and his voice was shaking and shrill.

He yelled, "When the hell are you taking this—this thing away? This is a huge inconvenience. I've had to keep my cattle in an overgrazed pasture because of all this. I've got lots of work to do today. How much longer is this going to take?"

Jake turned to Hamish Cross and said quietly …

"You can take the body away any time now."

Cross nodded and gave orders to his team. Then he led the angry man away and spoke to him quietly, apparently calming him down.

Chief Messenger explained to Jake …

"That's Guy Dafoe, who owns this property. He's an organic farmer—our local hippie, I guess you might say. He hasn't been around for very long. It turns out this area is good for raising grass-fed organic beef. Organic farming's been a real boost to the local economy."

The chief's cellphone rang and he took the call. He listened for a moment, then said to Jake …

"This is Dave Tallhamer, the sheriff over in Hyland. You may have heard there's a suspect in custody for the first murder—Philip Cardin. He's the victim's ex-husband, and a bad sort who didn't have an alibi at the time. Tallhamer thought he had him dead to rights. But I guess this new murder changes things, doesn't it? Dave wants to know if he should let the guy go."

Jake thought for a moment, then said …

"Not until I've had a chance to talk to him."

Chief Messenger squinted curiously and said, "Uh, doesn't being locked in a jail cell when this woman was killed pretty much let him off the hook?"

Jake suppressed a sigh of impatience.

He repeated simply, "I'll want to talk to him."

Messenger nodded and got back on the phone with the sheriff.

Jake didn't want to go into any kind of explanation right now. The truth was, he knew nothing at all about the suspect currently in custody, or even why he was a suspect. For all Jake knew, Philip Cardin might have a partner who committed this new murder, or else …

God knows what might be going on.

At this point in an investigation, there were always thousands of questions and no answers. Jake hoped that would change before too long.

While Messenger kept talking on the phone, Jake walked over to the victim's husband, who was leaning against a police car staring off into space.

Jake said, "Mr. Nelson, I'm very sorry for your loss. I'm Special Agent Jake Crivaro, and I'm here to help bring your wife's killer to justice."

Nelson nodded only slightly, as if he were barely aware that he'd been spoken to.

Jake said in a firm voice, "Mr. Nelson, do you have any idea who might have done this? Or why?"

Nelson looked at him with a dazed expression.

"What?" he said. Then he repeated, "No, no, no."

Jake knew that there was no point in asking the man any more questions, at least not right now. He was clearly in a deep state of shock. That was hardly surprising. Not only was his wife dead, but the way she had died was especially grotesque.

Jake headed back over toward the crime scene, where his forensics team was already hard at work.

He looked all around, noting how isolated the place seemed to be. At least there wasn't a crowd of gawkers hanging around …

And so far no sign of the media.

But right then he heard the sound of another helicopter. He looked around and saw that a TV news helicopter was descending toward the meadow.

Jake sighed deeply and thought …

This case is going to be tough.

CHAPTER SIX

Riley felt a sharp tingle of expectation when the speaker stepped in front of the 200 or so recruits. The man looked like he belonged to a different era, with his thin lapels and his skinny black tie and his buzz haircut. He reminded Riley of photos she'd seen of 1960s astronauts. As he shuffled through a few notecards, then looked out over his audience, she waited for his words of welcome and praise.

Academy Director Lane Swanson began much as she had expected …

"I know that you've all been working hard to prepare for this day."

He added with a half-smile …

"Well, let me tell you right now—you're *not* prepared. None of you."

An audible sigh passed through the auditorium and Swanson paused to let his words sink in.

Then he continued, "That's what this 20-week program is about—getting you as prepared as you can get for life in the Federal Bureau of Investigation. And part of that preparedness is learning the limits of preparedness, how to deal with the unexpected, learning to think on your feet. Always remember—the FBI Academy is called the 'West Point for Law Enforcement' with good reason. Our standards are high. Not all of you are going to get through this. But those of you who do will be as prepared as you can hope to be for the tasks that await you."

Riley hung on his every word as Swanson spoke about the Academy's standards of fostering safety, esprit de corps, uniformity, accountability, and discipline. Then he went on to talk about the rigorous curriculum—courses in everything from law and ethics to interrogation and evidence collection.

Riley felt more and more anxious at every word as the truth sank in …

I'm not a summer intern anymore.

The summer program seemed like some kind of teenage day camp in comparison to what she was now facing.

Was she hopelessly out of her depth?

31

Was this a bad idea?

For one thing, she felt like a kid as she looked around at all the other seated recruits. Scarcely anyone here was her age. She sensed by the faces around her that almost everybody here already had at least that much experience under their belts, and some of them considerably more. Most were over the age of 23, and some looked like they were verging on the maximum recruitment age of 37.

She knew that they came from all kinds of backgrounds and work fields. Many had been police officers, and many others had served in the military. Others had worked as teachers, lawyers, scientists, business people, and at many other occupations at one time or another. But they all had one thing in common—a powerful commitment to spend the rest of their lives serving in law enforcement.

Only a few were here fresh out of the intern program. John Welch, who was sitting a couple of rows ahead of her, was one of them. Like Riley, he had been given a waiver to the rule that all recruits had to have at least three years of full-time law enforcement experience to enter the Academy.

Swanson finished his speech …

"I look forward to shaking the hands of those of you who make the grade here at Quantico. On that day, you'll be sworn into service by FBI Director Bill Cormack himself. Good luck to all of you."

Then he added with a stern chuckle, "And now—get to work!"

An instructor took Swanson's place at the podium and began to call out the names of recruits—"NATs," they were called, meaning "New Agents in Training." As the NATs answered to their names, the instructor assigned them smaller groups that would be taking their classes together.

As she waited breathlessly for her name to be called, Riley remembered how tedious things had been when she'd gotten here yesterday. After she'd checked in, she'd stood in line after line, filled out forms, bought a uniform, and gotten her dorm room assignment.

Today was already turning out to be a lot different.

She felt a pang as she heard John Welch's name called out for a group that she wasn't chosen for. It might help, she thought, to have a friend close at hand to lean on and commiserate with during the tough weeks to come. On the other hand, she thought …

Maybe it's just as well.

Given her somewhat confusing feelings about John, his presence might prove to be a distraction.

Riley was finally relieved, though, to find herself in the same group as Francine Dow, the roommate she'd been assigned yesterday. Frankie, as she preferred to be called, was older than Riley, perhaps almost 30—a high-spirited redhead whose ruddy features hinted that she'd already experienced a lot in life.

Riley and Frankie hadn't gotten to know each other at all to speak of. They'd had time yesterday for little except getting unpacked and settled in their little dorm room together, and they'd gone their separate ways for breakfast.

Finally, Riley's group of NATs was summoned together in the hallway by Agent Marty Glick, the group instructor. Glick looked like he was in his thirties. He was tall and had the muscular build of a football player, and he wore a serious, no-nonsense expression.

He said to the group …

"You've got a big day ahead. But before we get started, there's something I want to show you."

Glick led them into the main entrance lobby, an enormous room with an FBI seal in the middle of its marble floor an enormous bronze badge on one wall with a black band across it. Riley had passed through here when she'd arrived, and she knew that it was called the Hall of Honor. It was a solemn place where martyred FBI Agents were memorialized.

Glick led them to a wall with two displays of portraits and names. Between the displays was a framed plaque that read …

National Academy Graduates who were killed in the line of duty
as the direct result of an adversarial action.

Small gasps passed through the group as they viewed the shrine. Glick didn't say anything for a moment, just allowed the emotional impact of the display sink in.

Finally he said, almost in a whisper …

"Don't let them down."

As he led the group of NATs away to start their day's activities, Riley glanced back over her shoulder at the portraits on the wall. She couldn't help but wonder …

Will my picture be there someday?

Of course there was no way to know. All she knew for sure was that the coming days would bring challenges she'd never faced before in her life. She felt staggered by a new sense of responsibility toward those martyred agents.

I can't let them down, she thought.

CHAPTER SEVEN

Jake steered the hastily-borrowed vehicle along a web of gravel roads from Dighton toward the town of Hyland. Chief Messenger had loaned him the car so Jake could get on his way before the media helicopter landed.

He had no idea what to expect at Hyland, but he was grateful to have escaped the invaders. He hated being besieged by reporters pummeling him with questions he couldn't answer. There was little the media relished more than sensational murders in bucolic, out-of-the-way places. The fact that the victim was a mayor's wife surely made the story all the more irresistible to them.

He drove with his window open, enjoying the fresh country air. Messenger had marked up a map for him, and Jake was enjoying the slow tour of country roads. The man he was on his way to interview wasn't going anywhere before he got there.

Of course the suspect in the Hyland jail might have nothing to do with either of the two murders. He'd been incarcerated at the time of the second victim's death.

Not that that proves his innocence, Jake thought.

There was always a possibility that a team of two or more killers was at work. Hope Nelson could had been taken by a copycat imitating Alice Gibson's murder.

Nothing like that would surprise Jake. He'd worked on stranger cases in his long career.

As Jake pulled into Hyland, the first thing he noticed was how little and sleepy the town looked—much smaller than Dighton, with its population of about a thousand. The sign he'd just passed indicated that only a couple of hundred people lived here.

Barely big enough to be incorporated, Jake thought.

The police station was just another storefront on the short business street. As he parked along the curb, Jake saw an obese uniformed man leaning against in the doorjamb, looking like he had nothing else to do.

Jake got out of the car. As he walked toward the station, he noticed that the big cop was staring at someone directly across the street. It was a man wearing a white medical jacket, standing there with his arms crossed. Jake got the odd impression that the two had

35

been standing there staring at each other silently for quite a long time.

What's this all about? he wondered.

He walked up to the uniformed man in the doorway and showed him his badge. The man introduced himself as Sheriff David Tallhamer. He was chewing on a wad of tobacco.

He said to Jake in a bored tone, "Come on in, let me introduce you to our house guest—Phil Cardin's his name."

As Tallhamer led the way inside, Jake glanced back and saw that the white-coated man wasn't budging from his spot.

Once in the station, Tallhamer introduced Jake to a deputy who was sitting with his feet up on a desk reading a newspaper. The deputy nodded at Jake and kept right on reading his paper.

The little office seemed saturated with a weird feeling of ennui. If Jake hadn't known it already, he wouldn't have guessed that these two jaded cops had been dealing with a grisly murder case.

Tallhamer led Jake through a door in the back of the office that led into the jail. The jail was comprised of just two cells facing each other across a narrow corridor. Both cells were occupied at the moment.

In one cell, a man in a rather threadbare business suit lay on his cot snoring loudly. In the opposite, a sullen-looking man wearing jeans and a t-shirt was sitting on his bunk.

Tallhamer took out his keys and unlocked the seated prisoner's cell and said …

"You've got a visitor, Phil. A bona-fide FBI Agent, he says."

Jake stepped inside the cell while Tallhamer stood just outside, keeping the cell door open.

Phil Cardin squinted hard at Jake and said, "FBI, huh? Well, maybe you can teach Deputy Dawg here how to do his goddamn job. I didn't kill nobody, let alone my ex-wife. If I did, I'd be the first to brag about it. So let me out of here."

Jake wondered …

Has anybody told him about the other murder?

Jake got the feeling that Cardin knew nothing about it. He figured it was best to keep things that way, at least for the time being.

Jake said to him, "I've got some questions, Mr. Cardin. Do you want a lawyer present?"

Cardin chuckled and pointed at the sleeping man in the opposite cell.

"He already *is* present—in a manner of speaking," Cardin said.

Then he yelled at the man …

"Hey, Ozzie. Sober up, why don't you? I need legal representation. Make sure my rights don't get violated. Although I guess that train's left the station already, you drunken incompetent bastard."

The man in the rumpled suit sat up and rubbed his eyes.

"What the hell are you yelling about?" he grumbled. "Can't you see I'm trying to get some sleep? Jesus, I've got a son-of-a-bitch of a headache."

Jake's mouth dropped open. The fat sheriff laughed heartily at his obvious surprise.

Tallhamer said, "Agent Crivaro, I'd like you to meet Oswald Hines, the town's only lawyer. He gets drafted into public defense duties from time to time. Conveniently enough, he got arrested a while ago for drunk and disorderly behavior, so he's right here at hand. Not that that's an unusual occurrence."

Oswald Hines coughed and grunted.

"Yeah, I guess that's the truth," he said. "This is sort of my home away from home—or more like a second office, you might say. At times like now, it's a handy location. I'd hate to have to walk anywhere else, the way I'm feeling at the moment."

Hines took a long, slow breath, staring blearily at the others.

Then he said to Jake, "Listen up, Agent Whatever-Your-Name is. As this man's defense attorney, I must insist that you leave him alone. He's been asked too damn many questions for about a week now. In fact, he's being held without cause."

The lawyer yawned and added, "Actually, I'd hoped he'd be gone by now. He'd better be out of here before I wake up again."

The lawyer started to lie back down when the sheriff said …

"Stay awake, Ozzie. You've got work to do. I'll go get you a cup of coffee. Do you want me to let you out of your cell so you can be closer to your client?"

"Naw, I'm good right here," Ozzie said. "Just hurry up with that coffee. You know how I like it."

Laughing, Sheriff Tallhamer said, "How is that again?"

"In a cup of some sort," Ozzie growled. "Go. Now."

Tallhamer went back into the office. Jake stood staring down at the prisoner for a moment.

Finally Jake said, "Mr. Cardin, I understand you don't have an alibi for the time of your ex-wife's murder."

Cardin shrugged and said, "I don't know where anybody got that idea. I was at home. I ate a frozen dinner, watched TV all evening, then slept the rest of the night through. I wasn't anywhere near where it happened—wherever that was."

"Can anybody corroborate that?" Jake said.

Cardin grinned and said, "No, but nobody can *corroborate* otherwise either, can they?"

Observing Cardin's snide expression, Jake wondered …

Is he guilty and taunting me?

Or does he just not understand the seriousness of his situation?

Jake asked, "How was your relationship with your ex-wife at the time of the murder?"

The lawyer called out sharply …

"Phil, don't answer that question."

Cardin looked across to the other cell and said, "Aw, shut up, Ozzie. I'm not going to tell him anything I haven't told the sheriff a hundred times already. It won't make no difference anyhow."

Then looking at Jake, Cardin said in a sarcastic tone …

"Things were just peachy between me and Alice. Our divorce was perfectly amicable. I wouldn't have hurt a hair on her pretty little head."

The sheriff had just returned and handed a cup of coffee to the lawyer.

"Amicable, shit," the sheriff said to Cardin. "The day of her murder, you went roaring into the beauty parlor where she worked, yelling right in front of her clientele that she'd ruined your life and you hated her guts and you wanted her dead. That's why you're here."

Jake put his hands in his pockets and said, "Would you care to tell me what that was all about?"

Cardin's lips twisted in an expression of savage anger.

"It was the truth, that's all—about her ruining my life, I mean. I've been down on my luck ever since the bitch threw me out and married that damned doctor. Just that day I got fired from my job as a short-order cook in Mick's Diner."

"And that was her fault somehow?" Jake said.

Cardin stared Jake straight in the eye and said through clenched teeth …

"Everything was her fault."

Jake felt a chill at the sound of hatred in his voice.

He's a real blamer, he thought.

Jake had dealt with more than his share of killers who couldn't accept responsibility for anything that went wrong in their lives. Jake knew that Cardin's fiery resentment was hardly proof of his guilt. But he could definitely understand why Cardin had been arrested in the first place.

Still, Jake knew that keeping him in custody was another issue, now that there had been another murder. From what Chief Messenger had told Jake back in Dighton, there was no hard physical evidence linking Cardin with the crime. The only evidence was a history of threatening behavior, especially the recent outburst at the beauty parlor where Alice had worked. It was all circumstantial ...

Unless he says something incriminating right here and now.

Jake said to Cardin, "I take it you're not exactly a grieving ex-husband."

Cardin grunted and said, "Maybe I would be if Alice hadn't done me so bad. Spent our whole marriage telling me what a loser I was—as if that toad she took up with was some kind of improvement. Well, I wasn't no loser until she divorced me. It was only when I was on my own that things started going bad. It's not fair ..."

Jake listened as Cardin kept griping on about his ex. His bitterness was palpable—and so was his heartbreak. Jake suspected that Cardin never stopped loving Alice, or at least wanting her. Part of him had always held out some vain hope that they'd wind up together again.

However, his love for her was obviously sick, twisted, and obsessive—not love at all, in any healthy sense. Jake had known plenty of murderers who were driven by exactly that kind of thing they called love.

Cardin paused from ranting for a moment, then said ...

"Tell me—is it true they found her wrapped up in barbed wire?"

Shaking his head with a smile he added ...

"Man, that's—that's *creative.*"

Jake felt a slight jolt at those words.

What did Cardin mean, exactly?

Was he admiring someone else's handiwork?

Or was he slyly gloating over his own resourcefulness?

Jake figured the time had come to try to draw him out about the other murder. If Cardin had an accomplice who had killed Hope

39

Nelson, maybe Jake could get him to admit it. But he knew he had to tread carefully.

He said, "Mr. Cardin, did you know a woman named Hope Nelson over in Dighton?"

Cardin scratched his head and said …

"Nelson … the name's familiar. Ain't she the mayor's wife or something?"

Leaning against the bars outside the cell, Sheriff Tallhamer grunted and said …

"She's *dead,* that's what she is."

Jake fought down a groan of discouragement. He hadn't planned to spring the truth on Cardin in so blunt a manner. He'd hoped to take his time about it, try to find out if he already knew what had happened to Hope Nelson.

The lawyer in the other cell jumped to his feet.

"Dead?" he yelped. "What the hell are you talking about?"

Tallhamer spit out some tobacco on the concrete floor and said, "She was murdered just last night—in exactly the same way Alice was killed. Strung up from a fence post, bundled up in barbed wire."

Suddenly seeming perfectly sober, Ozzie barked, "So what the hell are you holding my client for? Don't tell me you think he murdered another woman last night while he was locked up right here."

Jake's spirits sank. His tactic was spoiled, and he knew that any further questions were likely to be pointless.

Nevertheless, he asked Cardin again, "Did you know Hope Nelson?"

"Didn't I just tell you no?" Cardin said with a note of surprise.

But Jake couldn't tell whether his surprise was unfeigned or he was just faking it.

Ozzie grabbed the bars of his own cell and yelled, "You'd damn well better let my client loose right now, or you'll be facing one hell of a lawsuit!"

Jake stifled a sigh.

Ozzie was right, of course, but …

He picked a fine time to get competent all of a sudden.

Jake turned to Tallhamer and said, "Let Cardin go. But keep a close eye on him."

Tallhamer called for his deputy to bring Cardin's belongings. As the sheriff opened the cell for Cardin to leave, he turned toward

Ozzie and said …

"Do you want to go too?"

Ozzie yawned and lay back down on his bunk.

"Naw, I've done a pretty good day's work. I'd just as soon go back to sleep—as long as you don't need the cell for anybody else."

Tallhamer smirked and said, "Be my guest."

As Jake walked out of the station with Tallhamer and Cardin, he noticed that the white-coated man was still standing on the other side of the street in exactly the same spot as before.

Suddenly, the man went into motion, striding across the street toward them.

Tallhamer grumbled quietly to Jake …

"Here comes trouble."

CHAPTER EIGHT

Jake scrutinized the man who was rushing toward them just outside the police station. He saw outrage in the man's face and bearing, but didn't sense that it was aimed at him. And he was aware that Tallhamer wasn't bracing for action.

Meanwhile, Cardin had turned and hurried rapidly away along the sidewalk.

The angry man stormed up to Tallhamer. Waving an arm in the departing Cardin's direction, he shouted …

"I *demand* that you take that bastard back into custody!"

Seemingly impervious to the man's anger, Sheriff Tallhamer calmly introduced Jake to Earl Gibson, the town's only doctor and Alice Gibson's husband.

Jake started to shake hands and to offer his condolences, but the doctor's arms were still waving in circles as he ranted on at Tallhamer. He noted that Dr. Gibson was a remarkably homely man with a heavily pockmarked face that wasn't improved by the flush of fury. He remembered Cardin describing him as *"that toad she took up with."*

Indeed, Cardin was positively handsome by comparison.

Jake figured that Earl Gibson must have virtues that had attracted the dead woman despite his looks. After all, Gibson was a doctor, and Alice's ex was nothing more than a failed short-order cook …

Probably a pretty easy choice in a town with few options.

Gibson's anger only increased when he found out who Jake was.

"The FBI! What business does the FBI have even being here? You already caught my wife's killer. You had him locked away. There's not a jury in the world that wouldn't find him guilty. And now you just let him go!"

Sheriff Tallhamer shuffled his feet and spoke in a patient, almost condescending tone …

"Now, Earl, we talked about this just a little while ago, didn't we?"

Dr. Gibson said, "Yeah, we did. And that's why I stayed right here, waiting. I had to see this for myself. I wanted to stop it."

"We've got to let him go, and you know it," Tallhamer said, "Another woman was murdered last night over in Dighton, the same way as Alice was. I can vouch for Phil Cardin's whereabouts last night, and he sure wasn't anywhere near Dighton. He didn't kill that woman, and now we've got no reason to think he killed Alice, either."

"No reason!" Gibson said, sputtering with rage. "He threatened her life that very day. And don't insult me with all this nonsense about the victim in Dighton, and how Phil Cardin couldn't have killed her. We both know there's a perfectly viable suspect for the other murder."

Jake's interest was suddenly piqued.

"A viable suspect?" he asked.

Gibson scoffed at Sheriff Tallhamer and said, "So you didn't tell him, eh?"

"Tell me about what?" Jake asked.

"About Phil Cardin's brother, Harvey," Gibson said to Jake. "He takes Phil's side in everything. He threatened Alice too. He'd get her on the phone and tell her that he and Phil were going to get revenge. He called her the same day she was killed. And wherever he was last night, he wasn't in any jail cell. He's the one who killed that woman in Dighton. I'd bet my life on it."

Jake was truly startled now.

He asked Gibson, "Why do you think he'd kill someone in another town?"

Gibson said, "His motive you mean? Maybe he had something personal against that woman. He wanders around the state a lot so maybe he got involved with her, then followed his brother's example. But I think he most likely did it to protect his brother—to make people think he didn't kill Alice."

Tallhamer sighed and said, "Earl, we talked about this too a little while ago, didn't we? We've both known Harvey Cardin all our lives. He travels around because he's an itinerant plumber. He talks tough from time to time, but he's not like his brother. He'd never hurt a fly, let alone kill anyone in such an awful way."

Jake's brain clicked away, trying to process what he was hearing.

He wished Tallhamer had told him about Harvey Cardin from the start.

Small town cops, he thought. *Some of them are so sure they know everything about everybody in their district that they can miss what's important.*

Jake said to Sheriff Tallhamer, "I want to talk to Harvey Cardin."

The sheriff shrugged as if he considered it a waste of time.

He said, "Well, if that's what you want. Harvey lives only a couple of blocks away from here. I'll take you there."

As Jake started walking with the sheriff, he saw that Gibson was following along. The last thing Jake needed right now was a grieving and irate widower inserting himself into the interview of a possible suspect.

As delicately as he could, he said, "Dr. Gibson, the sheriff and I need to do this on our own."

When Gibson opened his mouth to protest, Jake added …

"I'll want to interview you in a little while. Where can I find you?"

Gibson fell silent for a moment.

"I'll be in my office," Gibson said. "The sheriff can tell you where it is."

Gibson turned and stormed angrily away.

Jake and Tallhamer walked the short distance to a tiny white house where Harvey Cardin lived. It was a ramshackle cottage with an overgrown lawn.

Tallhamer knocked on the front door. When no one answered, he knocked again, and there was still no answer.

Tallhamer said, "He's probably away, maybe working in some other town. We'll have to catch him some other time."

Jake didn't want to wait for "some other time." He peered through one of the glass panes in the front door. He could see some stark, simple furniture, but little else inside—certainly no personal touches to the decor. It looked like a the kind of place that was rented furnished, but there was no sign that anybody lived there.

Jake guessed that Harvey Cardin was out of town, all right …

But is he ever coming back?

His musings were interrupted by a man's voice from next door …

"Can I help you with anything, sheriff?"

Jake turned and saw a man standing in the yard.

Tallhamer said to him, "This FBI fellow and I are looking for Harvey Cardin."

The man shook his head and said, "You won't have much luck, I don't reckon. I saw him loading up his truck a week ago—just after his brother got arrested for killing Alice Gibson. It looked like he was taking everything he had, not that there was much of it to begin with. I asked him where he was going, and he said, 'Anywhere that's not Hyland. I've had it with this goddamn town.'"

Jake felt a jolt of alarm.

This possible suspect had already disappeared.

"Come on," Jake said to Tallhamer. "Let's go talk to some people."

*

Jake and Sheriff Tallhamer spent the rest of the day conducting fruitless interviews, starting in the neighborhood where Harvey Cardin had lived. All that Harvey's other neighbors knew was that they hadn't seen him since he'd driven away weeks ago.

They had no better luck with Alice's friends and acquaintances. Alice's female coworkers at the beauty parlor agreed that Phil Cardin had made a terrible, frightening scene there on the day before Alice was killed.

When Jake and Tallhamer stopped by Mick's Diner, the owner said that Phil Cardin had gotten himself fired from his job as a short-order cook for a whole cluster of reasons—skipping work, showing up drunk, and getting into fistfights with other employees.

None of them knew anything about where Phil's brother Harvey might be.

Finally Jake and the sheriff stopped by Earl Gibson's physician's office. The doctor was still seething about Phil Cardin's release, and was further angered to hear that Harvey had disappeared. Jake managed to calm him down enough to ask him some questions, but Gibson wasn't able to shed any light on who else might have wanted to kill his wife.

Their inquiries only deepened the mystery as far as Jake was concerned. He was looking for any indication that the two Cardin brothers had committed the two murders by turns, or even that the missing Harvey Cardin had committed both murders …

But if not?

Jake didn't have any alternative scenarios just yet. He'd gotten no gut instinct about anybody else in Hyland committing either of the two murders. Alice seemed well-liked by everyone they talked to that day, and nobody in Hyland seemed to know Hope Nelson except by name. Neither, apparently, had Alice Gibson. The two

45

women were from the same part of the state, but had spent their lives in different towns and different social circles.

When they found themselves back at the police station after a fruitless day, Jake told Tallhamer's deputy to keep a close eye on Harvey Cardin, especially to make sure he didn't try to leave town.

"One more stop," he told Tallhamer, "and then I'll give up for the day."

The sheriff drove Jake out to the first murder scene.

Dusk was falling by the time they got there. The fence post where Alice Gibson's body had been found dangling was marked by an X that Sheriff Tallhamer's deputy had painted on it. Like the spot where Alice Gibson's body had been found, the fence bordered on a gently rolling pasture.

Jake suppressed a sigh as he imagined the hideous bundle hanging there …

This'd be nice place to visit under different circumstances.

He figured it must have taken a remarkably sick man to leave such a grisly object in such a lovely location.

Was Phil Cardin such a man?

Might his brother be such a man?

Jake crouched down by the fence post and breathed long and slowly, hoping to catch some feeling about what had happened here. Jake was known for making intuitive leaps at murder scenes, oftentimes getting an uncanny sense of the mind of a criminal. Jake knew of nobody else who could do that—except for young Riley Sweeney, and her instincts were still erratic and undisciplined.

This morning at the other crime scene, Jake hadn't been able even try to make such a connection—not with all the hubbub going on around him and the arrival of a TV news helicopter.

Can I do it now? he wondered.

Jake closed his eyes and focused, trying to get some sort of gut feeling.

Nothing came.

When he opened his eyes, he saw that three black and white Black Angus cows had wandered over and were eyeing him curiously. He wondered—had they seen what had gone on that night? If so, had the horror of what they'd witnessed had any impact on them?

"If only you could talk," Jake said to the cows under his breath.

He rose to his feet, feeling thoroughly discouraged.

It was time to head back over to Dighton and check in with his

46

forensics team. He'd go over the day's notes and get some sleep in the town's only motel, then get a fresh start early tomorrow. Jake had left some unfinished business in Dighton, including a serious interview with Hope Nelson's husband, the mayor. Mason Nelson had been too incapacitated with shock for Jake to talk to him when they'd met at the other murder scene.

As for trying to track down Harvey Cardin's whereabouts, Jake knew that it wasn't a job for either the local cops or the forensics crew he'd brought along. He'd have to call for technical support from Quantico.

He said to Sheriff Tallhamer, "Take me back to my car, I'm leaving."

But before they could get into the sheriff's car, Jake saw a van approaching with a TV station's logo on it. The van pulled to a stop nearby, and a crew poured out with lights, camera, and a microphone.

Jake let out a groan of despair.

There was no way of getting away from the media this time.

CHAPTER NINE

Riley was disappointed when she went to the computer room after a day of tours, classes, and her first dinner in the Academy cafeteria. There was still no email from Ryan. For the moment she ignored the others in her box.

Last night she had emailed Ryan to let him know that she'd arrived at Quantico and was settling in. She hadn't heard anything from him in reply. She asked herself—should she send him another note, telling him about her day? Or should she give him a phone call?

Riley sighed deeply as she tried to come to terms with the truth …

He's still angry.

She wondered if maybe she'd made a mistake by catching the first train she could to Quantico. Maybe she should have returned home before she'd left to talk things out with him, find out where things stood between them. She couldn't imagine how they were ever going to do that as long as they were separated like this.

But she couldn't help thinking …

If I'd gone back home yesterday, I'd probably still be there.

She decided it was best not to try to do anything about it now. Maybe tomorrow morning she'd send Ryan another note.

One other email in the box was junk, which she deleted. But when she opened the remaining message, Riley was unsettled and alarmed.

"Brant Hayman," she whispered, with a shudder.

Hayman was the professor who had killed Riley's two college friends in Lanton. He had tried to kill Riley.

The email was from a Virginia circuit court summoning her to testify next week at his trial for murder, which was already in progress.

Riley gulped hard as she remembered how close to death she herself had come at Hayman's hands.

Doubtless she would have to face him when she gave her testimony.

Did she have the courage to do that?

She shrugged slightly and thought …

It's not like I've got any choice.

Besides, giving testimony against Hayman might give her some closure, make her feel that her ordeal was over at long last. She printed that email and left the computer room.

Back in their small dorm room, Riley's roommate Frankie, was sitting on her bed perusing materials in her orientation folder.

Frankie looked up and said with a slight grin …

"Still worried about whether your fiancé is pissed off with you, huh?"

Riley was startled. She and Frankie had talked very little since they'd first met. Riley certainly hadn't mentioned that she was engaged, let alone that there was any friction between herself and Ryan.

"How did you know?" Riley asked.

Frankie chuckled and said, "Oh, it doesn't take a detective. Your engagement ring was just about the first thing I noticed about you. And you went to the computer room three times last night, and once again this morning, and I'm willing to bet you came from there just now. It's what you might call classic 'worried girlfriend' behavior. So what's the guy's name?"

"Ryan," Riley said, sitting down on her own bed.

"Well, don't tell me," Frankie said, "Ryan's got ambivalent feelings about you going into this line of work, am I right?"

Riley shook her head sadly.

"'Ambivalent,'" she said. "Yeah, I guess that's one word for it—although outright disapproval is more like it."

Frankie let out a hearty laugh.

"Well, don't ask for my advice. I've got kind of a jaundiced view of men in general. I was married for four years—and good riddance, as far as I'm concerned."

Then Frankie pointed to Riley's ring and added …

"But I *do* think you should take that thing off and put it in a drawer, at least for the next few days. It's liable to distract you, and you're going to need all the concentration you can muster."

Riley looked at her ring and twisted it on her finger.

She said, "I don't think I can do that."

Frankie tilted her head and said, "Suit yourself. Anyway, tell me about yourself. There aren't too many kids your age starting at the Academy. What brings you here?"

Riley heaved a deep, long sigh.

Where do I begin? she wondered.

She showed Frankie the email from the circuit court and sketchily told the story of how she'd gotten mixed up in the murder case in Lanton. Then she described how she'd worked on the Clown Killer case earlier this summer. Frankie's eyes widened and she asked …

"You mean you *worked* with Special Agent Jake Crivaro?"

Riley was surprised at the question.

She said, "Well, it wasn't exactly my idea. I just sort of got mixed up in things. Agent Crivaro's kind of my … mentor, I guess you could say. I wouldn't be here if it weren't for him."

Frankie stared at Riley for a moment, then said …

"Wow. I mean you *do* know that Jake Crivaro's a living legend in the law enforcement profession, right?"

Riley didn't know what to say. She knew that Crivaro was known to be an exceptional agent, but …

A legend?

Frankie continued, "They say he's got the best instincts in the business. Like, hellish great instincts. I'm impressed. I mean, Jake Crivaro … *there's* a name you can drop around here if you want to impress people."

It felt strange to hear Frankie talk like this. Until now, Riley had felt anonymous here at Quantico—quite unlike when she'd gone into the summer program back in DC. Then all the other interns had known she'd already worked on two murder cases. She was possibly the only intern with that kind of experience, which stirred up quite a lot of envy and resentment. Here, she was one of the least experienced NATs around. Who cared that she'd gotten caught up in a couple of murder cases?

She remembered how Crivaro had praised her instincts when he'd talked her into going into the program …

"Do you realize how amazing that is, for someone with no training in law enforcement?"

Now Riley couldn't help wondering—what did it say about *her* that a living legend thought she had great instincts?

Careful, she told herself. *Don't get carried away.*

Also, she quickly decided that dropping Crivaro's name around Quantico wasn't a good idea. It was probably better to just stay anonymous to almost everybody, at least until she started to prove her own capabilities …

If that ever happens.

Riley asked Frankie, "What about you? I'm sure you've had a

lot more experience than I have."

Frankie stared at the wall for a moment, then said ...

"Well, yeah, I guess you could say that. I was a cop for several years in Cincinnati. It didn't end well—kind of like my marriage, you might say."

Sensing Frankie's uneasiness, Riley said ...

"You don't have to talk about it. I mean, it's probably none of my ..."

Frankie interrupted, "No, I'd probably better tell you. We're going to be in this thing together for the whole program. It's best that you know."

Frankie heaved a long sigh and said ...

"I spent six months working undercover, bringing down drug dealers."

Riley almost gasped with amazement. She'd seen sensational stories about undercover drug agents on TV shows, but she couldn't begin to imagine what that kind of work was really like.

Frankie hesitated for a moment, then said ...

"I was good at it, in case you're wondering. And I went the whole hog, living on the streets, pretending to be a homeless junkie. I'd approach a dealer or he'd approach me, and I'd make a purchase, then report him back to the drug squad, and they'd arrest him. The trick, of course, was to keep right on doing that without anybody figuring out my connection to the arrests."

"That must have been tough," Riley said.

Frankie shrugged slightly and said, "Like I said, I was good at it. 'Indigo' was my name on the street. And I learned all kinds of tricks and maneuvers. I can remember the first time a dealer got suspicious of me, asked flat-out if I was a cop. I was scared to death, but managed not to show it. I acted offended, said I wasn't an f-ing narc, and if that's what he thought of me, he could just get out of my face and not do business with me."

Frankie chuckled a little, then added, "I was relieved when it worked, and a little amazed too. One day I was sitting around with another homeless user who asked me, 'Is it true that undercover cops have to tell the truth if you ask them if they're cops? Is that the law?'"

Frankie scoffed and said ...

"Well, it's not the law. But I told the guy, 'I don't know. Let's go and ask somebody.' I walked with him right up to the nearest dealer, and I asked him whether undercover cops had to tell the truth or not. The dealer said no, and that we should always watch out for narcs, because they could be anybody you might meet. Anyway, that sort of behavior worked well for me. After a while, pretty much everybody stopped asking me if I was a cop."

Frankie frowned and shuffled her feet and added …

"You've probably heard all kinds of crazy stories about working undercover—that you've got some kind of license to break the law left and right, do all kinds of drugs, maybe even kill people, anything just to keep your cover, until you wind up becoming a criminal and an addict yourself. None of that's true. You're not supposed to do anything illegal. And that goes for taking drugs. That's not easy to pull off when you're surrounded by addicts who keep expecting you to do what they're doing."

Riley's mind boggled at how tricky and dangerous that must have been.

"How did you do it?" she asked.

"I developed my own tricks, learned how to fake it. I experimented around with incense and cologne until I found a recipe that smelled pretty much exactly like grass. I kept my clothes saturated with that smell, so people just sort of assumed that I was stoned all the time. It got to the point where nobody paid much attention to whether I was using or not."

Frankie's expression darkened as she continued …

"But one day along came this dealer who called himself Wormwood. From the minute I met him, I felt like he could see right through me. I should have known better than to try to sting him. For one thing, he had three big goons with him, like they were his bodyguards or something."

Frankie inhaled sharply and said, "Finally I scored some smack—heroin—off him. But before I could turn and walk away, he grabbed me by the arm pulled out an hypodermic and demanded that I use the stuff right in front of him. I stammered around, trying to make excuses, until one of his stooges pulled a huge knife and held it to my throat. I had to use right then and there, or else I'd get killed."

Frankie let out a long sigh.

"So—I did it. Before I stuck the needle in my vein, I was scared half to death. I figured Wormwood and his goons would probably kill me as soon as I was high. But then I felt the drug take hold and …"

To Riley's surprise, Frankie wiped away a tear.

"I didn't care if I lived or died," Frankie said.

Frankie choked back a sob and said, "Oh, Riley, you've got no idea what it's like—the euphoria, the bliss, like everything in this rotten world is suddenly perfect and beautiful. If I'd died right then, I'd have died happy."

Frankie paused for a moment to calm herself.

Then she said, "For some reason, Wormwood and his goons didn't kill me. I lay there like a dead woman on my cardboard mat surrounded by homeless junkies until the drug wore off. Then I headed straight to the police station and reported what I'd done. That's the correct procedure, and I didn't get a reprimand. In fact, I got praised for all the good work I'd done until then. It's understood that every undercover agent might face that situation sooner or later. You can't take drugs just to keep your cover, but you're allowed to if it's a matter of life and death. And it sure was a matter of life and death for me."

Frankie shrugged and added …

"That was the end of it. I got taken off the undercover gig, of course. They don't want any cops out there who've ever, ever taken a drug like heroin. It ruins you for good for that kind of work. It's too dangerous. You could get hooked for good."

Frankie squinted thoughtfully for a moment, then continued, "You know, until that happened, I thought I was doing good work. And as scary as it got sometimes, I enjoyed the thrill. But after I'd experienced that incredible high … I realized the whole mission was wrong—the 'War on Drugs,' I mean. It's a war that can't be won. There's got to be some way to deal with all that sickness and suffering. But locking people up isn't the way. All I'd really accomplished during that six months on the street was make life worse for people whose lives were already miserable."

Frankie nodded and said, "So that's why I came to the Academy. Maybe here I'll get the chance to start doing something to really help people. That's all I want from life."

Frankie sat staring off into space.

Riley was stunned by what she'd heard. As traumatic as her own ordeals at the hands of killers had been, they seemed like nothing in comparison to what Frankie had been through.

Finally Frankie laughed nervously and said, "Next time I get started, just tell me to shut the hell up."

"I'm glad you told me," Riley said.

Frankie got to her feet and said, "Come on, let's head on over to the commons room, maybe grab a snack and see what's on the tube."

Riley and Frankie walked down the hall to the commons room. Several other NATs were lounging around, nibbling on snacks from the vending machine, and watching a 24-hour news channel.

Right now on the TV, a reporter was standing in an open field. The banner across the bottom of the screen read …

FBI BROUGHT IN TO INVESTIGATE SECOND MURDER IN WEST VIRGINIA

The reporter held a microphone to a man's face.
Riley recognized him immediately.
She gasped and said to Frankie, "That's Jake Crivaro!"

CHAPTER TEN

As he drove the borrowed police car to Mayor Nelson's home just outside the town of Dighton, Jake couldn't get yesterday's clumsy misadventure with the media out of his mind. The memory still made him cringe.

The eager media crew had caught up with him when he was checking out the murder scene near Hyland. They'd engulfed him with their equipment, and a TV reporter had charged toward him, snapping out questions. Jake had done his best to play it by the book and not say anything that would cause a public panic.

"We don't have sufficient information to share at this time," he'd said when he was asked whether a serial killer was stalking this part of the state.

But the reporter had kept badgering Jake while he and the sheriff were trying to make their way to their car, demanding to know …

"What aren't you telling us? What are you hiding?"

Jake growled under his breath at that particular recollection. He knew the reporter's type all too well—a local hack who fancied himself some sort of crack investigator, anxious to make his name by harassing authorities and maybe someday winding up on the lineup of *60 Minutes*.

As Jake had tried to get away, the reporter stepped into his path so that he couldn't help bump into him—a deliberate move, Jake was sure. The reporter had staggered and almost fallen down, acting for all the world as though Jake had flat-out assaulted him.

Later that night, after he'd settled into a seedy motel room and was watching the TV news, he'd seen the story—an FBI Agent had attacked a reporter who was just trying to do his job.

And of course, Special Agent Erik Lehl had already called Jake to chew him out about that.

Well, Jake knew that Lehl had no use for excuses, and there hadn't been any point in trying to explain that it wasn't his fault. So Jake had followed orders. He'd called the TV station first thing this morning and abjectly apologized.

He wondered if his apology would make the news today.

That had been an inauspicious start to what was turning out to be a pretty lousy day.

Now it was only mid-afternoon, but Jake felt as though he'd already interviewed half of Dighton's inhabitants. He'd asked them all about the local victim, Hope Nelson, and her husband, the mayor.

He'd certainly gotten a variety of responses.

Most people, of course, were shocked by what had happened to Hope—shocked and afraid. Women especially talked about being scared to leave their houses after dark. As gently as he could, Jake had suggested that they were probably wise to stay inside.

Some people seemed to be truly grief-stricken and expressed nothing but admiration for the Nelsons. The high school principal, for example, appreciated how the couple had revitalized the town's economy by introducing grass-fed beef into the area. By switching from traditional to organic methods, a lot of nearby family farms had been saved from going under.

Other people didn't much like the changes. The town barber was sullen about the arrival of "goddamn hippie farmers" like Guy Dafoe. Jake could understand why a barber wouldn't want long hair and shaggy beards to become the local fashion.

Hope's employees at her farm supply store were still badly shaken, and Jake had a hard time reading just how they'd felt about their boss when she was alive. He was sure, though, that none of them wanted her dead.

In fact, Jake didn't sense that anyone in Dighton wished the Nelsons any serious harm. And nobody he asked had even heard Alice Gibson's name, which left any connection between the two murdered women a complete mystery.

He slowed the car, checked his directions, and then turned into the long, private drive leading to the Nelsons' home. It took him past big pastures where Black Angus cattle grazed on the other side of barbed wire fences.

Jake thought wryly …

Nice to see barbed wire put to its proper use.

The drive led to an impressive white farmhouse surrounded by maybe a half a dozen outbuildings. He pulled up in front of the broad, welcoming front porch.

An upright, well-dressed gentleman was standing on the porch waiting for him.

"Right on time," the man said approvingly.

Jake got out of the car and went to shake the hand of Mayor

Nelson. Jake observed that he barely resembled the stunned, stricken, and crumpled man Jake had met at the crime scene yesterday. Instead he definitely had the suave, slightly too-polished demeanor of a politician.

Nelson said, "I'm sorry for putting off meeting you until this afternoon. I've been busy with—well, the business of death, you might say. I'd forgotten what a bureaucratic ordeal the loss of a loved one could be. I've also been getting things ready for a small memorial service we'll be holding here tomorrow."

As the mayor led him through the front door, Jake noted that the mayor hadn't invited him to the memorial service. There was nothing suspicious about that. Grieving people tended to feel uncomfortable with an FBI Agent hanging around. Still, Jake normally made it a practice to attend victims' funerals whenever he could, just to observe the mourners and get a sense of their sincerity.

But there was no point in intruding upon tomorrow's service. If he wasn't wanted there, he'd only make things worse.

Walking through the wide hallway with polished wide-board wooden floors, Jake felt as though he were stepping back into history. They passed a table that Jake was sure must be an expensive antique. In a gilded frame above the table hung an oil landscape painting. Jake had no idea whether it was by someone famous, but it certainly looked old and valuable. The whole place seemed weirdly quiet except for the sound of their footsteps. Jake wondered whether there was anybody else in the entire place.

Finally the mayor ushered Jake into a room so different from the hallway that he had to stop himself from commenting. Apparently the mayor's den or study, this room was furnished with curved red leather sofas sitting on rugs woven with what Jake took to be rather inauthentic Native American designs. Prickly-looking modern lamps hung from the ceiling. A big white Longhorn skull was displayed on one of the paneled walls.

On another wall hung a cluster of photographs, all portraits of stern-looking men. The oldest looked like daguerreotypes, possibly dating back to the Civil War or even before. Jake realized those must be Mayor Nelson's male ancestors, probably including some of Dighton's founders. The Nelsons were clearly what passed for "old money" in this little town.

Nelson offered Jake a seat, then stepped over to a cluster of glasses and bottles on a nearby table. He poured some whiskey into a crystal glass and said …

"You're welcome to some fine old bourbon if you like—although I suppose since you're on duty …"

"Thanks, but no," Jake said.

Jake recognized the label on the bottle Nelson was pouring from. It was a rare and expensive 25-year-old whiskey that must have cost several hundred dollars.

Jake wondered—was Nelson showing off to him?

No, it seemed more likely that Nelson simply had a taste for what he considered the finer things in life.

Expensive whiskey and old cattle skulls, Jake thought.

As Nelson sat down near him, Jake said …

"First let me say that I'm very sorry for your loss."

Nelson said, "Yes, I believe you tried to tell me that yesterday. I'm sorry, I wasn't very … communicative at the time."

"That's more than understandable," Jake said.

Nelson heaved a long sigh and said …

"I suppose you're wondering if I knew anybody who might have wanted to kill Hope. I don't think so. Mind you, as rather prominent figures in this town, my wife and I haven't been universally liked. Small-town piques and differences, if you know what I mean. But I can't think of anyone who might harbor enough bitterness against us to do a thing like …"

His voice faded away, and he looked over at the portraits on the wall as if seeking sympathy from his ancestors. None of them looked very sympathetic as far as Jake was concerned.

Then he said, "This is all my fault."

Jake felt a twinge of expectation.

"How do you mean?" he asked.

Nelson stared into his bourbon and said, "After that woman was killed over in Hyland a week or so ago, I should have known … I should have made sure the town was alert to any danger, especially Hope."

Jake said, "There was no way for you to know. The local police in Hyland even thought they had a suspect."

"I suppose," Nelson said. "But I take my civic duties very seriously. Things like this … well, they just don't happen here in Dighton. And I do mean never, not as long as I can remember. Some years ago, some kids stole a car and committed some vandalism, just for a thrill. There have been no burglaries that I can think of, certainly no rapes or assaults. The only case of manslaughter happened when a couple of drunks got into a bar fight and one of them wound up dead—just a stupid accident, really."

Nelson hunched his shoulders and added …

"Still, I should have been more vigilant."

With a wave toward the portraits he added, "Duty is part of my inheritance, you might say. Hope felt much the same way. She had a rigorous work ethic. And she inspired others to work hard as well …"

Nelson fell silent. Jake could think of a number of questions he might ask. But from long experience, he could tell that Nelson was going to talk quite freely on his own—probably about his marriage, which was what Jake wanted to hear.

Then Nelson's whole face tightened, and he quietly gasped.

The truth is hitting him, Jake realized.

Jake had seen this among many people he'd interviewed over the years. Grief tended to come in terrible waves as the reality of a loved one's death became more and more of a reality.

In a choked voice, Nelson continued …

"I loved her—of course. But more than that, I admired her. She had a rare spirit—especially rare in a sleepy town like this. We got married when she was 18 and I was 35 …"

He chuckled a little and added …

"I know, that sounds stereotypically Appalachian—an older man marrying a teenager. But it wasn't like that. Some 15 years ago, when I'd just become mayor, Warren Gardner came through Dighton campaigning for his first term as West Virginia's U.S Senator. I supported Gardner, but most folks in the area were rather apathetic at first. It was Hope who turned his visit into a big local event, whipped up all kinds of support for him. She and I worked side by side during that campaign."

He smiled and shook his head and said …

"The whole time, I kept thinking, 'What a kid!' I'd known her all my life, but the Gardner campaign was when I fell in love with her, and she with me. When Gardner won the election, we celebrated by getting married. And in all the years since …"

He paused as if he couldn't find the words to describe their happiness.

Then he looked Jake in the eyes and said, "She's been—was—my partner in everything, and more than just politics. We did a lot of business in town, owned a lot of property. I managed the political end of things, but she was mostly in charge of money and business matters. She had more of a brain for that kind of thing than I do. And now that she's gone … well, I can't imagine how I'll manage on my own."

Nelson took a sip of bourbon and pointed to a photo on the table in front of them. It showed a handsome, smiling teenaged boy wearing a prep school uniform.

Nelson said, "That's our son, Ethan. He just started school at Liggett Academy this year."

Jake started a little.

Liggett Academy!

It was one of the most exclusive and expensive preparatory schools in the Washington, DC area. One or two past Supreme Court Justices had gone there.

Nelson continued, "Ethan's coming home for tomorrow's service. When I told him the news, he took it hard, of course. But he's tough and resilient, like his mom. He'll pull through it. As for me, I might be another story. I'm not so young, not so resilient anymore."

Jake asked Nelson a few more questions, but the mayor didn't offer any revealing answers. Jake thanked Nelson for his help, then got into his borrowed car and drove away from the house.

As he approached the open gate at the edge of Nelson's property, he saw a news truck parked just outside the open gate. The news crew was out and about, with all their equipment at the ready.

Jake groaned aloud. He'd been dodging them all day, but of course it had been easy for them to find out where he was right now.

The reporter that he'd bumped into yesterday stepped right in front of his car and Jake pulled to an abrupt stop.

Jake honked his horn. For a moment, nobody moved.

Jake reminded himself …

Running over him isn't an option.

Then, to his relief, the reporter stepped aside and out of his way, still holding out a mike and mouthing an inaudible question

Without a glance in the man's direction, Jake pulled past him and out onto the country road. When he checked his rearview mirror, he saw the team running around like cartoon characters, trying to load the equipment back in the van so they could follow him.

Jake allowed himself a smile. He'd be back in Dighton by the time they got themselves together.

His next stop would the Dighton police station, where he'd return the borrowed car, meet with his forensics team, and arrange for a helicopter to fly them all back to Quantico. Today the team had been to the crime scene near Hyland, but Jake knew they wouldn't have found any evidence there, not after a week of country weather with at least one rainfall.

Tomorrow morning he an appointment for a personal briefing with Special Agent in Charge Erik Lehl …

Not that I've got much to report.

Jake knew he was getting nowhere with this investigation.

I missed something, he thought.

But what was it? Something about the mayor? The man's grief and his love for his wife had seemed sincere. Besides, what connection could Nelson have had with the earlier murder?

Jake heaved a long, weary sigh. His usually reliable gut instincts simply weren't kicking in on this case. He almost wished he had a partner who could give him some feedback, maybe even some new ideas.

He remembered again the reporters asking him if there would be any more murders, and him replying that he didn't have sufficient information for a firm answer.

But at least one person did know—someone who enjoyed inflicting pain and wouldn't abandon his pleasures …

Unless I stop him.

CHAPTER ELEVEN

Riley fought back the dizziness that threatened to slow her down. She was short of breath and her heart was pounding. Still, she rushed ahead.

She was determined to complete this exercise.

Dashing across the gym floor, pausing to crouch beside a plastic cone marker, getting back to her feet, whirling in the other direction, running again—Riley would wind up sprinting a total of 120 yards. Running was hard enough after the grueling work she'd already done this morning, but all the stopping and starting and whirling really made the shuttle run difficult. When she skidded to her final stop, she bent over and put her hands on her knees, swallowing down welcome gulps of air.

Riley wiped her forehead, feeling pretty pleased with herself. Before the shuttle run, she'd completed the required two-mile run without any trouble. That wasn't really surprising. After all, back in DC she'd made the 1.5 mile run that was required for admission to the Academy. She'd also spent a lot of time working out in the gym over the summer. She felt confident about today's tests.

Then she heard the whistle and hurried to line up with the rest of her group at one end of the gym. The trainees stood at attention while instructor Marty Glick paced back and forth in front of them.

He didn't look pleased.

After several long moments of strained silence, Glick barked …

"I swear to God, you guys are a really sorry bunch of NATs, and right now I do mean of the insect variety. Some of you didn't even finish the runs so far—and those who did were as slow as molasses. What the hell am I supposed to do with you guys?"

After a pause, he added …

"Well? Can anybody tell me?"

Since the group was standing at attention, of course nobody could reply—or even shrug.

Riley wondered—was she included in Glick's criticism?

She thought she'd been doing just fine.

Had she been wrong?

Was she "as slow as molasses" as far as Glick was concerned?

Glick shook his head and looked at his clipboard.

He said, "We've still got pushups and sit-ups. You all need to do better."

One by one, he watched as each trainee performed as many regulation pushups as possible before stopping. By the time it came Riley's turn, she felt flustered and unsure of herself.

She drove her tired body as hard as she could, counting 14 pushups in all. When she finished and lay panting on the floor, Glick growled ...

"I'm discounting two of yours, Sweeney. You didn't lower yourself until your upper arms were parallel to the floor."

Riley's discouragement deepened. When it came her turn to do sit-ups she tried to summon up her remaining energy and determination.

This time the goal was to do as many sit-ups as she could do in a single minute—which she guessed would be an easier task than trying to keep on going until she couldn't do any more, like she had with the pushups.

When Glick started the stopwatch to time her, Riley put her hands behind her neck and went to work. With each sit-up, she had to snap upright until her back was perpendicular to the floor, then lower herself until her shoulder blades touched the floor.

She moved fast, getting in as many sit-ups as she could as fast as she could. For a few seconds she amazed herself by how many she was getting done.

But then the seconds seemed to drag out. She found it hard to believe that a whole minute hadn't already passed.

Was Glick tricking her about the time?

Riley was finding it harder and harder to pull her tired body upright.

Finally she heard the whistle signaling her minute was up.

She collapsed on her back and saw the instructor glaring down at her.

"Only 32," he grumbled. "The required number is 35."

Riley fought down a sigh of despair as Glick turned away, ready to time the next NAT.

After the last of the group finished the sit-ups, Glick called them into formation again.

"A lot of you did pretty damned poorly," he said. "Only a handful did really well. You're lucky I don't get to make the rules around here. If I had my way, those of you who failed today would be out of the Academy right now, for good. Whipping you NATs into shape is going to take time away from classes and training. I hate to see that happen."

He read out the names of the group, saying who had passed and who had failed.

Riley had failed.

With her spirits crushed and her body aching from head to toe, she slunk away to the locker room for a hot shower.

While she changed out of her gym clothes, Frankie Dow came up to her and said …

"Don't let it get you down. When you retake the test, you'll do just fine."

Riley sighed and said, "That's easy for you to say. I watched you breeze through with no trouble at all."

Frankie laughed and said, "Maybe it looked like that, but I didn't breeze through anything. That was one long, tough workout."

Riley and Frankie sat down together on a locker room bench.

Riley shook her head miserably said, "I had no idea I was so out of shape."

Frankie patted Riley on the back and said …

"You're not out of shape. I watched you go at it, and I'm sure you're at least as fit as I am. I know, you told me you've been working out all summer. But some of us do have an advantage. We've been training specifically to pass this test."

Riley's mouth dropped open.

"You've been *training* for this?" she said. "Like, you knew exactly what to expect?"

Frankie shrugged and said, "Maybe an unfair advantage. I know some people who've gotten through the Academy. They've told me all the tricks and secrets for surviving here."

"Including how to do sit-ups?" Riley said.

"That's right," Frankie said. "And believe me, it's not just a matter of strength."

"So what did I do wrong?" Riley asked.

"You started off fast to try to get in as many sit-ups as possible, right off the bat," Frankie said. "That doesn't work for sit-ups. You were wasting all your energy in just a few seconds, and you lost your momentum. Instead of rushing into it, you've got to pace yourself. If you do just one sit-up maybe every second and a half, you can keep that going and get through the whole exercise without wearing out. Once you get into the rhythm of it, you'll be surprised at how easy it is."

"Tell me more," Riley said.

But at that moment, Marty Glick came into the locker room and called everybody together for their first class. Frankie promised Riley to share everything she knew as soon as they got a chance.

*

The rest of the day was both exciting and daunting with brief introductory sessions in a wide range of topics—including law, ethics, and behavioral science. In a workshop on operational training, Riley learned some basics in handcuffing, searching, and disarming suspects.

Probably the most interesting session for Riley was the introduction to firearms. The only times she'd ever handled a gun were when she'd hunted with her father near the cabin where he lived in the Virginia mountains. He'd let her hunt squirrels and do some target practice, but only with a .22 caliber rifle.

The whole session was devoted to loading, cleaning, and taking care of a .40 caliber Glock semiautomatic pistol—an entirely new experience for Riley. The first actual target practice was going to be in the next couple of days. Riley wondered how well she would do on that.

Throughout the day, Riley stayed close to Frankie. Like many of the other NATs, her roommate already had experience in law enforcement, so some of what they were learning was already familiar to her. When they got back to their room after dinner, Frankie gave Riley a lengthy rundown of dos and don'ts and miscellaneous tips that could help with the coming 18 weeks of Academy life. Then they both headed on over to the rec room to catch the evening news on TV.

Tonight, there was nothing really new about the recent gruesome murders in West Virginia. The anchorwoman said only that the killer was still at large and definitely dangerous.

Then they replayed part of a tape from the previous night.

In last night's news segment, Crivaro had told the reporter several times …

"We don't have sufficient information to share at this time."

That reporter had seemed awfully pushy to Riley.

Finally, Crivaro seemed to have had enough of his badgering, and he knocked the reporter to the ground …

Or at least he'd appeared to. And of course the local station was playing that footage over and over again tonight.

Looking at it again, Riley found it hard to tell just how bad the incident had really been. Riley knew that Crivaro could be brusque and even temperamental, but she'd never known him to be physically aggressive. She suspected that the reporter had overdramatized the seriousness of his fall.

But the reporter and the anchorwoman had both made a big deal of the incident—even bigger, really, than the murder case itself.

Poor Agent Crivaro, Riley thought.

When she got to bed later that night, Riley found it hard to sleep. Her thoughts kept returning to Crivaro. She wondered how things were going with the case.

Working with him to hunt and stop two vicious killers had sometimes been scary and upsetting—but it had been thrilling as well.

She was surprised to realize …

I wish I was there.

Of course, that was out of the question.

It had only been by chance that Riley had been on those cases at all. She was here at Quantico to become the kind of agent who could legitimately partner with someone like Jake Crivaro.

Or at least so she hoped.

But she knew it was going to be a long, steep climb.

Flunking the physical exam had been a real blow to Riley's confidence. And the rest of the day's activities and classes had made her realize how much she still had to learn.

And now she couldn't help but wonder …

Am I really up to it?

What if I fail?

As she started to drift off to sleep, a procession of monochrome, gray and white faces began to pass through her mind. It took her a few moments to realize who those faces were.

They were the martyred agents whose pictures were displayed on the Hall of honor.

She could hear them whispering to her …

"Don't let us down."

Riley wanted to reply …

"I won't. I promise."

But how could she promise them that?

And if she failed, how was she going to live with herself?

Soon those faces and voices began to swirl around her, and Riley's nightmares began.

CHAPTER TWELVE

When Jake walked into Erik Lehl's office the next morning, he knew right away that the Special Agent in Charge was in a darker mood than usual. The tall, gangly man could be formidable when he was angry.

"Sit," Lehl said.

Jake obeyed uneasily. He was sure he was about to get a dressing-down from the chief.

Lehl swiveled in his chair for a moment, his long legs propelling him vigorously from side to side.

Then he stopped his rotations, stared directly at Jake, and said, "Tell me what happened."

Jake knew without being told exactly what his boss was asking. He wanted to know about Jake's altercation with the news reporter. The local TV station had been running that video footage over and over again, focusing on the frames that made it look like Jake had knocked the man down. Lehl had good reason to hate that kind of publicity.

Jake suppressed a discouraged sigh. He hated making excuses for himself, even when the excuses were true. Maybe he could just swallow his pride and accept the blame and be done with it …

"I'm sorry, sir," Jake said. "It won't happen again."

Lehl scowled at him and repeated, "Tell me."

Jake took a long, slow breath as he wondered …

Will he even believe the truth?

Finally Jake said …

"Sir, I didn't attack that reporter. He was badgering me with questions, which was OK, I'm used to it, and he was just doing his job. But when I tried to walk away, he stepped right in my path, and I couldn't help bumping into him. The camera made it look worse than it was. I'm sure I didn't knock him down. That was play-acting on his part."

Lehl steepled his long fingers and said …

"I see."

He paused and added, "I don't care whose fault it was. It can't happen again."

Jake gulped and said, "It won't, sir."

He hoped he could keep his word about that.

Lehl said, "Now, about what we discussed when we last met—don't you think you'd better look for a partner? Someone who could help keep you out of trouble, at the very least? And who might speed things up on this case? I don't much like the way you're going it pretty much alone right now."

Jake stammered a little, "I—I'll give it serious thought before I go leave Quantico."

"You'd better do more than that," Lehl said.

Jake he knew that Lehl was right. He was spinning his wheels right now with nobody around except a handful of forensics guys. But who could he get to work with him on such short notice? Who was available that he could actually work with?

Jake cringed inside as he remembered what Lehl had said to him the day before yesterday …

"It's about time for you to learn to play nice with others."

Jake hated to admit it, but it was true.

Then Lehl said, "Now tell me about how the case is going."

Jake filled Lehl in on his activities so far. He described his visits to the two crime scenes, and related the autopsy results on the victims' bodies—which hadn't produced any real surprises. The county medical examiner had found traces of chloroform in their lungs, so it looked as though they had been rendered unconscious, but only briefly. After that they had died slowly, and no doubt painfully.

He also described the various interviews he'd conducted so far in Dighton and Hyland, including with Philip Cardin in his jail cell and Mayor Nelson in his expensive home. He also told him about Philip Cardin's missing brother, Harvey, and how the Quantico technicians had so far failed to locate him.

Lehl asked him, "Do you think Harvey Cardin's a viable suspect?"

"I wish I knew," Jake said.

Jake wasn't surprised that Lehl frowned again …

Those are the last words he wants to hear right now.

Lehl fell silent for several long moments.

Then he said, "Tell me about the barbed wire."

Jake said, "The forensics team has analyzed it as well as they could. It's somewhat rusted, so they're sure it's been used, probably on an outdoor fence, and it's at least a decade or so old, and…"

Lehl interrupted, "What *type* of barbed wire is it?"

Jake was surprised by the specificity of the question.

He replied, "It's zinc-coated steel wire. The zinc has deteriorated, which explains the rust and gives the forensics guys an idea of how old it is."

Lehl asked, "Which class is it—1, 2, or 3?"

Jake's surprise grew a little.

"Class 1, I believe," he said.

Lehl nodded and said, "Standard low carbon wire. That explains the deterioration. I believe your guys are right about its age. I know the type well."

"Sir?" Jake asked.

Lehl swiveled in his chair again, then said ...

"I guess you didn't know I grew up on a farm in Nebraska. I spent a whole summer with my father fencing our entire property, digging postholes and stretching miles of barbed wire along the posts. A tough job, especially when it came to corner posts. The wire has to be stretched tighter than a drum."

Lehl took a long, slow breath and added ...

"God, I hate barbed wire."

Jake was truly startled now. It was almost unheard of for Lehl to express his personal feelings about anything at all.

Lehl added, "Still, I've been kind obsessed with it ever since I got all scratched up helping my dad that summer. I've studied its history—and its a damned ugly history. Before it was invented, nobody thought they could tame the Western plains."

Jake thought, *Maybe that would have been just as well.*

Lehl seemed to think the same ...

"Barbed wire fencing carved up the plains into tidy little squares of land. It led to all kinds of trouble between cattlemen and farmers, even some outright violence. And it was hell for Native Americans, who depended on hunting great herds of buffalo."

He squinted thoughtfully and continued ...

"Most people think the buffalo herds disappeared because of too much hunting. That's true as far as it goes. But barbed wire did more than its share, broke up buffalo grazing grounds so they starved to death."

Lehl's expression darkened as he said ...

"And then came World War I, when barbed wire made trench warfare all the more horrifying. And then came World War II, where it was used in the death camps ..."

Lehl smirked ever so slightly.

He said, "Back where I come from, folks sometimes call barbed wire 'the devil's rope.' An apt name for it, if you ask me. I guess you could say barbed wire pushes my buttons. I've never heard of a murder case involving it. But now that we've got one, I'm not surprised. Barbed wire is cruel and violent at its very core. It's hateful stuff."

Lehl paused, then repeated those words …

"'The devil's rope.'"

Jake gulped and said …

"I understand, sir."

But the truth was, he wasn't sure he *did* understand, at least not fully.

For one thing, he sensed that Lehl was leaving something important unsaid.

Jake summoned up his courage and asked …

"Sir, do you know something about this case that you're not telling me? Something I should know?"

Lehl was quiet for a few long seconds.

Then he looked Jake straight in the eye and said …

"Crivaro, you've got to solve this one quickly—and delicately."

Jake stared back at him, waiting for him to explain.

Delicately? he wondered.

Lehl said, "I've been getting some pressure from high places. I'd rather not go into any specifics …"

Jake gently interrupted, "Sir, I think I need to know."

"Very well," Lehl murmured reluctantly. "But what I'm about to say must never leave this room."

Jake's mind boggled.

Why would people in "high places" care about two small-town murders in rural West Virginia?

Jake listened with bated breath as Lehl began to tell him.

CHAPTER THIRTEEN

Vaguely familiar faces swirled all around Riley. Their mouths were moving, calling out to her. She struggled to see who they were and to hear what they were saying.

Then she realized, these were the faces of past FBI Agents who had been killed in the line of duty.

Now she could hear what they kept saying ...

"Don't let us down."

Again and again, Riley opened her own mouth to reply, but no words came out. She realized that was because she didn't know what to say.

Then the faces began to move away from her, but she could still hear their whispers ...

"Don't let us down."

As the faces swirled away into darkness, Riley felt herself getting smaller and younger.

Soon she was a little girl again, and she found herself in a familiar place ...

It was a candy store, and Mommy was spoiling her by buying her lots and lots of candy.

Little Riley laughed with joy.

It was wonderful to see Mommy again ...

But where has she been all these years?

But what did it matter?

It was so wonderful to have Mommy back in her life again—and spoiling her with so much candy!

But then a man stepped toward them—a man with strange, blank-looking features, like a mannequin she might see in a clothing store.

In a moment, little Riley realized ...

He's got a stocking over his head.

And he's got a gun.

She felt her whole body go cold with fear.

The man waved the gun at Mommy and yelled at her ...

"Your purse! Give me your purse!"

Riley looked up at Mommy, who had turned pale and was shaking all over.

Riley wondered ...

Why doesn't Mommy do what he says?

Didn't she understand what terrible danger they were in?

Riley wanted to warn her, but again no words came out of her mouth.

The man looked awfully frightened himself.

Mommy staggered a little, as if she wanted to run but couldn't make her legs move.

Then came a loud noise and a burst of flame from the gun, and Mommy fell to the ground, and deep red liquid was spurting out of her chest, soaking her blouse and spreading in a puddle on the floor.

Riley let out a wild shriek of grief and terror.

She screamed and screamed until she couldn't scream anymore.

Then she heard something behind her—a loud, deep crunching sound.

She turned around—and there was Daddy.

He had an axe in his hand that he was using to split small logs on a tree stump.

He was wearing his full-dress Marine officer's uniform.

She pointed down at Mommy's body and said ...

"Daddy, please do something! Help Mommy!"

Daddy frowned and split another log.

"It's too late to do anything, girl. She's dead. You let her down. You let her die."

Riley gasped with horror at his words.

Then she heard those voices around her again ...

"Don't let us down ... don't let us down ... don't let us down ..."

Riley called out to Daddy and those dead FBI Agents ...

"What can I do? I'm just a little girl."

Daddy chopped another log and said ...

"No, you're not. Not anymore. You're all grown up. It's time you acted like it."

Then Riley realized—it was true. She wasn't a little girl now. She was a woman in her early twenties.

But what could she do, even now?

She couldn't bring Mommy back to life.

As a deep and terrible darkness closed in around her, Riley shouted ...

"What can I do?"

Riley sat bolt upright in her bed, sweating and gasping.

A dream, she realized. *It was just a dream.*

Sunlight was pouring into the dorm room window.

She saw that Frankie wasn't in her bed. She knew that her roommate liked to get up and run laps before classes. But usually Riley was awake by then.

"Oh, my God!" Riley said aloud. "What time is it?"

She looked for her alarm clock on her side table, but it wasn't there. She jumped out of bed and saw the clock lying broken on the floor. She must have knocked it off the table when she was thrashing around during last night's nightmares.

She darted across the room to look at Frankie's clock.

Shit!

She was late!

The day's first activity would have started by now. All her classmates would already be there.

Riley scrambled into her clothes and dashed out into the hallway and down three flights of stairs. Once outside she hesitated for a moment to remember the way to her morning class.

Then she ran.

Finally, she came to a sign that read ...

WELCOME TO HOGAN'S ALLEY
CITY LIMITS

Underneath was the word "CAUTION" and other words in smaller print.

At the bottom in larger letters, the sign also said ...

HAVE A NICE DAY

Riley walked warily past the sign into the area called Hogan's Alley. On the introductory tour yesterday, she'd been struck by how oddly quaint the small town looked, with its barbershop, drugstore, pool hall, a movie theater called the Biograph, a hotel called the Dogwood Inn, rows of storefront businesses, and cars parked along the curbs. There was even a phone booth on one corner—a sight that was getting to be rare in these days of cellphones.

Yesterday there had been quite a few people roaming the

74

streets. But today she didn't see anyone right away. The morning sunlight was shining straight into her face, and it took a few moments for her eyes to adjust.

Then she noticed that she was hardly alone.

A police car was parked a little way up the street. Frankie herself was standing next to the vehicle with a couple of other NATs in Riley's group, all of them wearing FBI vests. Frankie was holding an electric megaphone, and the others had pistols in their hands. More NATs were hiding behind cars, and others crouched on rooftops. Some of them were armed with sniper weapons.

All the weapons seemed to be pointed at her.

Riley gasped, thinking ...

What have I walked into?

Then Frankie called out through the megaphone ...

"We've got the place surrounded, Ivor. This doesn't have to end badly. Just come out with your hands up."

Riley glanced to her left to see who Frankie was calling to. She realized she was standing on a street corner right next to the town bank.

As she watched, two people stepped out of the bank. One was a man, gripping a frightened-looking woman by her arm. He was holding a pistol to the woman's head.

"I've got a hostage!" he yelled back at Frankie.

Now Riley understood—the weapons weren't pointed at her, but at the front door of the bank.

Frankie hesitated for a moment, then called out on the megaphone ...

"I can see that, Ivor. I'll tell you what we're going to do. We're going to send in a hostage negotiator and ..."

The man named Ivor interrupted with a terrified-sounding cackle ...

"Not a chance! I'm the one in charge here! I'm going to walk right out of here quietly, and you're going to let me, or this hostage dies! Do you understand?"

A silence fell over the whole scene.

Nobody seemed to know what to do—including the man, who stood wavering indecisively with his terrified hostage.

Riley wondered whether anybody had even noticed her arrival on the scene.

Probably not, she thought.

She was off to one side and, after all, everybody here had other things on their minds. She still wasn't sure if any of her fellow NATs had noticed her presence. But she was sure the hostage-taker had no idea she was there.

Then a thought began to dawn on her …

Since the hostage-taker has no idea I'm here …

But no, it was a crazy idea …

Don't even think it.

After all, she'd just walked into this situation. What was going on right here was none of her business. She'd shown up too late to be part of it.

On the other hand …

She remembered things she'd heard people say about Hogan's Alley …

"Anything goes."

"No rules."

"All bets are off."

"You make the most of bad situations."

And maybe most important …

"You get an idea, you just run with it."

Riley had an idea, all right.

And maybe—just maybe—she could turn being late to her advantage.

While Riley was wrestling with her decision, the hostage turned her head, and her eyes met Riley's.

The hostage seemed to silently implore Riley …

"Help me! Please!"

Before she knew it, Riley was running down the sidewalk toward the criminal and his hostage. She thrust her fist straight in front of her and hit the criminal on his wrist, sending his gun flying away.

She took hold of the criminal with both hands and yanked him away from the hostage. Then she wrestled the man to the ground.

Something hit her in the side with a stinging "pop."

Her side was soaked yellow liquid.

A paintball, she realized.

She heard another pop, then she looked up in time to see the hostage get hit in the center of the chest, causing an explosion of blue liquid.

But where had those shots come from?

Riley turned and saw that another armed man had come out of the bank door, wielding his own handgun.

He had just shot both Riley and the hostage.

Suddenly the two criminals were standing side by side exchanging fire with the NATs. In a matter of seconds, the men were dripping with red, blue, and yellow dye. But before they'd been hit, they'd managed to splatter several of the NATs with paintballs from their own weapons.

Riley heard a female voice call out …

"Code Red!"

Riley knew that was a signal to stop the exercise—which had already come to a pretty grim conclusion.

Agent Aubrey Rogers, a tactical instructor Riley had met yesterday, came striding toward Riley.

She said, "Want to try that again, Sweeney? You didn't quite get *everybody* killed."

Riley slouched with embarrassment. Some nervous laughter broke out among the NATs, who were now walking toward Riley and Rogers.

"I wouldn't laugh, if I were you," Rogers called out sternly to the group. "Sweeney hit you with a surprise out of the blue. That'll happen in real life more than it happens here. This wasn't just Sweeney's screw-up. Did anybody here even consider the possibility that the hostage taker had an accomplice who was still inside the bank?"

Most of the NATs said no.

Rogers said, "Well, if you had thought about that, maybe this wouldn't have ended in a bloodbath. There were a dozen good ways to handle this situation. The whole bunch of you failed to think of any of them. That'll be all for today. But when you come back for your next session, I want each and every one of you to be able to tell me how you could have done better—even with Sweeney throwing a wrench in the exercise."

As the NATs started to walk away, Riley saw Frankie coming toward her, shaking her head with a grin. Riley grinned sheepishly back at Frankie and started to walk to meet her.

But Agent Rogers said sharply …

"Sweeney, you and I have got to have a little talk."

Frankie gave Riley a pitying look, and Riley followed Agent Rogers down the street. They passed by the three paid actors who had participated in the exercise—the two criminals and the female hostage. They were laughing and playfully wiping some of the dye off of each other's clothing.

As she and Rogers walked, Riley looked around at Hogan's Alley—which was, of course, an extremely detailed mockup of a small town, exactly like a movie set. One building wasn't just a facade, though. It housed a real classroom where trainees were taught tactics. Riley followed Rogers into the classroom.

Riley sat down at a desk, while Rogers paced back and forth in front of her, saying nothing for a few tense moments.

Finally Rogers said, "I hear you had trouble with your fitness test yesterday."

Riley gulped hard.

She hadn't realized that word had gotten around among instructors about her poor performance.

"I'll try to do better next time," she said.

Rogers' lips twisted a little and she said …

"Next time."

Riley felt overwhelmed with dread …

Oh, no.

Maybe there wasn't going to be a next time.

Maybe she was getting kicked out of the Academy right now.

Rogers pulled up a chair and sat down facing Riley. She said in a voice that sounded tight with anger …

"Sweeney, I swear to God, what you did back there was so stupid, it was almost good. But a miss is as good as a mile, as they say. And it *wasn't* good. It was miles away from good. You screwed up, and you screwed up really bad."

"I'm sorry," Riley said, almost in a whisper.

"Sorry doesn't cut it at the Academy," Rogers said.

She paused again, then said, "Hogan's Alley may look like a game, but it isn't one."

"I know," Riley said.

Rogers leaned toward Riley and stared at her.

"No, I'm not sure you *do* know. Let me repeat—Hogan's Alley *is not a game."*

Riley stared back at her silently.

Then Rogers continued, "Back in 1986, there was a bloody, four-minute gunfight in Miami. Two FBI Agents were killed and five were wounded. The Bureau realized that agents needed better tactical training—something realistic and hands-on, where they could act out life and death situations. That's why Hogan's Alley got built in the first place. That's why you and the other NATs come here to learn."

Riley felt as though her heart would sink through the floor.

Again, she thought she heard the voices of those dead FBI Agents …

"Don't let us down."

And now, on her second day of training, Riley felt like she had already let them down.

Rogers said, "I'm going to have to report this stunt you pulled. Meanwhile …"

Rogers was interrupted by the sound of the door opening behind Riley. Riley saw Rogers' eyes open wide with astonishment.

"Oh, my God," Rogers murmured. "Agent Crivaro!"

Riley turned and saw her mentor standing in the doorway.

Rogers stammered, "I hadn't expected … this is such an honor …"

Crivaro interrupted …

"I need to speak alone with Riley Sweeney."

CHAPTER FOURTEEN

Riley's initial surprise almost turned into a giggle of amusement. For several long seconds Agent Rogers just stood there staring dumbly at Jake Crivaro with an awestruck expression. The stern trainer who had so adamantly criticized Riley now seemed unable to speak.

Finally Crivaro said, "Did you hear me? I need to talk to Riley Sweeney alone."

Rogers stammered, "Y-yes sir. Absolutely, sir."

As Riley watched her instructor stumble nervously out of the classroom, she remembered what Frankie had said to her the night before last …

"You do *know that Jake Crivaro's a living legend in the law enforcement profession, right?"*

Riley had thought at the time that maybe Frankie was exaggerating.

But judging from Agent Rogers's reaction to his unexpected arrival, Frankie must have been telling the truth.

Crivaro stood and looked at Riley for a moment, as if he were trying to make up his mind what he wanted to tell her.

Sounding a bit evasive, he said …

"So. Hogan's Alley. They didn't have anything like this when I was in training here. What do you think of it?"

Riley fought down a sigh …

"Right now it's not my favorite thing in the world," she said.

Crivaro scoffed and shook his head.

"Yeah, I was watching the whole thing from around a street corner. Jesus, what a crazy thing to do. Didn't I tell you that you needed to develop some impulse control?"

Riley said, "I guess I'm not making much progress in that department."

Crivaro said, "No, it doesn't look like it."

Another silence fell.

Riley wondered …

Did he come here just to gripe about how I'm doing at the Academy?

If so, there didn't seem much point in hanging around for it.

She said, "I've got to go, or I'll be late to my next class."

Crivaro stepped toward Riley.

"You're not going to your next class," he said.

Riley's eyes widened with surprise.

"I beg your pardon?" she asked, feeling panic rise again. Was Crivaro here to finish the job of expelling her?

Crivaro said, "I talked to Marty Glick, your group instructor. I told him I'm borrowing you for a day or maybe two."

Riley could hardly believe her ears.

"You *what?*" she said.

Crivaro took a deep, long breath and said …

"Maybe you've heard about the two recent murders in West Virginia. The victims wrapped in barbed wire."

Riley started breathing normally again.

She said, "I've seen it on the TV news."

Crivaro let out an embarrassed chuckle …

"Yeah, and I guess you've seen *me* on TV, too. According to the media, I've got my own impulse control issues. But that thing with me and the reporter—believe me, it wasn't what it looked like."

Crivaro put his hands in his pockets and looked out the window at the make-believe street.

He said, "Anyway, I need your help. At this point in a case, my instincts usually kick in and I've got some kind of insight into the killer. That's not happening at all this time, and it worries the hell out of me. There's a serial murderer out there, and the only thing I sense is that he's liable to kill again before I can catch him. But if you come with me and check out the crime scenes, try to get into the killer's head … well, with your natural instincts, I'll bet you pick up on something in no time at all."

Riley was nearly overwhelmed by a cascade of confused and contradictory feelings. Part of her was flattered and proud that Crivaro had come to her instead of countless well-seasoned agents for help. But another part of her felt angry and resentful …

Who does he think he is, charging in here and dragging me away like this?

It didn't seem right.

"I can't do it," Riley said. "I just got here the day before yesterday, and I'm already failing at things. I've got to stay focused, get myself together, start doing better. If I don't, I'll get kicked out."

"You won't get kicked out," Crivaro said. "Glick told me about your problem with the fitness test. You'll ace it next time. And if you just stop doing stupid things, like running rampant into simulated crime scenes, you'll do fine. You're a smart girl."

Riley bristled inside …

"A smart girl?"

She knew Crivaro meant it as a compliment, but it felt condescending. And anyway, she wasn't nearly as confident as he seemed to be that she'd soon be doing better at the Academy. Getting kicked out seemed like a real possibility.

And besides …

"There's another thing," Riley said. "I got a summons from the circuit court for next week. I can't miss that."

Crivaro said, "Yeah, I got one of those too. We're both supposed to testify at Brant Hayman's murder trial. Don't worry, we should be done with this case by then. With some luck, I'll have you back here by tomorrow or the next day."

Crivaro looked at his watch and said, "Anyway, we've got to get going. You need to stop by your dorm room, put together whatever you might need in case you have to spend the night in West Virginia. Come on, let's go."

Crivaro walked out of the classroom.

Riley stood watching him for a few seconds.

I don't have to follow him, she thought.

I don't have to let him tell me what to do.

Then Crivaro turned and called out to her …

"Come on, kid. We've got lives to save."

Those words set off some kind of spark inside her …

"… lives to save …"

The words she'd heard in that dream last night—the words of those dead FBI Agents—rang through her head again …

"Don't let us down."

Suddenly, missing some time at the Academy didn't seem like a big deal.

The next thing Riley knew, she was trotting along to catch up with Crivaro.

*

A short time later, Riley was riding with Crivaro in an FBI vehicle, headed for West Virginia. As Crivaro drove and told Riley

82

more about the case, she looked through a folder filled with reports and crime scene photos.

She found both the folder's contents and Crivaro's words horrifying.

It seemed like only yesterday that she and Crivaro had hunted down the so-called "Clown Killer," the twisted murderer who dressed his female victims as clowns, and who had almost killed Riley herself.

Riley had never imagined that she would ever be faced with that kind of evil again, even if she spent a lifetime in law enforcement.

But these new murders were almost unimaginably vicious …

He wraps them up in barbed wire and lets them bleed to death.

Riley shuddered at the very idea.

After Crivaro finished his grim account of the case, he said in quiet voice …

"'The devil's rope.'"

"Pardon?" Riley said.

Crivaro said, "Erik Lehl told me that's what barbed wire is sometimes called—'the devil's rope.'"

"Sounds appropriate," Riley said, closing the folder.

They drove on in silence for a little while.

Then Riley noticed Crivaro glancing at her left hand.

"You're still engaged, I see," he said.

Riley almost felt like hiding the ring on her finger.

She remembered Frankie recommending that she take it off …

"It's liable to distract you, and you're going to need all the concentration you can muster."

She couldn't help but wonder …

Maybe I should have taken it off.

She said to Crivaro, "You sound surprised."

"Just making an observation," Crivaro said. "The guy you were with in DC? Maybe I can meet him when we get back from West Virginia."

Riley said, "Ryan doesn't live in Quantico. He still works for a law firm in DC. We have … he has an apartment there."

"Oh," Crivaro said.

Riley heard a lot of significance in that single syllable, as if Crivaro suspected that all wasn't well between her and Ryan.

Even so, it seemed like maybe he wasn't going to say anything further about it.

Riley didn't see any reason why she should either.

But she found herself wondering where things really were with Ryan. After two full days of not hearing from him, Riley had received an email from him yesterday. It had been a stiff but polite response to her earlier email, mostly about the work he was doing at Parsons & Rittenhouse.

He'd signed the note, "Love, Ryan," but she hadn't felt a lot of love in his message. And she simply hadn't known what to write in reply. She'd thought about calling him by phone either at work or at home, but she knew she'd only wind up leaving a voice message—and Ryan probably wouldn't call her back.

And if he did call back, were they really ready to talk out their differences?

She remembered something Ryan had said when they'd argued …

"Riley, you've almost been killed twice since I've known you."

Was her choice of a career a fatal obstacle to their future together?

She thought back to something Crivaro had told her once …

"Believe me, getting obsessed with the darkest parts of human nature wreaks havoc on relationships."

Crivaro had seemed almost like a father to Riley at times like those—more so than her actual father ever had. She'd felt like she could talk with him about things that nobody else would understand …

Finally, Riley took a deep breath and said …

"The truth is, I don't know where things are between Ryan and me. We had a fight before I came to Quantico, and we really haven't put things right since then."

"I'm sorry to hear that," Crivaro said. "Living apart like you two are can't be easy, especially when you're just getting started in life. I guess your future depends on how much you want each other to be happy, how much you'll put into that."

Riley sighed as she watched the Virginia landscape roll by outside.

She said, "I think the only thing I could do to make Ryan happy is to give up the whole FBI thing, settle down to some nine-to-five job that I don't bring home with me, start having kids as soon as possible."

Crivaro let out a grunt of disapproval.

"That doesn't sound so good," he said. "The life of an FBI

84

Agent is … well, not like that at all. It's crazy and unpredictable—and I don't need to tell you it's dangerous. As for having kids …"

Crivaro's voice faded away.

Then he said, "Well, I don't guess I've got any business giving you any advice. My own relationships never turn out too well—not even ordinary ones with my partners."

Then he chuckled and added …

"You know, Chief Lehl tells me I need to learn to play nice with others."

Riley laughed and said, "What a weird thing for a boss to say."

Crivaro shook his head.

"Not so weird," he said. "I put people off, I push people away, I expect too much, and I get impatient. I wonder if maybe …"

He paused, as if searching for the right words.

"Maybe I can't relate to people who aren't as passionate as I am, aren't as committed. My work is everything to me. My wife wasn't like that at all, and my son sure isn't. They couldn't understand why I would be. And that's not their fault. In fact, it's probably not a fault at all. They're perfectly normal, just like regular folks. She's settled into a happy marriage, and he's going into real estate. They're going to live stable, normal lives."

He laughed again and said, "Maybe I just can't *do* normal."

Riley smiled as a comfortable silence fell between them. She felt good, talking openly like this. And she sensed that Agent Crivaro felt the same way. He wasn't the kind of man who normally let his guard down, talked about his feelings.

Maybe we can do each other some good, she thought.

She was starting to feel really glad that Crivaro had yanked her away from Quantico, at least for a day or two—glad, and more than a little bit special.

Before too long they were driving up into the Appalachian Mountains, and they passed a sign for an exit to the town of Milladore.

She said to Crivaro …

"My dad lives in a cabin up in the mountains near that town."

Crivaro said, "A cabin in the mountains. Wow. That sounds great. I kind of envy him. Maybe I can meet him someday."

Riley frowned and said nothing.

She couldn't remember ever wanting to introduce her father to anybody.

If Agent Crivaro had a problem "playing nice with others," her father was much worse. He didn't get along with anybody at all—including Riley. Living the life of a hermit outdoorsman suited him just fine.

But she wondered … what would happen if she introduced Crivaro to her father? They were two crusty, cantankerous men. Her father had been as passionate about serving in the Marines as Crivaro was about being an FBI Agent. Maybe they'd really get along.

But Riley didn't feel ready to try to find out.

Maybe someday, Riley thought.

*

Not long after they'd crossed the state line into West Virginia, they pulled into the sleepy little town of Dighton, where Hope Nelson had lived. It was smaller than Lanton, the West Virginia town where Riley gone to college. It was more like Slippery Rock, the town where she had lived when she was a little girl.

It was hard to imagine that two brutal murders had taken place anywhere near here.

Agent Crivaro drove through the town without stopping and continued out into the country. Finally Crivaro pulled a car to a stop beside a pasture where several Black Angus cattle were grazing.

They got out of the car and walked toward the fence at the edge of the pasture.

Riley looked up and down the fence, until her eye lighted on one particular post.

Remembering the photos she'd looked at during the drive, she realized …

It was right here.

This was where she was Hope Nelson's body was found.

Riley hesitated.

Did she really want to sense anything about a ruthless killer who used barbed wire on his victims?

CHAPTER FIFTEEN

As she stood next to the barbed wire fence, Riley began to feel as though a deep and fearful darkness was closing around her. Although it was still mid-afternoon, it was easy to imagine how the place must have looked at night, when the killer had brought Hope Nelson's body to this out-of-the-way place. She shuddered slightly at the image that was forming in her mind.

Crivaro touched her on the shoulder and said …

"You know what to do."

Riley nodded. She did know exactly what she had to do next.

During the other times they'd worked together, Crivaro had discovered that they shared an unusual ability. They could sometimes tap into an earlier event and sometimes actually learn what a killer had felt and done. It was a gut sensation, a combination of perception, intuition, and imagination. He had taught her how to use that talent.

She remembered that the first time she'd done this, it had helped to close her eyes.

But this time she decided to keep her eyes open, in order to retrace the killer's movements as well as she could.

She walked back over to the road and said to Crivaro …

"He stopped his vehicle over here—probably a pickup truck or an SUV."

She imagined opening the back hatch or gate of the vehicle.

Inside was poor Hope's body, bound up tightly by duct tape and barbed wire and …

Anything else?

He couldn't very well have wrapped his arms around the spiky package without causing himself considerable injury.

She looked down at the ground between her and the fence.

She saw where the grass seemed to be matted down from something being dragged across it. But the earth wasn't gouged or torn up anywhere that she could see.

She said to Crivaro …

"I think the body was wrapped up in a blanket. He used the ends of the blanket to help him lower it out of the vehicle and drag it across the ground."

87

She walked along the matted path toward the fence post, trying to imagine herself hauling the heavy load along with her—scooting and lifting it in fits and starts. He was a strong man, she thought, but not necessarily very tall or heavy.

When she got to the fence post, she noticed a large sixteen-penny nail pounded part of the way into the top. Remembering the photos, she continued ...

"He let the blanket fall away from the bundle, then he pounded this nail here. He tied a length of slender rope to the bundle—clothesline, maybe. He passed the line around the nail in order to hoist the victim off the ground. Then he tied it fast. He stood here looking at his handiwork and ..."

Riley paused, wondering ...

And what?

A strange feeling started to come over her—or rather a lack of feeling.

It seemed like a kind of emotional numbness.

She stammered, "I think ... he felt spent. Whatever joy or excitement he'd felt while he'd been torturing her was over by the time he'd brought her here. She was dead now, so the thrill was gone. He was just finishing up. Or ..."

She paused again.

Crivaro said, "Or what?"

Riley sighed deeply and said, "Or maybe the numbness is just me. Maybe I'm just not connecting with him."

Crivaro patted her on the shoulder again.

"It's OK," he said. "Let's give it another try."

Riley walked through the exercise again, this time with Crivaro giving her more verbal prompts along the way. But it ended the same way—with a curiously empty feeling as she imagined how the killer might have felt while staring at his grisly handiwork ...

No pride, guilt, triumph, shame ...

"I just don't feel much of anything," she said, staring at the fence post again.

"That might be accurate," Crivaro said, "Maybe he didn't feel anything either. Like you said, the most exciting part was over for him. What he'd done here might have felt like a letdown, just some drudgery to get over with. Or ..."

Crivaro shrugged and added, "Or maybe you're right, and you're just not getting any connection. Don't be too hard on yourself. I didn't get anything here either. You're not trying to work

88

miracles here. There's nothing magical about it. It's all about intuition—and sometimes intuition doesn't come when we want it to."

Riley squinted thoughtfully and said, "What really matters is how he felt when he was really engaged with the victim, when she was still alive. I mean, was it just pure cruelty and sadism, like the Clown Killer? Or was it … something else? I wish we could go to where Hope was abducted, or where he wrapped her up and tormented her to death."

Crivaro let out a dismayed growl.

"Unfortunately, we don't have any idea where those two things happened. But don't worry, we can still check the other crime scene. You might get more of a hit there. Meanwhile, we'd better drive into town, check in with Chief Messenger, see if his men have found anything new."

Crivaro drove them back into the little town of Dighton. When they walked into the small police station, a couple of cops looked up from their desks. Crivaro asked them where he and Riley could find the chief, and they said he was in his office.

The office door at the back of the station was partially open as Riley and Crivaro walked toward it.

Riley heard a man's voice say …

"I'd expected Senator Gardner to be at Hope's memorial service yesterday."

Another man's voice snapped back …

"Why would you expect that?"

Sounding flustered, the first man said …

"Well, I just thought …"

The second man sternly interrupted, "Well, don't think about it. And don't talk about it. You know better than that."

Crivaro rapped lightly on the door and gently pushed it open. Two men were standing there, looking startled and upset.

The shorter of them was wearing a police uniform. Riley thought he looked a bit like Agent Crivaro. The taller of the two men was wearing an expensive-looking suit.

Crivaro introduced them as Chief Graham Messenger and Mayor Mason Nelson—Hope Nelson's husband.

As Crivaro asked for any news about the case, Riley felt a palpable awkwardness between the mayor and the police chief—and also more than trace of anxiety.

Riley's instincts hadn't kicked in at the crime scene, but right now her gut was telling her something quite clearly. Just now the chief had been saying something the mayor had disapproved of—and now they were both uneasy about having been overheard.

We walked in on something.

We heard something we weren't supposed to hear.

There was nothing new about the case to discuss, so Riley and Crivaro headed back to the car. As Crivaro started to drive away, Riley said …

"Something was going on back there."

"I don't know what you mean," Crivaro said.

Riley thought for a moment, recalling the chief's words …

"I'd expected Senator Gardner to be at Hope's memorial service yesterday."

Riley said, "Warren Gardner—isn't he one of West Virginia's U.S. senators? Yeah, he's always pushing some kind of religious agenda—school prayer, putting the Ten Commandments in government buildings, all that kind of thing."

"If you say so," Crivaro said. "I don't pay much attention to politics."

Riley said, "Just when we were walking in, Chief Messenger said something about the senator not coming to Hope Nelson's funeral."

"I didn't hear it," Crivaro said.

"Well, *I* sure did," Riley said. "And the mayor got upset that Messenger even mentioned it. And both of them seemed upset when we showed up at that moment."

"You're imagining things," Crivaro said.

Riley was surprised by the tightness in Crivaro's voice.

"No, I don't think I am," she said. "We need to go back there. We need to ask them …"

Crivaro interrupted sharply, "No, we don't. Whatever they were talking about was none of our business."

Riley began, "But I've got this feeling …"

Crivaro broke in again, his voice louder …

"Your feelings are out of whack today. You admitted it yourself. Whatever the chief and mayor were talking about, it's none of our business."

"But—"

"Leave it the hell alone, Riley. A detective's got to ignore stupid things that just don't matter, even when your gut tells you otherwise. You need to learn that. You've got a lot to learn."

Then in a low growl he added …

"Too much, maybe."

A long silence fell between them. Riley was startled by Crivaro's sudden coldness. After they'd driven for a little while, Crivaro took a turn onto the Interstate, taking them eastward, back toward Virginia.

Riley asked, "Aren't we going to the other crime scene near Hyland?"

"No," Crivaro said. "We're through for the day. I'm taking you back to Quantico."

Riley felt a chill at the note of finality in his voice. She wished he would explain why he was being so short with her. But she sensed that there was no use in trying to get him to tell her …

He's angry enough as it is.

As they drove on in silence, Riley remembered what the mayor had said to Chief Messenger …

"Well, don't think about it. And don't talk about it. You know better than that."

Despite Crivaro's objection, Riley felt sure that the exchange was important somehow.

She wished she knew why.

*

Riley and Crivaro said little to each other during the rest of the drive back to Quantico. She couldn't understand what had changed so much between them during the course of a single day. On the way to West Virginia, their conversation had been easy, relaxed, and more than friendly. Riley had spoken openly some troubling personal issues, and she'd thought that Crivaro had opened up to her as well.

In fact, he'd almost been acting like the father she'd always wanted.

But now …

Riley sighed deeply.

Now he seemed scarcely any different from her actual father—cold, bitter, angry, and silent.

When Crivaro dropped her off at the dormitory, Riley stood staring at the building with her go-bag slung over her shoulder. It wasn't very late, and she guessed that Frankie would be in their room studying. Riley felt as though she and Frankie had gotten surprisingly close during the short time they'd known each other.

Maybe I can talk to her about today, Riley thought.

But then she remembered the humiliating episode in Hogan's Alley—how Frankie had conducted herself with professional poise while calling out to the hostage-taker over the bullhorn.

Riley, by contrast, had rushed in where she wasn't supposed to be, and the exercise had ended in disaster. Even Frankie had gotten "killed" in the resulting melee.

Riley thought …

Frankie's got no reason to be sympathetic with me right now.

Riley sat down on the building's front steps with her bag at her side. The truth was, she didn't feel a lot of sympathy for herself right now. She'd blown her fitness exam yesterday, had made a fool of herself in Hogan's Alley, and …

She really didn't know what she'd done wrong in West Virginia to make Crivaro so angry. But maybe that was part of the problem …

I'm making mistakes without even knowing it.

She realized she couldn't bring herself to go inside and face Frankie right now.

She wasn't sure whether she could face anybody at Quantico tomorrow morning.

She made what felt like a fateful decision, then took out her cellphone and called for a cab.

She knew where she was going tonight.

What she didn't know was …

Am I ever going to come back?

CHAPTER SIXTEEN

Dusk had fallen by the time Jake Crivaro drove across the state line into West Virginia. During the entire drive, he'd been brooding about Riley Sweeney. He felt bad about being so cold toward her during the drive back to Quantico, and he was sorry he couldn't tell her the reason for it.

But that was impossible.

He remembered Erik Lehl's stern order during their last meeting …

"What I'm about to say must never leave this room."

And once Lehl had told him what he had to say, Jake understood exactly why it had to be kept secret.

Unfortunately, Riley had overheard the tense exchange between the mayor and the police chief. Chief Messenger had said …

"I'd expected Senator Alsop to be at Hope's memorial service yesterday."

And Mayor Nelson had gotten testy about it …

"Don't think about it. And don't talk about it. You know better than that."

Jake sighed and muttered under his breath …

"Why does that kid have to be so good?"

Any other rookie would have thought nothing of what she'd heard. But Jake knew all too well that Riley Sweeney wasn't just any other rookie …

She doesn't miss a trick.

In fact, he was pretty sure that her natural instincts were about as good as his own. That was why he'd pushed her into the Honors Internship Summer Program and then into the FBI Academy.

But now what was he going to do with her?

She's a diamond in the rough, he thought.

But she was a whole lot rougher than most rough diamonds, prone to rash decisions and sometimes too keenly sensitive and observant for her own good. Was Jake enough of a jeweler to shape that diamond into its potential shape?

Maybe not …

Maybe she's more than I can handle.

He noticed that he was approaching a freeway exit for the town of Milladore. Riley had pointed out that town during their drive to Quantico …

"My dad lives in a cabin up in the mountains near that town."

It occurred to Jake that he actually knew very little about Riley Sweeney—where and how she had grown up, the kind of experiences that had made her who she was. And he knew nothing at all about her father.

Without quite knowing why, Jake swung his car into the exit lane and continued on his way to Milladore. When he passed the sign for the town line, he quickly saw that this was a sleepy little Virginia town—similar to those in West Virginia where he'd been investigating the murders. Milladore was bigger than Hyland, he thought, but probably smaller than Dighton.

Not that it really mattered …

What am I doing here, anyway?

It occurred to him that he'd been driving for hours now, and maybe it was time for a little break. He parked in front of a little bar called Roy's Tavern. He walked into the smoky interior and saw that it was a slow business night. A couple of middle-aged men were playing pool, and another was sitting at the bar talking to the bartender. There didn't seem to be anybody else in the place.

Jake sat down at the stained and spotted wooden bar and ordered a beer. As the bartender filled a mug from a tap, Jake noticed that the man sitting next to him was eyeing his sidearm.

In a somewhat suspicious voice, the customer said …

"I take it you work with the law."

Jake nodded and took out his badge.

"Special Agent Jake Crivaro, FBI," he said. "Don't worry, though. I'm not here on business."

The bartender and the customer chuckled.

"Well, I guess we should be relieved," the bartender said.

The customer said, "If you don't mind my asking, what *does* bring you through Milladore? People don't often stop in this Podunk for no good reason."

Jake chuckled and lifted his mug.

He said, "I just wanted a beer. Is that enough of a reason?"

The bartender said, "Well, I guess you came to the right place."

Jake sat sipping his beer in silence for a few moments. He felt a growing itch of curiosity.

Then he asked, "Do either of you happen to know a guy named

Sweeney?"

The bartender and the customer looked at each other with surprise.

"Sweeney?" the bartender said.

"You mean Oliver Sweeney?" the customer said.

Jake shrugged and said, "I guess. The Sweeney I'm talking about lives in a cabin not far from here."

The bartender laughed and said, "Yeah, that would be Oliver Sweeney."

The customer squinted at Jake and asked, "Are you sure you're not here on law business? Because I can't remember anybody coming through Milladore asking about Oliver Sweeney. Did he maybe do something he shouldn't have?"

Jake felt his curiosity rising.

"Not that I know of," he said. "What can you tell me about him?"

The bartender started drying some glasses and said, "Not much, I don't guess. We don't see a lot of Sweeney here in town. He comes in to buy a newspaper, or shows up over at the local VFW from time to time—not that he's especially welcome there. He's got kind of a temper, that guy. Tends to get into fights."

Jake was fascinated now …

Riley's father—a brawler?

He asked, "How might I get in touch with him?"

The customer shook his head.

"I don't reckon you can," he said. "And I'm not sure why you'd want to. He's kind of hermit-like, doesn't have a phone. You'd have to go up on the mountain and roust him out of his cabin."

Then with a chuckle the customer added …

"That's a course of action I don't exactly recommend."

Jake's eyes widened with interest.

"Actually, I think I'd like to do just that," he said. "Can you give me some directions?"

The customer seemed reluctant.

"Oh, I don't know about that, mister," he said.

But the bartender was more obliging.

He pointed and said, "Drive out of town that way, and pretty soon you'll come to Elk Hill Road. Turn right and continue up into the hills for a couple of miles. Eventually you'll see a mailbox on your left with the initials OS and some numbers painted on it. That

95

marks the drive that leads up to Sweeney's cabin."

Jake swallowed the rest of his beer and put down money for a tip.

"Thanks," he said. "I'll be going now. You folks have a nice evening."

The bartender called after Jake as he walked away from the bar.

"Now wait just a minute, mister. You're not planning to go up there right now, are you?"

"Why not?" Jake asked.

The customer shrugged and said, "It's night, that's why not."

Jake felt a jolt of surprise.

This was starting to seem like the beginning of some Dracula movie …

What is this Sweeney guy, a vampire?

The bartender said, "Just wait till morning, why don't you? There's a little motel over on the edge of town. It's always got vacancies. Put up there for the night."

Jake smiled and said, "I'll do that. Thanks again."

Of course, as he left the bar and got into his car, Jake had no intention of spending the night here in Milladore. He needed to be back in Dighton before morning. He drove out of town until he came to Elk Hill Drive and turned left. It was a gravel road that wended its way along a sharply sloping hillside.

The night was overcast and very dark. Jake drove what seemed like more than the couple of miles the bartender had mentioned and felt like he was in the middle of nowhere.

Did I miss it? he wondered.

Finally, he spotted what he was looking for—a mailbox with the painted letters and numbers on the left. The road beyond the mailbox was dark.

He turned past the mailbox and continued along a twisting stretch of dirt road. For a while he was beginning to think that the guys at the bar had sent him on a wild goose chase.

Finally his headlights revealed a small cabin in a clearing. No lights were on inside. Again, Jake wondered if he'd been sent up here as a joke. But Riley had said her father lived in a cabin in the woods, and this sure was exactly that.

He parked, turned off the engine, and got out of his car.

In the darkness he heard the cabin door open and a snarling voice call out …

"Who the hell are you? What do you want?"

96

Jake called back in a pleasant voice …

"I'm just here on a friendly visit."

"I don't think so," the voice yelled back.

Just then Jake saw a flash from the front door and a heard the loud bang of a shotgun …

He's shooting at me! Jake thought.

CHAPTER SEVENTEEN

It was quite late as Riley walked briskly along the city sidewalk. The few other people who were out tonight didn't look particularly friendly, but the streets in this neighborhood were familiar and not any more threatening than they'd been …

Before, she thought.

Back in the summer, when I lived here full time.

With Ryan.

As she neared her destination, she wondered …

What do I think I'm doing here now?

She felt as though she'd been driven by some mindless impulse ever since Crivaro had dropped her off in front of the dorm. Instead of going back to her room, she'd caught a cab to the Quantico Amtrak station, taken the first train she could get to DC, then caught the subway that brought her here.

She discovered that she had no answer to her own question about what she was doing here. All she knew for sure was that she wanted to resolve *something* after such an awful day—her botched performance at Hogan's Alley that morning and then her failure to pick up any gut feelings at the crime scene in West Virginia.

Worse still, she didn't know exactly why Agent Crivaro was so angry with her, and he didn't seem interested in explaining it to her.

She thought that maybe Ryan had been right all along.

Maybe I don't belong in the FBI. Maybe going to the Academy was a big mistake.

Deep inside, she still didn't quite believe that, but she was driven by an overwhelming need to get something right. And there seemed to be only one thing she could hope to accomplish tonight—and that was to settle things with Ryan.

What "settling things" might mean, she had no idea.

All she knew was that his belated reply to the email she'd sent him on her first night at Quantico had been as cold as cold could be. It was time to find out where things really stood between them.

As she approached the apartment building, she saw that lights were on in their basement apartment.

She stopped in her tracks for a moment.

He's home, she thought.

Part of her had been hoping Ryan would still be at the law office working late tonight. That would give her some time alone in the apartment to figure out exactly what she wanted to say to him …

Because I sure don't know right now.

Riley took out her keys and opened the outside door to the building. Then she went down the stairs into the basement hallway and stood outside their apartment door.

She could hear jazz music playing inside. She figured Ryan must be sitting at the kitchen table working on stuff that he'd brought home.

She hesitated again and asked herself …

What am I going to say?

She fingered her engagement ring and considered a bold approach.

She'd just take off her ring and hold it out to Ryan and say …

"Do you want this back? Because it's time to decide."

She sighed as she realized she simply didn't have the guts to do that—and besides, it might have disastrous results.

But then, so might anything else she did or said.

She realized …

I've just got to play it by ear.

Riley took a deep breath to summon up her courage.

Should I knock?

Of course not, this is my apartment too.

She put her key in the lock and turned it and opened the door.

As the door swung open, Riley took a step backward at what she saw.

She dropped her go-bag on the floor.

Ryan was sitting on the couch, and a young woman was sitting close beside him.

They looked as surprised as Riley felt.

Ryan said, "Riley! I hadn't expected you home!"

Obviously, Riley thought.

But she couldn't think what to say, so she just stood there, staring.

Papers were spread out on the coffee table, along with legal pads bearing handwritten words and scribbles.

Ryan scrambled up from the couch, hurried toward Riley and tried to give her a hug.

She didn't hug him back.

The woman got to her feet too, and gave Riley a disarmingly warm smile. Like Ryan, she was wearing jeans and a t-shirt. She had short hair and a boyishly attractive face and was wearing reading glasses.

The woman said, "I'm glad to meet you, Riley. I'm Brigitte Carr, another entry-level lawyer at Parsons & Rittenhouse. Ryan and I have been doing a lot of work together."

Ryan was red-faced and obviously embarrassed, and of course Riley was deeply flustered. By contrast, Brigitte seemed remarkably cool and composed.

Before Riley quite knew it, she was shaking hands with the woman.

Ryan said, "Um—I'm glad to see you, Riley. What brings you home?"

Riley felt all her hopes for sorting things out with Ryan crashing all around her …

There's no way that's going to happen now.

Riley stammered, "I—I realized … I forgot to take some things with me. I came back to get them."

She dashed into their bedroom and shut the door. She realized she was hyperventilating, so she tried to bring her breathing under control.

What's going on here? she wondered.

She glanced around the room, looking for telltale signs that Ryan and Brigitte might be sleeping together. The bed was unmade, which was no surprise. Ryan seldom made the bed. She didn't see any suspicious items of clothing …

Was it possible that Brigitte really was here just to do some work with Ryan?

Without quite understanding why, she murmured to herself …

"Does it *matter* why she's here?"

Somehow, Riley felt that the woman's presence couldn't possibly be a good thing—not even if her visit was perfectly innocent.

The bedroom door opened and Ryan came in.

In an agitated voice he asked, "Riley, what's going on?"

Riley said, "I was wondering the same thing."

Ryan said, "This isn't what you're obviously thinking. Brigitte and I work closely together, and we've got a huge workload right now, and we needed to work late, so we decided to do it here. That's all that's going on. Really."

100

Riley looked into his eyes, trying to determine whether he was telling the truth.

She felt an odd shiver as she realized …

I can't tell.

It wasn't the first time her instincts had conked out on her today. But this felt worse than her failure to connect with the killer back at the crime scene in West Virginia. If she couldn't even tell whether her own fiancé was lying, what kind of FBI Agent could she ever hope to be?

She said, "Look, I came here to talk, find out where things were between us. Obviously this isn't a good time."

Ryan said, "No, I don't guess it is. You're right, we *do* need to talk, but …"

He shrugged and fell silent.

She could almost hear him saying the words, "Not now."

"I thought …" Riley began.

But she realized she didn't know exactly what she'd thought. Had she believed that everything was ever going back to some kind of normal between them?

Ryan said, "Just give us a little time to finish up. Then you and I can sit down and talk."

A storm of mixed feelings made Riley's head whirl. She couldn't understand why she was so upset, but she knew she couldn't stand to stay here another moment.

"I'm going now," she said with as much dignity as she could muster. "Let's talk sometime soon."

She hurried out of the bedroom and through the living room, toward the door.

Brigitte was still there, poring over the law papers. She glanced up over her reading glasses at Riley.

"Leaving so soon?" Brigitte asked.

"Yeah, I've got to get going," Riley said breathlessly.

"It was nice meeting you," Brigitte said cheerfully.

Riley picked up her go-bag and rushed out of the apartment.

Feeling lost and dazed, she headed straight for the subway stop and boarded the next train back to Union Station. As she took a seat, Riley struggled to understand what had just happened, what she had just seen.

Most of all, why she was so upset about it?

Were Ryan and that woman sleeping together, or … ?

"Stop it," she murmured aloud to herself.

At long last, a sad truth seemed to dawn on her.

It really didn't matter whether Ryan was having an affair. In a way, it would almost be better if he were.

What mattered was that he was sharing the evening with someone who shared his interests and goals …

In our apartment.

They were talking together about things that Riley knew nothing about.

And Ryan certainly knew and cared nothing about Riley's life.

The lesson of the last few days suddenly seemed starkly clear …

We don't have anything in common.

There wasn't even anything for them to talk over.

As the train started on its way, Riley looked again at the ring on her finger and thought …

I should have given it back.

But she couldn't very well stop the train and go running back to the apartment to do that …

Maybe I'll mail it to him or something.

Or maybe she could give it to him whenever she went back to the apartment to gather up her belongs—whenever that might be.

Right now, Riley's whole future felt like some kind of a black hole leading to nowhere.

CHAPTER EIGHTEEN

Jake felt a surge of adrenalin as he scrambled behind his car and pulled out his own sidearm. The gunshot blast had come from the cabin.

Now the strong beam of a flashlight clicked on from the doorway, searching around for him.

What have I walked into? he wondered.

He thought that he must have arrived at the wrong cabin in spite of following directions. Or maybe the guys at the bar had sent him into dangerous territory on purpose. Could this could be the hideout of a drug dealer or some other criminal?

Because if this was Riley's father, why would he be so hostile?

The rough voice from the cabin shouted …

"I'm asking one more time before I blow your head off—who are you?"

"My name's Jake Crivaro," he said.

He hesitated before adding …

"I'm a Special Agent with the FBI."

The man called back, "FBI? Well, you've sure as hell got the wrong man, then."

"I'm not here to arrest you," Jake yelled. "I'm not here on FBI business at all. Are you Oliver Sweeney?"

Jake heard a loud scoff from the doorway.

"That's *Captain* Oliver Sweeney to you—retired from the U.S. Marine Corps, 'Nam combat veteran, and if you ask around these parts, you'll hear I'm downright antisocial. Now get on out of here. I fired that first shot in the air. This is a Browning Citori stacked-barrel shotgun, and I've got another shell loaded, and my finger's feeling a little itchy on this pretty gold-plated trigger. I won't miss next time."

Jake called out, "Like I said, this is just a friendly visit.

"I'm not entertaining any visitors these days," the man called back.

The roving flashlight beam caught Jake's feet. Even though Jake was behind the car, he knew Sweeney could see him. If he stepped suddenly out in the open, he'd be an easy target.

This wasn't a good idea, he thought.

It would be best to try to slip away before things got out of hand.

"All right, suit yourself, I'm not here to make trouble," Jake said, holstering his sidearm. "I'll stand up slowly with my hands in view, so don't shoot."

Jake stood up with his hands held high and walked toward the car door.

Jake added, "I'll just get back in the car and drive on out of here. Have a nice evening, OK? Sorry for any inconvenience."

As Jake put his hand on the car door handle, Sweeney said …

"Wait just a minute. You didn't tell me what you're here for."

Squinting in the flashlight beam, Jake could now see that Sweeney had lowered his shotgun.

Jake said, "I thought maybe we could talk about your daughter Riley."

Sweeney laughed coarsely.

"What about?" he said. "You want to ask for her hand in marriage? You look a little old for her—not that I give a damn. She can marry whoever she pleases as far as I'm concerned."

With his hands still up, Jake began to walk cautiously toward the cabin.

"It's nothing like that," he said. "I'm sort of her mentor, you might say. She's training to become an FBI Agent, in case you didn't know."

"No, I didn't know," Sweeney said. "Last I heard she was still at college in Lanton. A couple of her friends had gotten murdered by some psychotic killer. She came up here and told me about it, I taught her a little Krav Maga so she could defend herself. I hear the killer got caught eventually."

"Catching the killer was mostly her doing," Crivaro said.

Jake was standing right in front of Sweeney now. He saw that the retired Marine captain was a big, muscular man who still maintained his military bearing. Jake thought he noticed a flicker of pride on his weathered face.

"You don't say," Sweeney said. "Come on inside, sit down and rest for a minute."

Jake followed Sweeney into the little cabin, its single room lit by a couple of gas lanterns. Jake took a seat in a rather uncomfortable straight-backed chair. Sweeney produced a bottle and a couple of glasses from a cabinet.

Sweeney poured the contents of the bottle into a glass.

He said, "I don't have anything to drink except some fresh-pressed cider. I get my own apples from an old orchard that's up the mountain a bit."

"That'd be fine," Jake said, taking the glass that Sweeney handed to him.

He took a sip of the cider and was startled by its tart, potent kick …

Hard cider.

Jake figured he'd better go easy on the stuff if he wanted to make the drive back down the mountain in one piece.

Sweeney pulled up another chair and sat facing him. In the flickering lamplight, Jake could see that he bore a startling resemblance to Riley.

Sweeney said, "So what did she do, drop out of school? If so, I'm glad of it. A degree in psychology—what the hell good is that?"

Jake almost began to explain that Riley hadn't dropped out of Lanton—that she'd graduated earlier this summer. But then he remembered …

He wasn't at her graduation.

For all Jake knew, Riley hadn't even invited him.

Jake said, "Your daughter's got some impressive natural abilities. I noticed that when she helped me catch the killer. She's got rare instincts, and I want to help her develop them. You see …"

Jake was about to explain Riley's ability to get into a killer's mind when Sweeney interrupted …

"I know. She's a hunter. Like me. I raised her that way."

Jake fell silent. He didn't know what to say.

Sweeney took a sip of cider, then said …

"Tell me, Crivaro. Do you have any kids?"

Jake shifted on his chair a bit uncomfortably.

He said, "Uh, yeah—a son named Tyson, about Riley's age."

"What kind of relationship have you got with Tyson?" Sweeney asked.

Jake's discomfort grew. Sweeney had hit him in a sore spot. Jake wasn't close to his son, and he hadn't heard from him in several months now.

"It's a good relationship," Jake said.

Sweeney smirked a little, and Jake noticed a twinkle in his eye that reminded him uncannily of Riley.

"Don't ever try to lie to a hunter," Sweeney said. "We've got those instincts you mentioned, and we'll see through you every

105

time. Come on, now. Tell me the truth about you and your boy."

Feeling embarrassed now, Jake said slowly …

"The truth is, Tyson and I … don't get along especially well."

Sweeney chuckled and said, "Glad to hear it. I never trust a man whose children don't hate him."

Jake winced a little. Tyson didn't *hate* him exactly. But Jake didn't want to elaborate about the matter, and he sure didn't want to get into an argument.

Sweeney said, "I've got two daughters who hate my living guts. I didn't set out to make them hate me—at least not the firstborn, Wendy. But hating me came so natural to her, I saw no reason not to give her good reason for it. By the time Riley came along, well …"

Sweeney's voice trailed off, and there was a far away expression in his eyes.

Jake almost felt as though Sweeney had forgotten he was there.

In the silence, Jake found himself thinking about something he'd found about Riley while researching her past—something Riley herself probably didn't realize that he knew.

Jake said, "Riley's mother got killed when she was little girl, didn't she?"

Sweeney winced sharply.

Jake realized he'd hit *him* in a sore spot now.

"Karen got gunned down in a candy store," Sweeney said in a whisper. "By some stupid thug who disappeared without a trace and is probably still alive today. That's how justice works in this world, if you don't mind my saying so."

Jake said, "And Riley was there when it happened, wasn't she? She saw it happen."

Sweeney nodded silently.

Jake said, "That kind of experience … it can haunt you for life. It leaves scars."

In a low snarl, Sweeney said, "Yeah, well—she gets no sympathy from me."

Jake was jolted by the harshness of those world.

"She was only six years old," Jake said. "Are you telling me you blame *her* for what happened?"

Sweeney barked with surprising sharpness …

"Of course I blame her. I blame everybody. I blame the man who fired the gun. I blame the store clerk who stood watching. I blame the cops for not finding the bastard who did it. And I blame *me."*

Sweeney said slowly, "But … you weren't even there when it happened."

Sweeney peered deeply into Jake's eyes, looking weirdly more like Riley every second.

He said, "What part of *blame* don't you understand, Agent Crivaro? I blame myself for what happened in 'Nam, too, because somebody sure as hell ought to shoulder that blame. We're all to blame—for something, for everything. And if we can't accept that and live with it, we don't deserve to live. I've got no damned use for anybody who doesn't blame himself for something. And if Riley still blames herself for what happened to her mother …"

Sweeney inhaled deeply and nodded.

"Well, it's good for her. Makes her a better hunter."

Sweeney's mouth dropped open. He was truly dumbfounded now.

Sweeney swallowed some more of his cider, then said …

"So tell me—how is she doing under your … tutelage?"

Crivaro realized that he had no idea how to answer that question.

When he'd dropped of Riley Sweeney at her dorm earlier today, it had felt like a permanent rift.

But was it really?

Instead of replying, Jake set down his glass and said …

"I'd better be going."

As he got up from his chair, Sweeney chuckled grimly and said
…

"She's failing that bad, huh?"

Crivaro stood staring down at the big, bitter man for a moment.

Then it occurred to him what he could honestly say about Riley
…

"She's a diamond in the rough."

Smiling, Sweeney said, "Well, don't polish her up too pretty. And don't smooth out all that roughness. She's going to need it."

"Thanks for the cider," Jake said.

As Jake walked out the door, Sweeney called out to him …

"Crivaro—I know something about you. Something you may not know yourself."

Jake turned and looked at him.

Sweeney said, "You're a good man."

Jake was swept by a chill of sheer perplexity. He felt as though he ought to return the compliment, or at least thank Sweeney for saying it.

But neither of those options seemed possible at the moment.

Sweeney added in a tight voice, "Stick by my daughter. She needs you. You can do her a lot of good. You're a lot better for her than I could ever be."

Jake nodded and climbed back in the car and started the engine. As he headed back along the crooked drive that led to the gravel road back to Milladore, he realized he was shaken deeply by the conversation he'd just had.

He remembered Sweeney's parting words ...

"You're a good man."

Jake shivered as a little as he wondered—what could that mean, coming from a man like Oliver Sweeney?

He played back Sweeney's words in his head ...

"I've got no damned use for anybody who doesn't blame himself for something."

Jake suddenly realized ...

That's me.

He saw right through me.

As much as he tried to deny it even to himself, Jake was haunted by failure—his failures as father, husband, colleague, and friend. As far as he was concerned, he hadn't done much good in any of those roles. As for his accomplishments as an FBI Agent, he'd brought a good many killers to justice, but he'd failed to bring in just as many others. Every time an innocent person died at the hands of a vicious killer, he couldn't help but blame himself.

He shuddered at the possibility that he and Sweeney were really quite alike.

But wasn't Sweeney some kind of monster?

Maybe, Jake thought.

Even so, he'd helped shape Riley Sweeney into what she was today ...

And that's not completely a bad thing.

He also remembered Sweeney saying ...

"Stick by my daughter. She needs you. You can do her a lot of good. You're a lot better for her than I could ever be."

It had sounded like an order. Coming from a military man like Sweeney, those words had a lot of force.

And suddenly, giving up on Riley Sweeney didn't seem like an option.

Besides, Jake realized he'd tended to underrate Riley until right now. She'd survived a life with this hard, bitter man—and she'd come out all the better for it. It would take a lot to defeat her, if anything ever could. And a kid like that deserved all the help he could give her.

Jake smiled as he recalled what he himself had just said about Riley …

"She's a diamond in the rough."

He thought …

Maybe not so rough after all.

She had abilities and resiliency and character far beyond her years.

Meanwhile, Jake had get his mind back on business. There was a murder case to solve in West Virginia.

A killer was still out there—and he might strike again at any minute …

If he hasn't already.

CHAPTER NINETEEN

The man crouched among some bushes at the edge of a town park. It was night and no casual observer would spot him here. This was a good place for him to watch and wait.

From his hiding place, he had a clear view of Wynnewood Community College just across the street. Through a window he could see a woman teaching a class of enthusiastic-looking students.

She'll be next, he thought.

The teacher didn't know it, but she had sealed her own fate that very afternoon. When she'd gotten out of her car and crossed the street while carrying an armload of books, she had almost bumped into him.

She'd frozen in her tracks at the sight of his scarred face and stared for a moment.

She'd blushed with embarrassment and blurted …

"Oh—I beg your pardon."

Then she'd rushed toward the school building where a group of students awaited her at the entrance. When she joined them, the students had looked in his direction, apparently saying something to her about the near collision. The teacher had shaken her head and said nothing, as if trying to pretend it hadn't happened. Then she'd led the group on into the building.

I know her type, he thought.

She fancied herself an exceptionally sensitive and compassionate person. She didn't like to think of herself as someone who judged people by appearances. And that was why she'd blushed with shame when she'd caught herself staring at him. His appearance had horrified her—irrationally but quite naturally. And she couldn't help but feel that she was to blame.

Stupid woman, he thought.

Didn't she know that everybody judged everybody else, especially by appearances?

It was human nature.

He didn't especially mind how children pointed at him and laughed and sometimes openly called him names …

"Moonface! Moonface!"

They were being cruel, of course, but they were also being true to their natures.

But as they grew up, they learned hypocrisy and falseness.

They tried to swallow down their meanness, pretended to be better people than they were, lied to themselves …

They stop being children, he thought.

It angered him. This woman angered him in a way that neither of the other women had angered him. Not that anger had anything to do with what he planned to do her tonight. That would be all about pleasure, not anger. It would be about release from the pain he'd carried inside him for so many years.

She'd been in the school building since long before sunset, and she hadn't come outside once.

Devoted to her work, he thought.

Despite his anger toward her, he admired her for that.

This was the third class he'd watched her teach, and yet he still had no idea exactly what her classes were about. He was too far away to see exactly what she was writing down on the blackboard.

But the classroom window was open, and now that things were especially quiet in Wynnewood, he could faintly hear the woman's voice wafting over the lawn and across the street to where he was hiding.

He couldn't make out any words she was saying, but he could tell that it was a gentle, lilting, cheerful voice. Her voice alone seemed enough to keep her students smiling at her.

He wondered …

What will her voice sound like when it happens?

He hadn't noticed much change in Alice's voice one way or the other. It had sounded reedy and whiny when he'd approached her, and much the same when she'd awakened from the dose of chloroform and realized he was wrapping her up with barbed wire.

But the next woman had been different. Her voice had become timid, childlike, and rather sweet when she'd recovered from her chloroform stupor and realized what was happening.

Would this woman still sound nice a little while later, when her real torment began?

He hoped so.

He would find it disappointing if the music he heard in her voice right now finally gave way to more strident tones.

Of course, it all depended on how things worked out tonight. The truth was, he wasn't sure how he was going to carry out the abduction this time. When class let out, how was he going to catch her alone before she got to her car?

Maybe tonight's not the night, he thought.

Maybe he needed to spend another day or two stalking her, looking for some pattern in her movements that offered a better opportunity.

He looked at his watch and figured it was about time for her class to be over. But both she and her students were chattering with excitement about whatever topic they were discussing.

How long will they drag this out?

He told himself to be patient …

Like a spider.

He'd spent many long hours watching how spiders captured and devoured their prey. He was fascinated by how a spider used its web as a sort of extension of its nervous system, sensing the moment an insect got stuck in its silken stickiness, then moving in and injecting its numbing venom …

Just like my chloroform.

… and finally wrapped the writhing creature up in strand after strand of silk—rather lovingly, he thought—to be liquefied and eaten at the spider's leisure.

He smiled at the memory …

How wise nature is.

He did his best to be like a spider.

And yet …

Something troubled him about how his previous two endeavors had ended. After the tender act of wrapping up the women in barbed wire, partaking of their delicious terror and pain, he'd go away for awhile. And when he'd come back and find them dead, drained of blood, what did he feel?

Nothing.

Just an empty numbness.

The bundles might as well have been sacks of laundry. That was why he hadn't bothered to keep them. Each time he'd gathered the prickly cocoon in a blanket, carried it to his truck, transported it to a fence post, and hung it up to hang there for someone else to find.

Numbness.

Surely no spider felt that way after its own prey was cocooned so nicely. Sometimes, watching a spider finish its work, he thought he sensed a feeling of fulfillment, satisfaction, and achievement radiating from that web-sized nervous system.

He'd felt that same satisfaction himself, long ago when he'd claimed his first victim. In fact, that early satisfaction had hung on for many years, and he'd kept that bundle as a trophy—no, more than a trophy, more like a shrine where he could relive the euphoria of he'd experienced back then, bask in its lingering glory.

But eventually the shrine had lost its magic. He didn't know why, but he no longer got that precious uplift from it anymore. That was why he'd taken his more recent victims—in hopes of creating a new and vital shrine.

It was a shame that it hadn't yet happened …

But maybe this time will be different.

If so, this woman would be his last victim—perhaps forever.

As he crouched there thinking and reflecting, he finally saw the students rise from their desks, and the teacher began to pack her books and papers into her briefcase.

He breathed a sigh of relief.

At long last, the class was over.

The students filed out of the room, and the teacher turned off the light and disappeared after them. For a few moments, the whole building was dark. Then the front door opened and the students poured out, still clustered around the teacher and chatting with her eagerly about today's studies.

His spirits sank as he realized …

I can't catch her alone.

The students were going to stay with her all the way to her car.

How many days was he going to have to spend stalking her to find his opportunity?

She got into the car, and the students waved as she started to drive away. Then the students turned and walked away, probably on their way to a local bar. Meanwhile the teacher was driving slowly in his direction.

He felt a surge of excitement as it dawned on him …

I can stop her!

But he didn't have a moment to lose.

He reached into his leather bag and took out the bottle of homemade chloroform and drenched a rag with it.

Then just as the car rounded the corner toward him, he stepped right in front of it.

The tires squealed as the woman slammed on the brakes—but not quick enough to stop her from bumping into him.

Perfect, he thought.

He wasn't hurt in the least, but she didn't know that.

She jumped out of the car shouting with alarm …

"Oh, my God! I'm so sorry! I didn't see you! Are you all right?"

He shook his leg a little and said …

"I'm not sure. I think so."

As she walked toward him, he could see her cringe guiltily as she seemed to recognize his scarred face. Once again, she quickly repressed her disgust.

"I'll drive you to the hospital," she said.

"No, I don't think you need to," he said, limping a little. "But maybe you could walk with me to my truck, just to make sure."

"Oh, I'd be glad to," she said.

Clutching the rag in one hand, he put the other on her shoulder, feigning a need of support.

Perfect, he thought again.

This time will be so much better than the others.

CHAPTER TWENTY

Riley heard a woman's voice, but she couldn't understand the words that echoed weirdly all around her.

Who is that? she wondered. *What does she want?*

Whoever it was, she sounded as if she had something direly important to say to Riley.

Riley almost asked aloud …

"Speak more clearly. I can't understand you."

But she felt too groggy to speak and too stiff to move. She ached all over and her head was tilted back, resting on something hard.

She opened her eyes and found herself staring upward at an ornate ceiling that arched high above her head.

The train station, she realized.

She was sitting on a bench in Union Station in DC with her go-bag and handbag clutched in her lap. The woman's voice she heard was broadcasting announcements about train departure and arrival times.

But Riley couldn't remember what she was doing here.

Maybe it's just a dream, she thought.

Then all that had happened last night flooded back into her mind. She'd arrived at the apartment to find Ryan with some strange woman—whether a friend, coworker, or lover, she still didn't know.

Maybe all three, she thought. In any case, they had seemed very comfortable together.

She'd quickly fled the apartment and taken the subway here to Union Station. But she'd been too late to catch any trains back to Quantico, so she'd fallen asleep sitting awkwardly on this bench.

She glanced at her watch and saw that it was now morning.

Well, at least I slept a good long time, she thought.

The cavernous grand hall was coming to life with noisy announcements and people hurrying about in all directions. Riley looked around until she saw a screen with train schedules. She still had about 25 minutes before she could catch the next train to Quantico.

But was there any point in going back to the Academy? Even

after her absence yesterday, she'd barely missed full day of activities. But even so, things had been going so badly, and she felt hopelessly far behind.

But where else am I going to go? she thought.

She looked at her cellphone and saw that Ryan hadn't tried to call her. Going back to the apartment didn't seem like an option. She might as well catch that train to Quantico and either sink or swim there. If she failed completely, then she'd decide what to do with her life.

Meanwhile, she was hungry. She got achingly to her feet and headed for the food court, where she bought coffee and a cheese Danish. The news was showing on a large TV screen.

She saw some reporters eagerly surrounding a distinguished-looking gray-haired gentleman. One of the reporters was speaking to the camera …

"We're meeting West Virginia Senator Warren Gardner just outside Grace Family Church here in Washington …"

The name caught Riley's attention …

Where have I heard that name recently?

Then she remembered—it had been back at the police station in Dighton.

She listened closely to the TV reporter, who was holding out a microphone to Senator Gardner …

"Senator, is it true you're about to announce right here in this church that you're sponsoring a new bill?"

The senator grinned and said, "You don't know, do you? Just wait and see. It won't be long now."

Ignoring a chorus of questions from the rest of the reporters, the senator and several plain-clothed bodyguards went on into the church, followed by some reporters with TV cameras.

The reporter spoke into the camera again …

"Rumor has it that the senator is going to announce the sponsorship of a bill to require the teaching of the Ten Commandments in public schools throughout the U.S."

The news anchor asked, "But isn't that bill going to be a nonstarter? It'll surely never make it out of committee, much less get a full vote in the Senate."

The reporter said, "That's what my sources tell me. It seems possible that the senator is doing this only to appeal to his base …"

As the anchor and the reporter kept talking, Riley remembered what she'd overheard at the police station. As she and Agent

116

Crivaro had approached the office, they'd heard the chief say to the mayor …

"I'd expected Senator Gardner to be at Hope's memorial service yesterday."

And the mayor had testily replied …

"Don't think about it. And don't talk about it. You know better than that."

She also remembered the anxious faces of the mayor and the chief when she and Agent Crivaro had walked into the office and they'd realized they'd been overheard. Their behavior had seemed awfully suspicious at the time.

Again she thought that there had to be some special reason why a U.S. Senator might be expected to attend a funeral in a little town in West Virginia. Did it have something to do with the case?

Crivaro hadn't seemed to think so.

In fact, he'd been angry with Riley for even suggesting the idea …

"Leave it the hell alone, Riley."

But could she leave it alone?

Now that she'd been reminded of the case, she realized how upset she was about how Crivaro put her out of action.

Maybe I can get something done after all, she thought.

But she knew she had to hurry. She left the rest of her Danish and coffee unfinished and ran out of the building. Outside, she caught the first cab she could get.

*

A few minutes later, the cab dropped Riley off in front of Grace Family Church. The front entrance was still surrounded by reporters, and there were plenty of other bystanders gathered there as well.

It looked like she'd gotten here just in time. The front door opened, and the senator came back outside flanked by his security people. Reporters charged toward him, asking dozens of questions at once.

With a smug smile on his face, the senator waved the reporters away.

He said, "I think everybody just heard my message loud and clear. It's time we put God back into the classroom. And I'm going to make sure that Congress makes it happen. I'm on my way to the

117

Capitol right now to formally introduce my bill on the Senate floor. Now if you don't mind, I've got to get going."

The reporters and onlookers showed no sign of wanting to disperse. They bunched around him asking whether he really thought his bill was constitutional, if it could pass both Houses of Congress, or if it was just a stunt to cater to his voters.

Riley knew she had to get closer to him if she was going to find out why she'd heard his name back in the police station.

How could she possibly get this man to answer her questions?

Blend into the group, she decided.

She took out her notebook and a pencil and pushed her way through the crowd until she was very close to the senator.

Holding up her notebook, she called out …

"Senator, do you have any comment to make about the recent murder of Hope Nelson in Dighton, West Virginia?"

The senator stopped dead in his tracks.

He stared at Riley with a startled expression.

"What did you just say?" he asked.

Riley felt a sharp tingle. She knew that she'd hit a nerve somehow.

She said, "A constituent of yours named Hope Nelson was murdered on Saturday. Do you have anything to say about that?"

For a moment, Riley thought she saw a trace of panic in the senator's eyes.

Then he seemed to try to gather his wits.

He said, "It's a tragedy, of course. Crime in this country is completely out of control. We're too soft on crime."

Riley pushed her way directly in front of Senator Gardner and said.

"What about the murder of Alice Gibson a week earlier in Hyland?"

Gardner's eyes looked angry now.

"Another tragedy."

Riley felt in her gut now that she was onto something. She was determined not to give up.

She said to the senator, "Did you have any personal connection with either of the victims?"

The reporters surrounding Riley and the senator seemed suddenly intrigued by this line of questioning. They acted like they already knew about the two murders in West Virginia. But apparently this was the first time they'd heard anyone suggest a link between Gardner and either of the victims. Gardner's defensive reaction really got their attention.

It was clear that Riley had aroused their curiosity.

"I think you should answer the woman's question," one reporter demanded.

"What do you know about the murders?" another yelled.

"What aren't you telling us?" shouted yet another.

The newly-besieged senator huddled for a moment with his security people.

Then one of the bodyguards stepped close to Riley.

"The senator would be happy to talk with you," the burly man said.

Before Riley quite realized what had happened, he took one of her arms and steered her out of the group of reporters.

Another bodyguard hurried over and grabbed her other arm. They almost lifted her off her feet as they hustled her away from the crowd.

Riley was too startled to protest. She could hear the senator telling the reporters that he had promised this person an interview and was going to fulfill that promise now. He said he would hold a press conference with all of them later in the day.

The two men firmly shoved Riley into the back of a limousine.

The climbed in too and sat on each side of her.

The senator and other guards quickly joined them in the spacious vehicle.

In a matter of seconds, she found herself seated face to face with the frowning senator.

The driver of the limo pulled away from the crowd and headed on down the street.

Riley's head was whirling with surprise and alarm.

What have I gotten myself into? she wondered.

CHAPTER TWENTY ONE

As the limousine continued on its way, Riley fought down the terror that threatened to overwhelm her. She tried to convince herself that she wasn't in danger for her life—not like when she'd been bound in the Clown Killer's lair about to be injected with a fatal dose of amphetamines.

This is different, she thought.

Surely neither the senator nor the bodyguards intended to kill her.

The very idea was ludicrous. After all …

He's a U.S. Senator—not some common criminal.

But why had she been snatched up like this? What did they want with her?

It didn't help that Senator Gardner, sitting on a seat facing her, was frowning with malignant fury.

He growled, "Who do you work for?"

Riley stammered with confusion and fear …

"I—I don't work for anybody."

"Then you're not a reporter?" Gardner said.

Riley gulped hard at her mistake. She should have lied. She should have tried to bluff things out, made up some news organization she supposedly worked for. But it was much too late to try that now. It had been stupid of her not to prepare such a ruse before she'd even approached him …

Actually, the whole thing was probably stupid in the first place.

Pointing at Riley's handbag, Senator Gardner exchanged looks with the bodyguards who sat flanking her.

Obeying his silent command, one of the bodyguards grabbed her bag and scrounged roughly through it until he located her wallet. He quickly found Riley's FBI Academy ID card and showed it to Gardner.

Gardner squinted at the card and said, "FBI?"

The guard said, "According to this ID, her name is Riley Sweeney. She's just an agent in training, sir. At the Academy in Quantico."

Gardner's eyes widened as he stared at Riley.

"Nonsense," he said.

Riley shivered deeply.

This isn't good, she thought.

"It's true, sir," she said in a shaky voice. "I just started at the Academy this week."

Gardner glared at her silently for what seemed like a long time.

Then he said, "Tell me everything you know."

Riley felt overwhelmed by sheer perplexity.

She wanted to ask …

Everything I know about what?

In fact, she really knew nothing at all—except that she'd heard the senator's name mentioned in a police station in Dighton, West Virginia. Should she tell him at least that much? No, somehow she suspected that would get her in even more trouble.

She said, "I'm sorry, sir, but I don't know anything."

Gardner pointed an accusing finger at her and said …

"You're lying. Why were you asking me those questions back there?"

Riley's brain clicked away, trying to think of some plausible excuse.

She said, "I was just curious, I guess. I'd heard about the two murders, and since you're a senator from West Virginia, I just wanted to know … how you felt about all that."

"I don't believe you," Gardner said.

Riley suppressed a groan of despair …

Of course he doesn't believe me.

I wouldn't believe me either.

But given the circumstances, she didn't dare ask the questions that she'd really wanted answers to—for example, did the senator have anything to do with the two murders?

She knew she'd better keep her mouth shut about all that …

If I want to get out of this safe and sound.

Gardner's face twitched as he said …

"Erik Lehl put you up to this, didn't he?"

Riley tried to think … where had she heard that name before?

She thought maybe she'd heard Agent Crivaro mention Erik Lehl at one time or another …

Like maybe he's Crivaro's boss.

She said, "I don't know anybody named Erik Lehl."

At least that's the truth, she thought.

Gardner turned his head and told the driver of the limo to pull over to the curb. When the car came to a stop, he ordered one of the guards to open the door.

"Get out," he said to Riley. "But from now on, keep your questions to yourself. And don't think you've heard the last of this."

Riley gasped with relief as she hopped out of the limousine and watched it drive away down the busy street.

The whole world felt shaky as she stood there on the street corner, trying to understand what she'd just been through. All she knew was that she'd stumbled into something scary and dangerous—something she'd better not try to tangle with on her own.

Should she call Jake Crivaro and tell him what had happened?

Somehow that didn't seem like a good idea.

Perhaps it would only get Crivaro into trouble as well.

She looked around to get her bearings and realized the limo had let her off within walking distance of Union Station. She figured maybe the best thing to do was to catch a train back to Quantico, see if she could make her way back into the program, and try to forget about this weird and terrifying incident.

But as she walked on to the station, the senator's words rang through her head …

"Don't think you've heard the last of this."

*

Jake was eating breakfast in a restaurant in Dighton with his forensics team, discussing what little progress they all were making. Suddenly his cellphone rang. He felt a twinge of worry when he saw that the call was from Special Agent in Charge Erik Lehl.

This probably isn't good, he thought.

When he took the call, Lehl said …

"Crivaro, what the hell have you done?"

Jake was startled by the anger in the normally reticent man's voice.

He stammered, "Sir, I—I don't understand."

Lehl continued, "I thought I made myself clear when we talked in my office. What I told you about Senator Gardner was not to leave my office."

Jake was truly baffled now.

"I promise, sir, I didn't talk about it with anybody."

"That's not what Gardner tells me. I got a call from him just now. He says that protégé of yours, Riley Sweeney, badgered him about it in public this morning in DC. Then I checked with the FBI Academy and found out she hasn't been there since yesterday morning. They told me you took her out of her classes and she'd been working with you in West Virginia. You must have told her. How else could she have found out?"

Jake stifled a sigh.

He was starting to understand at least part of what had happened.

He began, "Sir, let me try to explain …"

Lehl interrupted, "Oh, you're going to explain, all right. But not over the phone like this. I want to hear it from you face to face. A helicopter is on its way to you now to pick you up. I expect to see you in my office ASAP—and you'd better have that girl in tow with you. I want to talk to her too."

Lehl tersely gave Crivaro details about the helicopter that was on its way, then ended the call.

Jake looked at his what remained breakfast. There was no time to finish eating—and besides, he'd lost his appetite. He asked one of his forensics guys to drive him to the spot where the helicopter was due to land. On the way there, Jake called Riley's cellphone.

When he heard her scared-sounding voice he asked …

"Riley, where the hell are you? What did you just do?"

Riley said, "I—I'm on the way out of DC. I'm not quite sure what just happened. How did you find out?"

Jake let out a groan of annoyance.

"I found out in just about the worst possible way," he said. "Special Agent in Charge Erik Lehl called me to chew me out about it. Now we're both in trouble. And I need to know what it's all about."

He heard Riley take a sharp breath.

"I talked to Senator Gardner," she said.

"Where? When?"

"In DC. In front of a church where he was making a political announcement. I pretended to be a reporter and …"

Jake blurted, "You *pretended* to be *what?*"

"I just wanted to know, that's all. Remember what we overheard in the police station in Dighton? You know, when the mayor asked the chief about the senator not coming to the funeral? It was driving me crazy. I knew it must mean something. So I asked Senator Gardner whether he had anything to say about the murders in West Virginia and …"

Her voice trailed off.

"And what?" Jake asked.

"Well, if he had any personal connection with the two victims."

Jake felt his mouth drop open.

What a mess, he thought.

This whole thing was worse than he'd even imagined.

Riley continued, "A couple of his bodyguards grabbed me and dragged me to his car. He asked me questions. He was really angry. Then he let me out. He said I hadn't heard the last of it. I don't know what it was all about. But Agent Crivaro, I'm onto something important. I just know it."

Jake shook his head miserably.

You're onto something, all right, he thought.

And now all hell was breaking loose.

He said, "Riley, I told you to leave it the hell alone."

"I know, but—"

Jake interrupted again, "I meant what I said. I had good reasons for saying that. You've got to learn to follow orders."

Riley was quiet for a moment.

Then she said, "I'm sorry."

"Oh, you're going to be a lot more than sorry," Jake said. "So am I, for that matter. What were you doing in DC anyhow?"

"Um, I went to see Ryan, but ... don't ask."

Jake didn't want to know anything about Ryan. Instead he asked, "Exactly where are you right now?"

"I'm on a train to Quantico."

"Stay in the station when your train arrives. Somebody will be there to pick you up."

He heard Riley gasp.

"Am I going to be arrested?" she asked.

Jake growled, "Not yet. But the day is still young."

He ended the call, then readied himself to call in a couple of agents to meet Riley at the Quantico train station. Jake knew that he and Riley were both in for a grilling by Special Agent in Charge Erik Lehl ...

And it's not going to be pretty.

Jake wondered—was he even going to have a job later today?

*

When Riley got off the train in Quantico, she spotted them

124

right away—two men wearing business suits and sunglasses, too stiff and robotic-looking to be ordinary civilians. Sure enough, they came up to her flashing their FBI badges, asking whether she was Riley Sweeney.

When she said yes, they whisked her away to a car they'd left waiting in front of the train station.

Yet again, Riley felt as though she were dreaming.

It was the second time today she'd been snatched up by men who seemed markedly less than friendly.

At least these guys are with the FBI, she thought.

Surely she'd be safe in their custody—at least for now.

They drove her to the vast BAU complex, escorted her through the broad lobby, up an elevator, and through a maze of hallways. Finally they arrived in a plain little room with a table and three chairs and a large, rectangular window that Riley guessed to be a two-way mirror.

Riley wondered—was anybody on the other side of that mirror?

One of the agents asked her, "Do you have a cellphone?"

Riley nodded.

The other agent held out his hand and said, "We'll take that, if you don't mind."

Riley gulped.

That doesn't sound like a request, she thought.

She took out her cellphone and handed it to the agent. Then the two men left her alone in the room.

Riley sat there, feeling stunned by the sudden silence. Was she alone, or was somebody watching her every move through that mirror?

What have I gotten myself into? she wondered.

She remembered asking herself that question earlier, but she still had no idea of the answer.

She remembered Crivaro saying …

"Now we're both in trouble."

Was he in the same situation at this very moment—sitting in another interrogation room in this same building waiting for something to happen?

It didn't seem likely.

After all, wasn't Crivaro still in West Virginia?

The truth was, she really didn't know where he'd been when he'd called her.

Long minutes began to drag out. Riley especially missed her cellphone. She had no connection to the outside world, and that really scared her.

But who would she call if she still had her phone?

There wouldn't be much point in calling Crivaro.

Maybe Ryan, she thought.

She felt a wistful pang at the idea. She couldn't thinking—wouldn't it be nice to be able to call Ryan right now, tell him that the whole FBI Academy thing had been a foolish mistake, that she knew better now and was coming home, and that from now on she'd be exactly the kind of wife he wanted her to be … ?

What a stupid idea, she thought.

After all, like her father had once told her …

"You're just not cut out for a normal life. It's not in your nature."

Besides, what about the woman who'd been with Ryan in their apartment?

The more Riley thought about it, the more sure she felt that Ryan had decided to move on with his life without her. If so, what was she going to do with her own life? It seemed likely that her time at the FBI Academy had ended almost as soon as it had started. And Riley couldn't think of anything else she felt the least bit passionate about …

But maybe passion's overrated.

After all, Crivaro had told her that his own passion for his work had been the ruin of all his relationships …

"I put people off, I push people away, I expect too much, and I get impatient."

Of course, it must have taken years for Crivaro to alienate all the people he most loved and cared for.

Riley had already done that, and she was only 22 years old.

After a while, Riley began to fidget uncomfortably in her chair. She was awfully stiff and sore after a whole night sitting asleep on a bench in Union Station. She wanted to get up and pace, but felt oddly afraid to even move.

She still wondered whether she was being watched through the two-way mirror. If so, did she need permission to even get up and stretch a little? She almost called out to ask whoever might be there. But she was scared to do even that.

She didn't know how long she'd been sitting there alone when the door finally swung open.

126

Jake Crivaro came in, looking both worried and angry.

As he sat down at the table beside her, she blurted …

"Agent Crivaro, I swear to God, I've got no idea …"

Crivaro interrupted, "Save it. You'll get a chance to tell your side of the story. It had better be good."

A few seconds passed, and the door opened again. Another man came inside—a tall, gangly man with a dour expression. The chair seemed almost too small for him as he sat down across the table from Riley and Crivaro.

The man stared at Riley for a moment, then said …

"I don't think we've met. I'm Special Agent in Charge Erik Lehl. And you, I believe, are Riley Sweeney—an academy NAT who has gotten way, way out of her depth."

Lehl folded his hands on the table, glanced back and forth between Riley and Crivaro, and said …

"And now—which of you wants to start explaining things?"

CHAPTER TWENTY TWO

As Lehl sat waiting for one of them to speak, Riley thought that Agent Crivaro looked uncharacteristically intimidated. But she sure didn't want to be the first to say anything.

Jake finally said, "I guess this whole thing is my fault, sir. I felt like I needed help on the West Virginia case. As you know, Riley Sweeney has worked with me on two murder cases. She's … well, she's very talented, among other things."

Lehl nodded and said, "Go on."

Crivaro shifted in his chair and continued …

"I pulled her out of her classes yesterday and took her with me to West Virginia. While she was there, she got … curious about a conversation she overheard about Senator Gardner. She sounded a little too curious for her own good. So I brought her back to the Academy in Quantico that very night."

Riley felt a jolt of surprise.

This was the first hint she'd gotten that Crivaro had hauled her back to Quantico on account of her questions about Senator Gardner.

Lehl drummed his fingers on the table.

He said, "Let's start right there—with Agent Crivaro leaving you at the Academy. Why didn't you stay put there? What were you doing in Washington the next day?"

Riley said, "My fiancé lives in Washington. Actually, I … I do too, I guess. We rent an apartment there together. But the night before I came to the Academy, Ryan—my fiancé—and I had a fight. So after Agent Crivaro dropped me off, I decided to take a train back to Washington and try to straighten things out with Ryan and …"

She paused and wondered …

Do I need to go into everything that happened then?

Did she have to explain that she'd found Ryan with another woman?

Surely such details didn't matter right now.

Instead she said, "Well, things didn't go well with Ryan when I got there. So I headed back to the train station and slept there all night, figuring I'd get a train back to Quantico in the morning. After

I woke up and I was eating breakfast in the station, I saw on TV that Senator Gardner speaking at that church, and ... well, I got curious."

Lehl squinted at her and said, "Curious?"

Riley swallowed hard and said, "Look, it's like Agent Crivaro said—we overheard something. When we walked into the police station in Dighton, we heard Mayor Nelson and the police chief talking about the senator. Chief Messenger said he was surprised the senator hadn't come to Hope Nelson's funeral. The mayor was upset that he'd even mentioned it. And both of them looked worried when they realized they'd been overheard."

Riley shrugged nervously and added, "Well, that seemed strange to me, that's all. I felt like maybe it had something to do with the case. Agent Crivaro told me to forget all about it. And I guess I should have, but ..."

Lehl interrupted, "Yes, you emphatically should have."

"I know now, and I'm sorry," Riley said.

Lehl leaned across the table toward her with a curious expression.

He said, "So Agent Crivaro didn't tell you anything about Senator Gardner? He didn't tell you *why* you should mind your own business about him?"

Riley was surprised by the question.

"No," she said. "He didn't tell me a thing. And I still don't *know* anything else."

Lehl leaned back again, seeming to study Riley's face closely.

He said, "So when you walked up to Senator Gardner and asked him those questions, you were just following some kind of gut impulse."

Riley felt a flash of relief that he seemed to understand.

"Yes, that's right," she said. "I was just going on pure ... instinct, I guess."

Lehl's mouth twisted a little, almost into a smile.

He said, "You've got some interesting instincts there, Riley Sweeney. It's too bad you don't know how to put them to better use."

Riley's spirits sank again. She knew she wasn't going to like whatever he said next.

Lehl said, "I checked in on how you were doing at the Academy. I'm afraid the reports I got weren't exactly favorable."

Riley stifled a sigh ...

No, I don't suppose they were.

Lehl continued, "When you went to West Virginia yesterday, you left the Academy under Agent Crivaro's authorization. But that authorization ended the moment he dropped you back off at Quantico. You should have reported for your classes the next morning. Instead you went AWOL. Worse, you conducted an interview without bothering to get any sort of official approval."

Riley had to bite her tongue from saying "I'm sorry" again.

At this point, she knew it wouldn't help at all.

Lehl crossed his arms and said, "You're expelled from the Academy."

Riley felt as though her heart and just fallen through the floor.

She noticed that Crivaro looked quite upset as well—but hardly surprised.

Lehl turned his attention to Crivaro and said …

"What are your plans for the rest of today?"

Crivaro shrugged slightly and said, "As long as I'm here in Quantico, I might was well check in with my tech team. They've been trying to track down Harvey Cardin, the brother of the man who was originally held in Hyland under suspicion of killing Alice Gibson. Harvey left town under suspicious circumstances. If the tech guys still haven't found him, maybe I can push them along, get them moving."

Lehl nodded and said, "You do that, Agent Crivaro. I'll keep a helicopter ready for whenever you want to head back to West Virginia."

Without another word, and without even looking at Riley, Special Agent in Charge Erik Lehl left the room.

Riley and Crivaro sat at the table in silence for a moment.

Finally Riley began, "Agent Crivaro …"

Crivaro interrupted, "I know. You're sorry. So am I."

Then he, too, got up and left the room.

Riley sat alone for a few long moments, feeling lost and desolate and on the verge of tears.

What do I do now? she wondered.

All she knew for sure was that she had to leave the Academy for good.

She left the room and headed on out of the building.

*

Later that evening, Riley was back in her dorm room packing up her belongings when Frankie came in.

"How'd things go in West Virginia?" Frankie asked.

Riley sighed as she put more clothes into her suitcase.

"I guess you haven't heard," she said. "I've been expelled."

Frankie's eyes widened.

"No kidding?" she said. "Just on account of that Hogan's Alley stunt? That's harsh."

Riley said, "No, there's more to it than that. I screwed up, Frankie. I screwed up royally."

Closing up her suitcase, Riley told Frankie about her grim meeting with Crivaro and Lehl.

"You poor kid," Frankie said when Riley was finished. "It sounds like you stumbled onto something serious about the senator. I wonder what it is."

"Yeah, well, I don't much care anymore," Riley said, sighing again. "Agent Crivaro and Agent Lehl obviously know something nobody else is supposed to know, including me. And if I hadn't been so stupid, I'd just left the whole thing alone."

Riley stood staring at her packed suitcase for a moment.

Then, to her own surprise, she burst into tears.

Frankie put her arm around Riley and sat down on the bed beside her.

"Kid, what's the matter?" Frankie said, her voice full of concern.

Her voice choking with sobs, Riley said ...

"Oh, Frankie—I don't even know where I'm going to *go* now."

"What do you mean, you don't know?" Frankie said, handing her a tissue. "Just go back home to your apartment in DC."

"It's not that simple," Riley blubbered.

Then she explained what had happened when she'd walked into the apartment last night.

Frankie shook her head and said, "That son of a bitch."

Riley said, "Frankie, it's not like I really *know* he's—he's involved with that woman."

Frankie scoffed ...

"Oh, he's *involved* with her all right. I've had more experience with men than you have, so believe me, I know what I'm talking about. You're lucky to have found out this early on."

Frankie patted Riley on the back and continued ...

"This is what you're going to do. Take your suitcase and go

somewhere new. Don't worry about your belongings back in that apartment. You can get all that stuff sometime later. Just pick out someplace and go and start all over again. Richmond, maybe. That's a good city."

"But what will I do there?" Riley said.

Frankie shrugged and said, "Whatever you want to do. You're free. But in the long run, I'll bet anything you're not through with law enforcement. You might be a little too wild for the FBI, but you'd still make one hell of a cop. You've obviously got real talent. Even your screw-ups prove that."

Riley laughed a little. Before she could ask Frankie for further advice, there was a knock at the door.

Frankie went to the door and opened it, then gasped aloud.

Riley looked and saw that Jake Crivaro was standing in the doorway.

He looked at Riley sternly and said …

"Get your go-bag ready. We're headed back to West Virginia."

CHAPTER TWENTY THREE

As Crivaro came on into the dorm room, Riley jumped up off the bed. She looked like a mess and she knew it. She wiped at her eyes with a tissue, embarrassed for him to see that she'd been crying. But it couldn't be helped.

Frankie just stood there staring at the legendary Jake Crivaro with her mouth hanging open.

As Riley dabbed at her eyes, she was trying to register what Crivaro had just said.

Had he really told her they were going somewhere?

Crivaro snapped impatiently …

"Did you hear me? There's been another murder in West Virginia. Grab your bag. We've got to get going."

Riley couldn't believe her ears.

She stammered, "But … I thought … I …"

Crivaro smiled ever so slightly.

He said, "You just got kicked out of the Academy, right?"

Riley nodded.

Crivaro added, "So, have you got anything better to do right now?"

"No, I—I guess not," Riley said.

"Good. Because there's a chopper waiting for us over at the airstrip."

Moving in a daze, Riley obediently picked up her go-bag and followed Crivaro out into the hall. She turned back and saw Frankie standing just outside their room, beaming proudly at her. Riley remembered what Frankie had said just before Crivaro had arrived …

"I'll bet anything you're not through with law enforcement."

Riley thought …

Maybe Frankie was right.

Still, it was hard to imagine what route she was going to take to that kind of a career now that she was out of the Academy. She had to make the best of this new and completely unexpected opportunity …

I can't screw this up.

As he drove them the short way to airstrip, Crivaro said …

"Don't get the wrong idea about all this. You've stirred up hell of a lot of trouble, and it'll be a while before you hear the last about it."

Riley looked at him with surprise.

"I stirred up trouble?" she said. "How?"

Crivaro chuckled a little.

"I take it you haven't seen the TV news this evening," he said.

"No, why?"

"Well, when you asked the senator those questions this morning, you piqued the curiosity of all the *real* reporters who were also hanging around outside that church, doing their jobs. They started looking into things—and sure enough, they found out the truth real fast."

"The truth about what?" Riley asked.

"About the very thing Special Agent in Charge Lehl was trying to keep quiet. Fifteen years ago, Warren Gardner was traveling through West Virginia, campaigning for his first term as U.S. Senator. During a stop in Dighton, he got an 18-year-old campaign volunteer pregnant. Can you guess who that teenager was?"

Riley only had to think for a couple of seconds.

With a slight gasp, she said, "Hope Nelson."

Crivaro nodded and said, "Hope *Gentry* back in those days. Things didn't work out too badly for her. The mayor of Dighton knew all about the affair and pregnancy, but he fell in love with her even so. He married her and wound up raising her son as his own. Gardner kept supporting the kid financially, making sure that he went to the best schools and all."

Crivaro paused for a moment, then said …

"If that was all there was to it, I don't guess it would be much of a scandal. But Gardner's got a closet full of skeletons—apparently there's more than one love child in his home state. At least one of them by a girl who was underage when he got her pregnant."

Crivaro scoffed and added …

"Mind you, we're talking about the same Senator Gardner who wants to teach the Ten Commandments in U.S. public schools. So naturally, he's been trying to keep all this quiet for years now. And when he heard about Hope's murder, he was afraid the FBI might accidentally blow the lid off their relationship. So he personally called Chief Lehl and gave him an earful, told him to make sure his agents watched their step."

Riley's eyes widened as the whole thing became clearer in her mind.

She said, "So *that* was what the mayor and the police chief were talking about when we overheard them. The chief must have known all along about the affair and the baby. So he'd thought maybe the senator would show up at Hope's funeral. But of course, he didn't."

Crivaro nodded.

"You're getting the idea," he said.

A new question started nagging at Riley …

"But why did Chief Lehl go along with the senator? Why did he agree to try to keep things quiet?"

"Good old-fashioned political bullying," Crivaro said. "Gardner's a high-ranking senator on some prestigious committees, and he's got a lot of pull over the BAU's purse strings. Lehl had good reason not to want to piss him off—especially over something that wasn't really BAU business to begin with."

Crivaro grunted and said, "But it seems like that ship has sailed. After that stunt you pulled outside the church, those reporters were onto the story like a school of piranhas. Within hours they'd figured out at least some of the truth, and it's already all over the media. What they've reported is just the tip of the iceberg, though. A lot more will come out over the next few days, you can be sure of that."

Riley felt a little dizzy at the enormity of what she'd done.

"Oh, my God," she murmured. "Is the BAU going to lose funding because of me?"

Crivaro shook his head and said, "Oh, I kind of doubt that will be a problem now that everything will go public. It's more likely that Senator Gardner's days as a political powerhouse are pretty much over. This is probably the end of the line as far as his senate career is concerned."

Crivaro chuckled and added, "It couldn't happen to a nicer guy as far as I'm concerned. A bastard like Gardner deserves to rot. And I'm pretty sure Chief Lehl feels the same way."

As Crivaro pulled into the airstrip parking area, he wagged a finger at Riley and said …

"But none of this had anything to do with the murders in West Virginia. So let this be a lesson to you. Orders are orders. When I tell you to leave something alone, leave it the hell alone."

"I will, I promise," Riley said. "And thanks for giving me

135

another chance."

"Don't mention it," Crivaro said. "Besides, it was Chief Lehl's idea."

"What?" Riley said with a gasp of surprise.

"He suggested it when he contacted me about the new murder," Crivaro said. "I guess he didn't act like it, but he was actually pretty impressed by you. And believe it or not, he thinks you might be a good influence on me. 'Maybe she'll teach you to play nice with others,' he said."

Crivaro grunted again and added, "Don't get your hopes up about that. Others have tried and failed lots of times. I'm pretty damned incorrigible."

Crivaro parked the car, and he and Riley rushed toward the waiting helicopter. Within seconds they were airborne and on their way to West Virginia.

*

The helicopter descended toward a weird and unsettling light in the midst of the deep nighttime darkness. Then the copter's own powerful lights came on and Riley could see that they were landing in a meadow. She knew that this must be the crime scene near the West Virginia town of Wynnewood.

When the copter was down and the engine off, Riley and Crivaro climbed out.

One edge of the meadow was lit by halogen lamps.

At first the piercing white light made everything looked flat and bleached, like a badly processed photograph. As Riley's eyes adjusted, she saw a couple of parked police cars and a medical examiner's van, and several people were milling about.

Then she spotted what they had come there to see.

The light picked out a grotesque bundle hanging from a fence post.

The victim, Riley realized with a shudder.

CHAPTER TWENTY FOUR

Riley felt chilled deep inside. Her legs became weak and wobbly. The sight of the bundled victim hanging from the fence post was having an unexpected effect on her.

Steady, she told herself as she struggled to stay on her feet.

You've seen dead people before.

In fact, she'd seen much bloodier murder scenes before. She'd also seen photos of the other two victims in exactly this condition. So why did she find this one to be so uniquely shocking?

Surely, she thought, it must be the kind of death the victim suffered.

And the sheer depravity of whoever did this to her.

She heard Crivaro say to her …

"Come on, we've got to talk to people."

Riley and Crivaro stepped across the fence in a spot where the rusted barbed wire had been pressed down for human traffic. A man with white hair and a thick mustache came toward Crivaro.

"I see we meet again, Agent Crivaro," the man said. "Too bad, I was kind of hoping we'd never see each other again. Certainly not under these circumstances."

"Yeah, me too," Crivaro said.

Crivaro introduced Riley to the man, who was the county medical examiner, Hamish Cross. Crivaro told Cross that Riley was "an agent in training."

Whatever that means exactly, she thought.

Still, it was a little bit encouraging to hear those words. It sounded like she still had some connection to the FBI instead of being tossed out completely.

Hamish Cross then introduced them to Wynnewood's police chief, Vachel MacNerland, an intense-looking man with a sharp chin and large, bulging eyes.

"I'm glad you're here," MacNerland said to Jake and Riley. "Ever since those other women got killed, I've been hoping and praying it didn't happen around Wynnewood next time. No such luck.

"Is the victim a local woman?" Jake asked.

"Her name was Anna Park," MacNerland said. "She moved

137

here a couple of years ago from across the state in Huntington. She lived alone in Wynnewood, didn't have any family here. She taught English at our community college, and she was one of our most popular teachers, students just loved her."

MacNerland turned and looked over at a woman standing nearby.

"You need to meet Clara Jarrett," he told them. "She owns the property."

He led them to the woman who was wearing round spectacles and a plain gingham dress that made her look like an old-time frontier woman. She stood with her arms crossed, staring at the body with an expression of what seemed to be bitter distaste, as if somebody had vandalized her property with graffiti.

After the chief introduced the agents, she said, shaking her head …

"I never thought I'd see anything like this," she said, shaking her head.

Chief MacNerland explained, "Clara is one of the many organic farmers we live in these parts."

Clara pointed toward a couple of small buildings across the pasture.

"I raise mostly chickens, over there," she said.

Sure enough, now that she listened closely, Riley could hear clucking sounds.

"They're disturbed by all the commotion out here," she said. "I'll let them out when it's daylight and after this is all cleaned away. They'll settle down then."

Clara added, "It was the cattle that got me up. I keep just a couple of cows in this pasture. I knew something was wrong a good while ago when I heard them bellowing at the top of their lungs. I came down from the house and found them running around like they were scared half to death."

Pointing at the corpse, she said, "Then I found this. Naturally I called Chief MacNerland right away. And I moved my cows into the barn."

She shook her head again and added matter-of-factly …

"Cattle get spooked by the smell of blood. Can't say I blame them, when it comes to something like this. I'd heard about the other two women, over near Dighton and Hyland. I sure never expected to find anything like this on my own property."

Riley again found herself staring at the bundled-up corpse.

It hardly seems real, she thought.

The victim had been tightly compressed into a fetal position. Her head was twisted so that her dead, terrified eyes looked directly into Riley's.

Riley walked over to the corpse and crouched down beside it.

She actually reached out to touch it, but then realized …

This is a crime scene.

Don't touch anything.

But then she heard Crivaro speak from beside her …

"It's OK to touch her, just slightly. It might trigger your instincts. That's what you're here for."

As Riley touched the face, she felt what seemed almost like an electric jolt, then pinpricks of pain all over her body.

As she cringed from the pain, Crivaro said in a gentle, encouraging voice …

"That feeling you're getting—you're empathizing the victim, not the killer. That's natural. I feel some of that myself right now. But you're not likely to get much insight that way. You know the next step—get into the killer's head. Take a few deep breaths. Close your eyes. Try to relax. Visualize what he did. Try to see it through his eyes. Engage all your senses."

Riley breathed long and slowly, but it wasn't so easy to relax.

After all, her task now was to fathom the unfathomable.

Keeping her eyes closed, she tried to imagine the killer going through these last steps—dragging the wrapped-up bundle across the shoulder of the road to this spot, hammering the large nail into the top of this post, unwrapping the blanket from the bundle, then hoisting it up and tying into place, and finally …

She paused as she continued to feel the cold flesh under her fingertips …

Maybe he touched her, like I'm touching her now.

The body had already been dead and drained of blood, so it had been cold like it was right now.

How did it make him feel to actually touch his horrible handiwork?

She felt as though the energy was draining from her body.

She sighed a deep, despairing sigh and said aloud to Crivaro …

"I feel like I did last time I tried this. Sheer exhaustion. Numbness. Maybe even … disappointment."

Her eyes were still closed. She heard Crivaro say …

"Good. I think you're probably right. Try to go back further, to when the victim was still alive and he was torturing her."

Riley shivered and murmured, "Oh, Agent Crivaro, I don't know if I can …"

Still speaking gently, Crivaro said, "You can do it, Riley. Try opening your eyes now."

Riley opened her eyes and found herself staring at the bundle again.

She felt a renewed jolt at the sight of that dead, staring face bleached out in the glare from the halogen lights.

This was much different from when she'd been to the crime scene where Hope Nelson's body had been found.

The intense light and her fingers on the flesh made this seem too, too real.

She spoke slowly …

"I think … he must have killed her in some place that he considered safe, somewhere out of the way, a lair that only he knew about."

She studied the bundle for a moment, noting how the body seemed to have been tightly bound in duct tape before it had been wrapped in barbed wire.

She remembered something she'd read in the reports of the earlier murders.

She asked Crivaro, "The other victims had been subdued with chloroform, weren't they?"

"That's right," Crivaro said. "It's a good guess that this one was too."

Riley moved her hand around, letting her fingers rest on some duct tape.

She said, "He couldn't have bound her up with the tape after she woke up. He did it when she was still unconscious. But he had the barbed wire all ready, laid out and arranged under the body as he bound her up. And when she started to regain consciousness …"

Riley shuddered deeply …

"That was when he began to tie the barbed wire into place. And he was vividly aware of her terror and pain. And terror and pain … *that* was what this was all about for him. He got tremendous satisfaction from the woman's suffering. And yet …"

She paused for a moment, then said …

"It wasn't sadism … exactly. Not really an act of cruelty. Well, it was cruel in its way, but it wasn't … gloating or malicious. I know that doesn't make sense …"

"Go on," Crivaro said.

"It was all about *his* pain, not his victims' pain. I …"

She felt on the verge of understanding something truly terrible about the killer.

But then her feelings began to ebb, and she felt her whole body slacken.

"I'm losing it," she said to Crivaro. "I'm not getting anything else."

Crivaro touched her on the shoulder and said, "That's OK. You did good. It's a good start. We can work with those impressions. We can build on them. Come on, let's go talk to the police chief."

She rose unsteadily to her feet. As she and Crivaro approached the police chief, Riley glanced back at the bundle and remembered what Crivaro had said barbed wire was sometimes called …

"The devil's rope."

Those words seemed horribly appropriate.

Something dawned on her as she remembered that empty numbness she felt sure the killer had felt as he left his victim here …

He's not done yet.

The killer wouldn't stop killing until the entire experience satisfied him from beginning to end …

And that's never going to happen.

Never.

CHAPTER TWENTY FIVE

Riley was aware that Chief MacNerland was gawking at her as she and Agent Crivaro walked toward him.

She realized …

What I was doing just now must have looked pretty strange.

But then, it couldn't have looked any stranger than it had felt. In fact, it had felt worse than strange. It had been horrifying.

Riley wondered, could she ever get used to trying to find her way into the mind of a murderous monster?

Did she *want* to get used to it? How deep into that darkness would her strange talent take her?

Crivaro asked Chief MacNerland …

"What do you know about how Anna Park was abducted?"

"We've got at least some idea," MacNerland said. "She was teaching a class at the community college last night. A while after the class was over, a local man came across Anna's car, abandoned right near the school. The driver's door was open and the motor was still running and the headlights were on. Apparently she was abducted when she came out from her last class and was starting to go home. Whoever took her must have gotten her to stop the car and get out of it. The guy who found the car called us right away."

MacNerland shook his head and added …

"I knew right then that she was in serious trouble. I was just hoping it wasn't … this."

Crivaro asked, "Were there any witnesses to the abduction itself?"

"No," MacNerland said. "But several of Anna's students came out of the building with her. They walked her to her car, then headed off in a different direction. We've already rounded up the students, and we've been interviewing them at the station."

"I'd like to talk to some of them too," Crivaro said.

"Be my guest," MacNerland said. "Several of them have gone home already, but I think three or four of them are still at the station. I'll take you right there."

As MacNerland drove them into town, Riley saw that Wynnewood was larger than Dighton. It was more like Lanton, the Virginia town where she had gone to college. Still, Wynnewood was very much a typical Appalachian small town, and its streets seemed almost eerily peaceful and quiet at this time of night.

But Riley was sure that the town wasn't nearly as tranquil as it looked right now. Word must have gotten out about Anna Park's disappearance, and then about her murder. Behind closed doors, the citizens of Wynnewood were surely trembling with fear.

When they got to the police station, Chief MacNerland led them into a small conference room. The four students who hadn't gone home yet were sitting at a table being interviewed by a cop who was taking notes.

Riley and Crivaro sat down at the table, and MacNerland introduced them to the students. Riley was a bit surprised at the range of their ages and backgrounds. But she reminded herself that the school was a community college. People of different types and ages went there for different reasons and with different expectations.

The youngest, Jane Hunter, had graduated a year ago from the local high school. She was trying to get course credits to help her continue her college education elsewhere—in Glenville, maybe.

Then there were Rudy and Lark Chesterfield, a couple in their fifties. They were retired "empty nesters," they said, and they enjoyed doing a variety of things together, from playing bridge to taking ballroom dance classes. Anna had been teaching a class in romantic poetry, which they thought would be fun to study together.

"And we were right," Lark added. "Anna was *such* a wonderful teacher."

Rudy shook his head sadly and said, "She had so much to offer. What happened to her was ... so horrible."

The last student was a convenience store manager in his thirties named Fred Combes. He seemed to be especially distraught.

"This is my fault," he said. "I should have insisted that she join us after class. Or I should have stayed there until she drove away."

Jane touched Fred gently on the hand and said, "How can you say that? This wasn't your fault. This wasn't any of our fault."

Then turning to Riley and Crivaro, Jane explained, "After class, we asked Anna to come to the local bar, so we could keep talking about the poetry of John Keats. We were all very excited about what she'd been teaching us about him. She thanked us for the invitation, but she said she wanted to drive on home."

Fred seemed close to tears now.

He said, "She wanted to go home and write, she said. That was her ambition. She wanted to be a writer. She'd taken the job at Wynnewood Community College to support herself while she wrote. She liked Wynnewood, she said, because life was so peaceful here, and she could really devote her spare time to writing."

In a choked voice he added …

"I should have insisted. I shouldn't have let her drive home alone."

At first Riley was a bit startled by Fred's seemingly irrational sense of guilt. But as he kept talking, it dawned on her …

He was in love with Anna.

He'd taken the class just to be close to her.

And now this terrible thing had happened to her.

Riley felt a stab of sympathy for him.

Then Lark Chesterfield began to murmur softly …

"When I have fears that I may cease to be
Before my pen has gleaned my teaming brain …"

Her husband joined in and they kept reciting in unison …

"Before high-piléd books, in charactery,
Hold like rich garners the full ripened grain …"

The couple's voices faded, and then Fred Combes continued alone …

"And when I feel, fair creature of an hour,
That I shall never look upon thee more …"

This was too much for poor Fred. He broke down and sobbed uncontrollably. Jane put her arm around him and added in a gentle voice …

"… on the shore
Of the wide world I stand alone, and think
Till love and fame to nothingness do sink."

Fred kept on crying, and Lark and Rudy both had to wipe away their tears as well.

Riley and Crivaro looked at each other with surprise, not sure

144

what had just happened.

Still comforting Fred, Jane said to Riley and Crivaro …

"Anna was teaching us that poem in class that night. It's a sonnet by John Keats, and it's about how he was afraid of dying young, before he'd done all the writing that he thought was in him. He had good reason to be afraid. He died really young."

Composing herself a little, Lark added …

"Anna cried when she read that poem to us. She'd recently turned 25, she said—the same age Keats was when he died. She, too, had 'fears that she might cease to be' before she got to do everything she wanted to do in life—especially all that she wanted to write. But she felt safe here in Wynnewood—'on the shore of the wide world,' as she put it. And she felt so, so grateful to have such a nice, peaceful place to live."

Riley felt a lump form in her throat.

Don't cry, she told herself.

She knew that would be completely unprofessional. But keeping her emotions to herself wasn't easy right now. She remembered Chief MacNerland saying about Anna …

"She was one of our most popular teachers, students just loved her."

Now Riley could see just how true that was. She could also understand why. Anna Park had brought her most personal thoughts and feelings to her work. She'd inspired all four of these students so deeply, they'd memorized a sonnet just because of how much it had meant to her.

Riley wondered …

Did I ever have a teacher who inspired me like that?

She quickly realized that she once had. That teacher had been a psychology professor back at Lanton, Brant Hayman. But Hayman had turned out to be a murderous monster who had almost killed Riley. In fact, she was due to be a witness at his murder trial the day after tomorrow.

Riley felt sure that Anna Park hadn't been anything like Hayman. She hadn't hidden any inner evil, any need to manipulate and murder those around her.

She'd been a good, generous, and brilliant woman who had died much too young.

Riley's sorrow was starting to turn to anger.

She didn't deserve this, she thought.

These people don't deserve this.

It was a horrible injustice that Anna Park had been snatched so brutally out of their lives. Nobody should have to face that. Not a little child losing a parent and not an adult losing someone they valued.

Riley found herself brooding silently as Agent Crivaro kept asking the group questions, trying to determine whether any of them had seen or heard anything that might serve as a clue about Anna's murder. It quickly became apparent that they hadn't. Agent Crivaro thanked the four people, and Chief MacNerland sent them home.

Chief MacNerland called a local motel and reserved two rooms for Riley and Crivaro. Then he lent them a car so they could drive there and get some sleep. It would be dawn soon enough.

Riley and Crivaro didn't say a word to each other during the short drive to the motel. They checked in at the front desk, then headed back outside and started toward their rooms.

Crivaro called out and stopped Riley …

"Wait. We've got to talk a minute."

Riley turned and looked at him.

"What is it?" she asked.

"You're angry," Crivaro said, walking toward her again.

Riley hadn't realized how much she was showing her anger. Not that she thought it mattered.

In a tense voice she said, "Yeah, I'm mad as hell. A kind and caring young woman got killed, leaving some really good people to grieve. They'll probably never get over losing her—especially poor Fred, who was obviously in love with her and thinks it was all his fault. Sure, I'm angry about it. So what?"

Crivaro shrugged slightly and said, "So—get over it."

Riley was truly surprised now.

She said, "Isn't it good to get angry at times like this? Isn't getting angry part of our jobs, part of what drives us?"

Crivaro smiled knowingly, as if reflecting on long personal experience.

He said, "No, it doesn't do you a damn bit of good, believe me. It's human. It's natural. At times like now, you're going to feel angry. *I* feel angry. But when we get up in the morning, we'd better be over it, or else neither one of us will be worth a damn as detectives."

"I don't understand," Riley said.

Crivaro shuffled his feet and said, "The way I look at it, anger's like sneezing. Sometimes you can't help sneezing. Sometimes you've got to sneeze and get it out of your system. But it's stupid to think there's anything righteous or good about a sneeze, and it's the same with anger. It'll just cloud your judgment, stop you from thinking straight."

Crivaro patted Riley on the shoulder and added …

"So go in your room, and scream into your pillow, or pound on the floor if you have to. But get it out of your system. Get done with it."

Without another word, Crivaro walked to his own room and went on inside.

Riley went into her room and realized she was hyperventilating and shaking all over from sheer rage.

She remembered what Crivaro had just said …

"Get over it."

She now knew he was right. Feeling this way might be natural, but it sure wasn't helpful. But what was she going to do about it? She doubted that screaming into a pillow and pounding on the floor would do any good.

But she knew she had to do something.

She collapsed on the bed, and before she knew it, a torrent of uncontrollable emotion poured over, and she was sobbing her heart out.

That's it, she thought as she wept.

That's what I need.

She cried and cried for long minutes, until she was too exhausted to feel much of anything except a numb, tired kind of sadness. Then she took a shower and got ready to go to bed.

When she climbed under the covers, she heard her phone buzzing on the nightstand.

She picked up her phone and saw that the call was from Ryan.

Strangely, she simply didn't care.

Ever since the ugly scene at their apartment last night, she'd been desperately anxious to hear from, or to call him, to try to straighten things out between them.

But right now, at this moment, she didn't care if she saw him or heard his voice ever again.

All she wanted was to catch the fiend who had killed those three women in such a hideous way.

She ignored the buzzing phone and rolled over and went to sleep.

Morning light was peeking through the curtains when Riley was awakened by a sharp knock at the motel room door.

"Who is it?" she called out tiredly.

"It's Crivaro," came the reply. "Open up."

Riley scrambled out of bed and opened the door and saw Crivaro standing there.

"We've got to leave right now," he said. "I just got a phone call from Chief Tallhamer over in Hyland. He thinks we've got a break in the case."

CHAPTER TWENTY SIX

As he pulled out of the motel parking lot, Jake Crivaro began filling Riley in on the news he'd just gotten. He was glad to see that she seemed excited and alert, despite just having been rousted out of bed.

Jake reminded her, "You've heard me talk about Philip Cardin, the guy who was arrested and held for Alice Gibson's murder, right?"

"I remember," Riley said. "You had to let Phil go because he was in jail when Hope Nelson was murdered. But his brother, Harvey, had recently left Hyland under suspicious circumstances."

"Which left a couple of interesting possibilities once you consider the prospect of both brothers being killers," Jake said. "Nobody knew Harvey's whereabouts after his disappearance. He could have been near Dighton during that time. Harvey might have killed Hope Nelson. For that matter, he might have killed both Hope and Alice. Or he and his brother might have partnered up for the murders, taking turns with them. Phil might have killed Alice, and then Harvey might have killed Hope while Phil was still in jail."

Jake could see Riley shake her head.

She said, "That's a lot of stuff to consider."

"I know," Jake said. "But as long as Harvey was missing, there wasn't much we could do to follow up on those possibilities. I'd put a tech team in Quantico to work trying to hunt Harvey down, and they turned up nothing. Meanwhile, Chief Tallhamer kept a close eye on Phil Cardin, made sure he didn't do anything suspicious or try to leave town."

Riley said, "So what happened? Did Harvey come back to Hyland?"

Jake said, "Yeah, Chief Tallhamer's cops picked him up last night. In fact, they took Phil back into custody as well. According to the chief, both brothers were behaving pretty suspiciously. Tallhamer will fill us in on details as soon as we get there."

"Wow," Riley said quietly. "So maybe the case has been solved without us having to do much of anything."

Jake heard a note of disappointment in her voice. He thought he understood why. Between getting kicked out of the Academy and

149

whatever issues she was having with her fiancé …

The poor kid needs a win right now.

Riley needed to accomplish something, and the bigger the accomplishment the better. He was tempted to tell her that he wasn't at all sure this was really a break in the case. If the Cardin brothers turned out to be innocent after all, he and Riley still had their work cut out for them. And he'd need Riley's special gifts more than ever.

But it was best not to say so right now …

Don't want to get her hopes up.

Besides, Jake really did hope this case was solved and over with. He and Riley had to be in Lanton tomorrow to testify at the trial of Brant Hayman, the college professor who had killed two of Riley's friends and had almost killed Riley herself.

Jake had testified at plenty of murder trials himself, but he knew this would be a new experience for Riley, and possibly a traumatic one. It wouldn't be easy for her to recount her friends' deaths and her own ordeal at Hayman's murderous hands. Jake figured it would be best if Riley didn't have their current case hanging over her when she had to do all that.

As they drove on in silence, a worry started nagging at Jake. There was something he hadn't yet told Riley, and he knew he probably ought to tell her. But how would she take it? Would she feel angry, confused, betrayed, or … ?

Jake swallowed down his concerns …

I'd better just come out with it.

He cleared his throat and said …

"Riley, I've got something I need to tell you, and I'm not sure you're going to like it."

Riley turned and looked at him expectantly.

Jake said, "After I dropped you off in Quantico the night before last, and when I was driving back to West Virginia, I …"

Jake swallowed hard.

"I drove up to your father's cabin and paid him a visit," he said.

Riley gasped and said …

"You *what?*"

Jake shook his head and said, "I know it sounds crazy …"

"Yeah, it kind of does," Riley said. The expression on her face revealed more shock than her words did.

Jake stifled a discouraged groan. He was starting to wish he'd kept his mouth shut. But there was no taking back his words now, and she would likely find out sooner or later anyhow.

Riley asked, "How did you even find the place?"

Jake said, "I asked for directions in a bar in Milladore."

"And you went up on that mountain in the middle of the night?" Riley asked.

Jake nodded.

Riley said, "And he didn't blow your head off with his Browning Citori stacked-barrel shotgun?"

Jake chuckled, feeling oddly relieved by the question.

"Oh, he emptied one barrel, but he fired in the air. I managed to talk him out of killing me."

"You're lucky," Riley said.

As Jake remembered scrambling behind the car for safety and drawing his own weapon, he thought …

Yeah, I guess I was lucky.

"Why did you do that?" Riley asked.

Jake shrugged a little and said, "I was curious, that's all."

"Curious about what?" Riley asked.

Jake didn't reply. He wasn't sure what to say.

Riley asked, "Curious about me?"

Jake smiled a little and said, "You're an enigma, Riley Sweeney. I'm just trying to make sense of you."

Jake glanced sideways and saw that Riley's mouth was hanging open.

After a moment, Riley said, "So how did your visit go?"

"OK," Jake said. "Your dad makes some tasty hard cider."

"Did you find out what you want to know?" Riley asked.

Jake paused and remembered …

Yes, I learned a lot.

He'd gotten some insights into how Riley had been shaped by her father's expectations. He remembered Sweeney's words …

"She's a hunter. Like me. I raised her that way."

Jake had also come away from the encounter feeling more impressed by Riley than he'd ever been.

But he didn't want to go into any details about that strange encounter. And he hoped Riley wasn't going to ask a lot of questions.

Riley finally said with a sigh, "Well, I guess it only makes sense that you'd meet sooner or later. You're a lot alike, the two of you."

Jake winced inside.

He wasn't sure he liked being compared to that wild man in the hills.

Besides, Jake remembered again how Sweeney had told him …

"I never trust a man whose children don't hate him."

Considering Jake's troubled relationship with his son, those words had cut way too close to home.

Did he and Oliver Sweeney have too much in common for Jake's liking?

Then Riley said in a near whisper …

"Agent Crivaro … thanks."

Jake glanced at her with surprise.

"Thanks for what?" he said.

Riley laughed a little and said, "I don't know exactly. Just … thanks."

They both fell silent. As Jake continued to drive, he kept puzzling over just why Riley had thanked him. Little by little, something began to dawn on him. Perhaps Riley was grateful that he'd simply gone out of his way to learn more about her, to understand her better.

After all, in a way he was acting like a father. He realized that even as weak as his own parenting skills might be, he was still the kind of father she'd never had.

Jake felt his throat tighten with emotion.

He hadn't given it much thought before, but he was definitely feeling paternal toward this young recruit. Maybe if he became a good guiding influence on her, he might feel less guilty about how things had turned out with his son.

But he quickly told himself …

Be careful.

Mentoring and parenting were two different things, after all. They might not make a good mix. He'd already had to be tough on Riley, more like a boss than a father, even to the point where they'd both thought their relationship was over.

Besides, what kind of relationship was still in the cards for them? Riley had gotten herself kicked out of the Academy, and Jake couldn't very well keep on partnering with an uncertified civilian kid. Sooner rather than later, she was going to have to start finding her own path through life …

Still, maybe I can be part of it.

He found himself remembering that moment when he was leaving the cabin and Sweeney had called out to him …

"Crivaro—I know something about you. Something you may not know yourself."

When Jake had turned to look at him, Sweeney had said …

"You're a good man."

Jake half-smiled to himself and thought …

Wouldn't it be nice if that were true?

*

During the rest of the drive to Hyland, Riley found herself thinking about what Crivaro had just told her. The idea that he had ventured up into the hills near Milladore by night just to visit her father boggled her mind.

Still, when she'd thanked him, she'd really meant it.

Right now, when so many things were going wrong in her life, it felt good to know that someone was not only looking out for her, but was genuinely curious about what made her tick.

How long had it been since anyone had treated her that way? Ryan certainly hadn't shown her much consideration or concern lately. It seemed an odd thing that she felt closer to this cantankerous FBI agent than she did to her own fiancé …

But that's how things are.

She was glad to have Crivaro in her life right now, and it made her sad to realize they'd probably have to part ways before very long.

At least they'd still be together tomorrow, when they both had to testify in Brant Hayman's murder trial. The closer the time came for Riley face her one-time teacher and would-be killer in court, the more frightened she was by the prospect. She knew she would need Crivaro's emotional support to get through it.

When they reached Hyland, Riley was startled to see how small the town was—much smaller even than Dighton, with maybe just a couple of hundred people …

The kind of town where nothing ever happens.

But Riley knew that something had definitely happened near here—a hideous murder that she guessed would haunt the residents of Hyland for a long time.

Crivaro parked in front of the little storefront police station, and they got out of the car. There was only a handful of pedestrians in sight. Riley could hear Crivaro breathe a sigh of relief.

"No reporters—at least not yet," he said. "I guess they haven't gotten wind of these new arrests, thank God."

A man stepped out of the police station as Riley and Crivaro approached—a startlingly unattractive man with a pockmarked face. He was wearing a white medical jacket.

The man walked toward them with a smirk on his face.

He said, "Well, if it isn't our FBI man again. And you've brought along a little helper. I guess it's no surprise that you got here just in time to be of no use at all. The chief's got the murderers in custody. It's like I said all along—the Cardin brothers were guilty as hell. I don't yet know which of those two bastards killed my poor Alice, but it won't be long now before I do know—no thanks to you."

Without another word, the man brushed past Riley and Crivaro and continued on his way.

"Who was that?" Riley asked Crivaro as they stood staring after him.

Crivaro said, "That was Dr. Earl Gibson—the husband of the first murder victim. When I met him before, he was sure the Cardin brothers were the killers, and he was furious when Phil Cardin was released from jail. I guess he could have been right after all."

Riley and Crivaro walked into the police station, where two uniformed men stood talking. The larger of the two was chewing a wad of tobacco—Chief Tallhamer, Riley guessed. She was surprised when she recognized the shorter, stockier man. It was Graham Messenger, the chief of police over in Dighton.

Crivaro introduced Riley to the two men—once again as "an agent in training." Then he asked them to fill him in on what had happened.

Nodding toward Tallhamer, Messenger said, "I'm afraid my colleague Dave here called you on a needless errand. Dave called me too, and I showed up here just a little while ago myself."

Tallhamer pointed to a doorway in back of the station and added, "I took Dave back there to see the brothers in their jail cells, and we all had a serious talk. The Cardin boys are our killers, all right. I wasn't sure when I called you, but I am sure now."

Then Messenger crossed his arms and said, "So we won't be needing the FBI's help anymore. You can head on back to Quantico."

Riley saw Crivaro's mouth drop open at this remark. She knew, of course, that Crivaro and his forensics team were here solely at Messenger's request. It was entirely up to Messenger whether they stayed or left. But Crivaro obviously hadn't expected such an abrupt dismissal.

Crivaro asked Tallhamer, "How did you apprehend them?"

Tallhamer explained, "Harvey Cardin pulled into town late last night and went straight to his brother's apartment. When my men busted in on them, they were packing up to leave town together once and for all. I guess they knew they'd get caught for sure if they hung around too long."

Messenger chuckled a little and said, "Of course, the way the brothers tell it, it was all perfectly innocent."

Riley heard another voice bark out …

"It *was* innocent. And you can't prove otherwise."

Riley turned and saw a bleary-eyed man walking unsteadily toward them. Crivaro whispered to her …

"That's Ozzie Hines, Phil Cardin's lawyer."

Riley's eyes widened with surprise …

His lawyer?

She could smell alcohol on the man's breath even from several feet away.

Hines wagged his finger at the two police chiefs and said …

"You heard what Harvey said just now. He left town in the first place because he was sick to death of Hyland and how he and he and his brother both get treated here. The only reason he came back was to talk Phil into going away with him, this time for good. That's why they were packing up to go. Neither one of them ever killed anybody."

Tallhamer and Messenger smiled condescendingly at Hines.

"Come on, Ozzie," Tallhamer said. "That doesn't hold water and you know it."

Messenger added, "When we asked Harvey where he'd been and what he'd been doing during the last week or so, his answers were all muddled. He can't even make up his mind about his own alibis."

Ozzie Hines was red-faced with anger now.

He said, "Tallhamer, Messenger—the two of you interrogated my client before I could get over here. You know that isn't kosher. You violated his Fifth Amendment rights. The same with his brother, and I'm representing him now too. Nothing they said will be admissible in court."

Tallhamer and Messenger laughed raucously.

"Now isn't *that* a load of crap!" Tallhamer said.

"Phil and Harvey knew their rights when they talked to us," Messenger added. "They just got tired of waiting around until you could sober up enough to find your way here."

Riley saw that Crivaro's eyes were darting back and forth between the two police chiefs.

He said, "I think Sweeney and I should talk to the suspects ourselves."

Ozzie Hines let a growl of defiance.

"Well, you *can't* talk to them, Mr. FBI man. Nobody else is talking to them, and they're not talking to anybody—not until I say otherwise, which will probably be never."

Hines turned and strode shakily but brashly back through the door into the jail.

Tallhamer and Messenger nudged each other, chuckling heartily.

"Poor Ozzie Hines," Tallhamer said. "That poor drunk's out of his depth for sure. He knows right well he doesn't have the stuff to handle a real live murder case—especially one where both of his clients are obviously guilty as hell."

Messenger added, "Yeah, he was talking tough just now, but it was all just bluster. He's probably back there right this minute trying to persuade the Cardin boys that they're going to have to make some kind of a deal, starting with a guilty plea."

Crivaro's eyes narrowed as he said, "I think Sweeney and my forensics team and I should stay on the case for a while longer."

Messenger shrugged and said, "Why? It's like we told you, we've got the Cardins dead to rights."

Tallhamer let out a mocking laugh and said to Messenger …

"I guess Agent Crivaro's feeling a little put out, what with us hillbillies solving the case before he and his smart Fed team could make any headway with it. It's got to be a little rough on his pride."

"It must be at that," Messenger said. "I'm truly sorry, Agent Crivaro. But really, it's time for you and your good people to head on back to Quantico."

Riley could see Crivaro's body tense up all over as he tried to think of something else to say. But he knew that nothing he could say would change the two men's minds.

Instead, Crivaro said to Messenger …

"All right, then. But that's your car I've got out there. Sweeney and I have got some separate business over in Lanton tomorrow, nothing to do with this case. Would it be OK if we borrowed it for another day?"

"As long as you bring it back in one piece," Messenger said.

Crivaro turned to Riley and said, "Come on, let's go."

As Riley and Crivaro headed out of the police station and got back in the car, Riley asked …

"Are we really through with the case?"

Crivaro scoffed as he started the car engine and pulled out of the parking place.

"You tell me, Riley. What's your gut telling you right at this moment. Do you really think those two jokers have got two killers dead to rights?"

The answer came to Riley right away …

"No. I don't think so."

"I don't either," Crivaro said as he drove down the street. "Nobody can make us go anywhere. My forensics guys are still in Wynnewood, and that's where they're going to stay for the time being. Meanwhile, you and I have got to testify in a trial in Lanton tomorrow. That's not too far away, just across the mountain. We can get a couple of rooms for the night. We can get back here in a hurry if we have to."

As they rounded a corner to head on out of town, Riley saw a man in a white jacket walking along—Dr. Earl Gibson, she quickly realized.

When Gibson saw who was in the car, his gaze connected with Riley's. His stare was strange and hostile.

Riley felt chilled to the bone, but she didn't know just why.

It was more than the fact that his appearance was so startlingly homely.

Something is deeply wrong with that man, she thought.

But whatever that something was, she figured it was none of her business.

She tried to put the doctor out of her mind as Crivaro drove them on out of Hyland.

CHAPTER TWENTY SEVEN

As Riley sat in the court room awaiting her turn to testify, she kept having to remind herself that this wasn't another dream. Getting plunged into the last phases of a long murder trial felt weird and disorienting.

She wished she'd been here during at least some of the proceedings—Brant Hayman's not guilty plea, the questioning of other witnesses, the presentation of evidence, testimony of experts, and all the rest of it.

Instead, she felt lost and confused and downright scared. She wondered if she'd have the courage to testify.

Meanwhile, she hadn't realized that a murder trial could seem so strange and surreal. It wasn't as though anything outwardly weird was happening. To the contrary, what disturbed her was how everything seemed so formal and regimented.

The courtroom itself was stately and museum-like, with its high ceiling, its polished, dark wood paneling, its stiff wooden furniture, its imposing judge's bench, and its pew-like seating for spectators.

Riley remembered the killings all too well, and those memories brought back feelings of horror, helplessness, and sheer confusion—so different from the atmosphere here and now.

She almost wondered …

Am I in the right place?

Is this really a murder trial?

Or is this really a dream after all?

After Riley and Crivaro had arrived here in Lanton yesterday, they'd gotten a good night's rest in their motel rooms. Before coming to the courthouse this morning, Crivaro had told her over breakfast …

"Hayman has got no defense. The evidence against him is solid. There's no possibility of reasonable doubt. The only question is—why did he plead 'not guilty'? He might have cut a plea deal if he'd cooperated with prosecutors. Now he'll almost certainly face the death penalty."

Indeed, according to what Riley had been told, everyone in the courtroom was stunned when Hayman's pleaded not guilty. Even his own lawyer had seemed badly shaken.

Right now Mona Brogden, the prosecuting attorney, was questioning a cop on the witness stand. The cop was presenting especially damning evidence. The police had seized notes that Hayman had written about each of the murders—notes that he must have intended to destroy after he had completed a twisted "experiment" in mass trauma.

He'd written those notes before and after the murders—first describing before the fact exactly how he intended to kill his victims, then later relating how each murder had actually unfolded, carefully noting any deviations from his original plan.

The cop's testimony made Riley feel just a little less worried.

Surely those notes alone proved Hayman's guilt.

Then Hayman's lawyer, Kirby Larch, rose to cross-examine the witness. He showed little conviction as he suggested that Hayman's notes had been nothing more than an academic exercise—an attempt on his part to imagine what the killer might be experiencing. It was a weak defense, and Larch seemed to know it.

But as Larch took his seat again, Hayman smiled a knowing smile.

Is he up to something? Riley wondered.

Has he got a surprise up his sleeve?

So far, Hayman didn't seem to have noticed her presence in the courtroom. She'd forgotten what a handsome, charming man he was, dressed even now in a casual, academic-style corduroy outfit.

He didn't look like a man who had brutally murdered two young coeds by slashing their throats in their dorm rooms.

But then, she'd misjudged him from the very start.

She remembered taking her first class with him. She'd been a freshman then, and he was still a graduate assistant, not yet a professor. She found him to be the most exciting, stimulating, and inspiring teacher she'd ever had. It was because of him she'd decided to major in psychology.

After the cop was dismissed from the stand, Agent Crivaro was soon called to testify. Crivaro had warned Riley that his own testimony was liable to seem bland. His task, he'd said, was simply to relate his own actions as a law enforcement officer, not to vent his personal outrage toward the man on trial.

As Crivaro answered the questions of the prosecuting attorney, Riley was impressed by how clearly and succinctly he told his story—how he'd come to Lanton at the request of the local police after the second murder took place, and how he and his team had employed their best skills in trying to find the killer.

Crivaro also told how he had met Riley and soon sensed that she had the potential to be a BAU profiler. He described how she'd worked with him during the case—sometimes with valuable insights, sometimes making rookie mistakes, but always doing the best she could.

Then he told how Riley, without meaning to, had led him straight to the killer, and how he'd narrowly saved her from becoming his next victim. Finally he described how he'd subdued and arrested Brant Hayman.

The prosecution lawyer thanked Crivaro for his testimony. Then she turned the witness over to the defense lawyer for cross-examination.

Still displaying a distinct lack of enthusiasm, Kirby Larch asked Crivaro …

"Are you *sure* my client was trying to kill Riley Sweeney when you burst into his office? Couldn't it possibly have been the other way around? Might my client only have been acting in self-defense?"

Crivaro couldn't help but scoff aloud at the question.

"I know what I saw," he told Larch. "If I'd gotten there a moment later, Hayman would have killed her. And that was exactly what he was trying to do."

"Thank you," Larch said. "I've got no further questions, your honor."

Again Riley was surprised. Why hadn't Larch pushed harder to cross-examine Crivaro? Did he really think there was no point in trying to challenge Crivaro's testimony?

Crivaro stepped down, and Riley gulped hard as she realized …

Now it's my turn.

She remembered how Brogden had prepared her for this moment a little while ago, helping her rehearse what she was likely to have to say.

"Just tell the truth," Brogden had said.

It sounded so simple. So why did it feel like such a daunting task right now?

The bailiff called Riley to the stand, and she raised her right hand to affirm the truth of her testimony. Then Mona Brogden stepped toward the witness stand and said in a gentle tone …

"Ms. Sweeney, how are you today?"

Riley almost said "fine" before she reminded herself a bit

wryly …

I'm under oath.

And I'm not exactly "fine."

Instead she said …

"I'm nervous and scared."

Brogden nodded and said, "I know, and I understand that. I'm sorry that you have to relieve such a terrible ordeal. But your testimony is very important today."

"I understand," Riley said.

Always maintaining a kindly and sympathetic tone, Brogden asked the same questions she'd asked Riley during the preparation—questions about Riley's discovery of the body of her friend Rhea Thorson in the victim's own dorm room, her subsequent interactions with the local police, and then finding the body of her best friend Trudy Lanier in the room they shared together.

As she described all this, Riley felt almost as though she were leaving her body, looking over the proceedings from a distance, relating events that had happened to somebody else. She was relieved that Hayman still wasn't making eye contact with her. He seemed to be going to some trouble to ignore her presence. Riley couldn't guess why.

She talked about Crivaro's arrival in Lanton and how they'd done their best to work as a team. Finally she explained how she'd come to the mistaken suspicion that a kindly older psychology professor was the real murderer, then had gone to Brant Hayman's office to share her thoughts with him.

That had been when Hayman had revealed his true nature.

He'd brutally attacked Riley, and once she'd been subdued, he'd told her about his twisted purpose. He was conducting a scientific study of mass grief and terror, using the Lanton campus as a laboratory. He himself was committing the murders in order to provoke the reactions he wanted to study.

The plan, he'd told her, was going smoothly until she'd come along just now.

That was why he had to kill her too, he'd said.

She'd done her best to defend herself, but he'd gotten the better of her. He began to strangle her with his necktie, and she was losing consciousness when Agent Crivaro had burst through the door to save her.

Finally Brogden asked her, "Ms. Sweeney, is there any chance

161

that you misconstrued the situation? You said that you tried to defend yourself. But are you *sure* Prof. Hayman was really trying to hurt you? Might he have felt as though he had to defend himself from you?"

"Oh, no," Riley said. "I know what happened. He was really trying to kill me. And he openly admitted to killing my two friends."

Brogden turned to the judge and said, "I have no further questions, Your Honor. The defense may cross examine the witness."

To Riley's surprise, Kirby Larch stood up beside his client and said …

"The defense has no questions for this witness, Your Honor."

Again, Riley sensed that Larch considered his client's case to be hopeless.

And yet …

Shouldn't he at least go through the motions of trying to defend him?

Larch sat whispering with Hayman for a few moments.

Then the lawyer got to his feet and said to the judge …

"Your Honor, if the court has no objection, I wish to call Prof. Brant Hayman to the stand."

The air suddenly echoed with confused and startled voices.

Riley, too, was taken completely by surprise.

Why on earth did Hayman want to testify?

What could he possibly say that wouldn't wind up being self-incriminating?

Although Riley was no lawyer, it seemed like a truly insane tactic.

The judge rapped his gavel and called the court back to order.

Then the judge said, "I'll allow it."

Hayman rose from the table and walked to the witness stand, where he affirmed that his testimony was going to be true.

As he sat back down, he looked straight at Riley for the first time.

And he smiled with look deep satisfaction, as if he relished the thought of whatever was about to happen next.

Riley shuddered deeply.

So far, nothing about the trial had made any sense, including the defendant's plea of not guilty …

But now …

Riley felt pinned under his gaze like an insect in a display case.

She felt absolutely certain that Brant Hayman was about to do or say something that nobody could possibly have expected …

And it has something to do with me.

CHAPTER TWENTY EIGHT

Riley tried to disengage herself from Hayman's gaze. But somehow, she couldn't bring herself to look away from him. She found herself remembering how captivating a presence he'd been in a classroom, how a whole hour could pass without her realizing it. Other students had told her they'd felt the same way.

Back then, she'd enjoyed the strange spell he could cast on a group of students.

It had seemed like a positive and exciting thing.

Even as he sat there on the witness stand, a prisoner accused of murder, the man had a similar magnetism.

But now it seemed scary and positively dangerous.

After a few moments, Kirby Larch asked his client …

"Prof. Hayman, was Ms. Sweeney's account of your encounter in your office accurate?"

Still looking directly at Riley, Hayman smiled and said …

"Not at all. She attacked me, not the other way around. In fairness to her, though, she thought she had a good reason. She thought I'd killed her two friends, and she was angry, and I couldn't make her listen to reason. She's a surprisingly strong young woman and …"

He paused and shrugged and said …

"Well, I did what I had to do to defend myself. When Agent Crivaro burst into my office, it must have looked like I was the aggressor. The truth was, I was relieved that he arrived. I truly feared for my life."

Kirby Larch scratched his chin and said, "Then the conversation Ms. Sweeney says took place between you, when you supposedly admitted to killing her friends as part of an experiment—that didn't take place at all?"

Hayman looked at his lawyer and said, "No, I never said any such thing."

"Why do you think she'd make something like that up?" Larch asked.

The prosecuting attorney jumped to her feet and shouted, "Objection! The defendant is being asked to speculate on Ms. Sweeney's motivations. He's not a mind-reader."

Larch said, "No, but he *is* a psychology professor. Your Honor, the question goes to the previous witness's credibility. In his own defense, my client deserves to have his say in this matter."

The judge frowned for a moment.

Then he said, "I'll allow it."

Hayman turned his disturbing stare back on Riley again.

He said, "Odd though this may seem, I don't think the young lady was lying. Her story is a rather extreme case of confabulation—a belief in fabricated imaginary experiences. In her mind, she has been building and elaborating on this story for quite some time. I noticed that she had this tendency when she was my student. She has a remarkable imagination—and an unfortunate tendency to take her own imaginings as fact."

Riley bristled with anger.

He's making me sound like I'm crazy, she thought.

Was anyone in the courtroom going to believe him?

The possibility scared her.

His voice, manner, and appearance were so compelling, and he seemed both sincere and authoritative.

She almost thought *she'd* believe him if she were someone else in the courtroom.

Hayman continued …

"The truth is, I'm afraid I let our relationship get a little out of hand. I think I became more than a teacher to her. I became a sort of mentor."

Riley felt a chill all over as she realized …

That's true.

His impact upon her as a freshman had been enormous.

She cringed as she remember confessing as much to him one day …

"I've always meant to tell you … you really inspired me to major in Psychology."

Hayman added, "Not that I saw anything wrong with that, at least not at the time. Riley Sweeney struck me as a talented young woman—rather brilliant, actually. I was flattered that she held me in such high regard. But I hadn't realized … well, that she had personal issues. My guess is that she had or has a troubled relationship with her father. She's been looking for a substitute father figure for a long time."

Riley felt frozen with mortification.

Why did he have to be so insightful about her?

165

She wanted to put her hands over her ears …

If I keep listening, I'm liable to think I'm crazy.

Hayman then glanced back and forth between Riley and Crivaro and said …

"I've been trying to follow Riley's life since … well, since this whole terrible thing happened. I've kept up with her even during my incarceration. She's been training to become an FBI Agent, I hear. And she's found another mentor—the witness who spoke before her, Special Agent Jake Crivaro. My guess is that he's a somewhat more appropriate influence on her than I could be, being a somewhat older man."

Riley could see Crivaro's face redden with rage.

Everybody else in the courtroom seemed utterly transfixed, including the prosecuting attorney.

Hayman locked eyes with Riley again, as if he were talking to her and her alone …

"Tell me, Riley—how is this new case of yours going? Something to do with 'the devil's rope,' I hear."

Riley shuddered …

He really has *been following my life.*

Hayman continued …

"Two men were arrested yesterday, weren't they? Two brothers. But you've got doubts that they're really guilty, don't you? You should pay attention to those doubts. Follow your instincts. But be fearless about it. Sooner or later, those instincts will lead you into a world of your own darkest nightmares. If they haven't already."

Almost as if she'd snapped out of a trance, the prosecuting attorney jumped to her feet …

"Objection! Your Honor, this has gone much too far!"

"I agree," the judge said with a growl, rapping his gavel. "The defendant—the *witness*—is dismissed."

But Hayman didn't move from the witness chair.

Still staring at Riley, he smiled and said …

"Think, Riley—about pain, shame, self-hatred, and especially ugliness."

Riley felt ready to explode.

She simply couldn't take this anymore.

She jumped up from her seat and hurried out of the courtroom. Then she stood in the hallway, gasping and hyperventilating. In just a few seconds, Crivaro came dashing through the door and took her by the shoulders.

"Riley, sit down. Take some deep breaths. It'll be all right."

Riley sat down with Crivaro on a wooden bench.

Fighting back her tears she said …

"It won't be all right. He's going to get off. He's going to be found not guilty."

Crivaro squeezed her hand and said in a firm voice …

"No, he won't. I promise."

"How can you know that?" Riley asked.

"Think about it, Riley. He's not even trying to defend himself. If he were, he'd be talking about those notes he'd written, trying to explain them away. But he knows that's impossible. His fate is sealed. My guess is the verdict will be in by tomorrow."

Riley felt stunned and baffled.

"Then what was he trying to do … just now?"

Crivaro stared off into space, as if trying to answer that question for himself.

Finally he murmured …

"Riley, you're not going to like this."

"Tell me," Riley said.

Crivaro shook his head and said, "It's about *you*. All of this. The plea of not guilty, the trial, everything. All he wanted was a moment to look into your eyes and make you question your own sanity."

"But why?" Riley asked.

Crivaro shrugged.

"Do you really have to ask?" he said. "Riley, you led me right to him. It's because of you that he's been brought to justice. You and your fine instincts. It's been eating him up inside, the whole time he's been in jail—that he let a college kid wreck all his brilliant plans. He'll never be able to get back at you, never truly even the score between you. But …"

Riley felt as though she was starting to understand now.

She said, "But by going on trial, and getting to face me in the court room, he could mess with my head one last time."

She sighed and added …

"And he succeeded."

"Not really," Jake said with a chuckle. "It was pretty desperate on his part. He doesn't have any power over you—not now. I mean, he took his only opportunity and did his worst, and you still seem pretty sane to me."

167

Riley fell silent for a moment.

She thought hard about what Crivaro was saying.

She felt sure that it was true …

As far as it goes.

But she sensed that Crivaro was missing something.

Hayman must have had some purpose in mind other than simply making her feel like she was going crazy.

But what was it?

She remembered something that he'd said about her …

"I was flattered that she held me in such high regard."

She murmured aloud …

"He wanted to finish mentoring me."

Crivaro gave her a startled look.

"Huh?" he said.

Still trying to grasp the truth, Riley remembered those last words she'd heard Hayman say …

"Think, Riley—about pain, shame, self-hatred, and especially ugliness."

Those words clanged about in her mind, mixing with images she'd encountered in recent days.

Riley gasped and said to Crivaro …

"We've got to go back to Hyland. Right now."

"Why?" Crivaro said.

"I know who killed those women," Riley said. "It wasn't the Cardin brothers."

CHAPTER TWENTY NINE

While Jake drove the car back to Hyland, he listened eagerly to Riley's new theory. She was sure Brant Hayman had given her a hint during his final moments on the stand, just before she'd rushed out of the courtroom. And now she believed she knew what he'd been getting at.

She said, "Those words Hayman used—pain, shame, self-hatred, and ugliness. Those are characteristics of the killer himself. He's been living with them all his life. And now he's trying to escape all those feelings by inflicting them on others. The victims die an incredibly painful death—but more than that, they're degraded, disfigured, even humiliated."

Jake crinkled his brow skeptically.

"It's an interesting idea," he said. "But how did Hayman come up with it?"

Jake heard Riley let out a bitter sigh.

"He's brilliant," she said. "I know we both hate to admit it about a cold-blooded killer, but he's got incredible insights into criminal pathology. And he got a kick out of sharing one last insight with me before he heads off to death row. It was like he got to teach one last lesson."

Jake shook his head and said, "Riley, I don't know if I ..."

Riley interrupted insistently.

"Think about it, Agent Crivaro. Do you remember when we went to the crime scene to look at Anna Park's body? I got a powerful feeling about the killer—that what he was doing was all about pain. But it wasn't just about his victims' pain. It was also about his own."

Jake began to sense some truth in what Riley was saying.

He said, "And the killer is in pain because ..."

"He's ugly," Riley said. "He's lived with humiliation and shame and self-hatred all his life."

Suddenly it felt as if a light flashed on in Jake's head.

He remembered a phrase Phil Cardin had used to describe his ex-wife's new husband ...

"... that toad she took up with."

Jake also remembered how he himself had reacted when he'd

first seen the man's face …

"My God," he murmured, glancing over at Riley. "You think Dr. Gibson is the killer."

Riley nodded vigorously.

"I'm all but sure of it. When we drove out of Hyland yesterday, I saw him walking down the street. When he saw me, he stopped and stared. It was a really weird look—hostile, I thought at the time. But now I realize, it was a guilty look too."

Jake's brain clicked away as he considered this possibility.

It makes sense, he thought.

And these days, he had to admit, Riley's instincts were functioning better than his own.

He said, "Riley, I need you to call Chief Tallhamer on your cellphone."

Riley asked, "Should I tell him to release the Cardin brothers?"

"No, it's too soon for that," Jake said. "Tell him we need Dr. Gibson's office address. We're going to pay him a visit."

*

In a town as small as Hyland, it was easy enough to find the address that Tallhamer had given them. Dr. Gibson's office was actually a wing attached to his modest but attractive house on the edge of town. The place was somewhat isolated, set among rolling hills and patches of forest.

Jake pulled into the driveway, then he and Riley got out of the car and walked to the door that led into Gibson's office. They entered a small foyer, where a white-clad woman was sitting at a desk—Gibson's nurse/receptionist, Jake guessed.

Before the receptionist could say a word to them, the office door opened, and Dr. Gibson came out with a middle-aged female patient. He was handing her a prescription and giving friendly dietary advice for dealing with high cholesterol. The woman gave them a curious glance, then thanked the doctor f or his help and left.

Then Dr. Gibson stood looking at Jake and Riley.

Jake remembered how bitter and angry Gibson had seemed when he'd confronted them in front of the police station saying …

"I guess it's no surprise that you got here just in time to be of no use at all."

But now his pockmarked face lit up with an almost eerily pleasant smile.

170

"The FBI people again, I see," he said. "I'm sorry—I may have heard your names, but I've forgotten."

Jake produced his badge and introduced himself and Riley.

Gibson smiled enigmatically and said to them …

"I'm really rather glad you stopped by."

Then Gibson turned to the woman at the desk and said …

"Julia, I believe Mrs. Norris was my last patient for the day, am I correct?"

"That's right, doctor," the woman said.

Gibson nodded at her and said, "And I doubt there will be any drop-ins. Why don't you close up for the day, Julia? Take the rest of the afternoon off."

Julia smiled and said, "Thanks, doctor. I'd like that."

As Julia scurried around preparing to leave, Gibson said to Jake and Riley …

"That's one of the perks of being a small-town doctor—lots of unanticipated leisure time. It's not exactly a lucrative business, but at least I don't have to deal with the same pace and pressure as big city doctors. Let's go over into the house and you can tell me why you're paying me a visit."

They walked through a door that led directly into the living room of the main house. It was a large, pleasantly decorated, and impeccably neat area with plush furniture and fancy valances on the windows.

Dr. Gibson invited them to have a seat on the cushiony sofa, then sat in a big soft-looking chair himself.

He folded his hands together on his knee and said, "I believe I owe you an apology for my behavior yesterday. Grief brings out the worst in people—I've seen it among people I deal with, especially when they've lost a loved one. I'm embarrassed to fall prey to it myself. You're only here to do your job, after all, and murder investigations can't be pleasant work. I'm sure we can all breathe a sigh of relief that my wife's killers are safely in custody. Would you like something to drink—some iced tea, maybe?"

Something about Gibson's hospitality struck Jake as forced and insincere. But of course if Riley was right, Gibson was just putting on a show of friendliness.

"No, thank you," Jake said. "We're just here to wrap up some loose ends."

"Certainly," Gibson said. "How can I be of help?"

Jake hesitated. He wasn't sure how to proceed. How could he

draw the man out, find out if he really was the killer? What sorts of questions could he ask without giving himself away?

Jake and Gibson sat looking at each other for a moment.

Then with a wry twist to his smile, Gibson said …

"I believe you've got some questions about *me,* don't you Agent Crivaro?"

Jake felt a slight chill as he realized …

He knows why we're here.

And now—was the man going to play some sort of game with them? Jake decided to keep quiet and find out how the doctor would proceed.

Gibson crossed his arms and leaned back in his chair.

He said, "I suppose you'd like to look around the place. Do you have a warrant?"

Jake shook his head.

"Well, it doesn't matter," Gibson said with an expansive gesture. "As far as I'm concerned, you're free to look wherever you like."

Gibson got up from his chair and added, "Come on. I'll show you something that might interest you."

Jake and Riley exchanged wary glances, then got up and followed Gibson toward a pair of doors on the other side of the room. Gibson swung both doors open, revealing another room almost as large as the one they were in.

A formal dining room, Jake thought. But he saw nothing that looked like dining room furniture.

The doctor stood back and motioned Jake and Riley inside.

Followed by Riley, Jake stepped into the room.

At first the strange clutter he saw was confusing.

Was this some kind of exercise room?

But why was there so much leather, and why were there so many spiked objects?

Then Jake's mouth dropped open as the realized what he was looking at.

The room was packed with racks and shelves full of unsettling sexual paraphernalia—whips, harnesses, handcuffs, gags, clamps, and various kinds of contraptions and equipment that he couldn't even imagine the uses for.

But most disturbingly, those coils lying loose almost everywhere on the floor …

Barbed wire!

Suddenly Jake heard a loud gasp from behind him.

He whirled around in time to see a wicked grin on Gibson's face as he stood holding Riley from behind, pulling a length of barbed wire around her throat.

CHAPTER THIRTY

Riley was yanked backwards by a hard loop around her throat.

Barbed wire, she realized, as her attacker pulled her whole body against him.

A split-second before, she had seen coils of barbed wire scattered on the floor. Now she could feel two sharp barbs, spaced widely across her neck.

She stood very still, watching to see what Crivaro would do.

He had drawn his weapon, but Riley knew that Dr. Gibson was using her as a shield. She didn't doubt that Crivaro's aim was good enough to shoot the man in the head if he chose to. He looked like he was evaluating the risk. But judging by his expression, he didn't want to take the shot.

And at the moment, she didn't much want him to.

As she tried to think through what was happening and what to do about it, Riley was surprised to feel a strange calmness settle over her.

The real question at the moment was …

What does he want?

In effect, he had just taken her hostage. But to what purpose? What did he want in exchange for releasing her? Whole seconds had already gone by, and Gibson hadn't made the slightest hint of what he had in mind.

Finally he said to Crivaro in a tight, desperate voice …

"What do you think would happen if I pull this wire across her throat, so that a barb tears its way across it? What kind of damage? Would the wound go deep enough to cut her windpipe? Or a carotid artery? Or both? Maybe, maybe not. But I'm curious enough to give it a try—unless you stop me."

What is he asking Crivaro to do? Riley wondered.

Then she felt him maneuvering and rotating their bodies into a different position. In a moment, the doctor was no longer using Riley's body to shield him. Instead, he had made himself entirely visible to Crivaro.

Riley struggled to understand …

Doesn't he realize he's giving Crivaro a clear shot?

Then it dawned on her …

That's what he wants!

Dr. Gibson was trying to commit "suicide by cop."

Riley decided she couldn't let that happened.

She locked eyes with Crivaro, who was still pointing his Glock steadily at the doctor. With a movement of her eyes alone, she signaled Crivaro not to take the shot. Seeming to understand, Crivaro nodded slightly.

Now it's all up to me, Riley thought.

Her calmness deepened, as if time were slowing down and she had no reason to hurry. A memory came back to her—a fighting lesson her father had given her up at his cabin not long ago.

It was part of a fighting system called Krav Maga, and the techniques he had taught her were brutal and merciless.

He'd told her …

"Sheer aggression is the key thing."

During the lesson, her father had put Riley in a hold much like this.

She remembered exactly how she'd escaped it …

I've just got to do the same thing right now.

Without another moment's hesitation, she slammed a fist backward into Gibson's groin. As he let out a groan of pain, she spun around and grabbed him by the hair with one hand. Making a fist with the other hand, she smashed him in the face.

As her assailant collapsed onto the floor, she remembered her father saying …

"You don't stop until he's debilitated—or dead."

Her adrenaline surging wildly now, Riley seized the nearest object in reach—a whip with a hard wooden handle. She crouched beside Gibson and raised the whip to slam it handle-first into his face when she heard Crivaro call out …

"Riley! Don't kill him, damn it!"

Crivaro's voice snapped her out of the savage spell.

The aggression ebbed from her body, and she saw Dr. Gibson trembling at her feet, his nose bloody from where she'd punched him. She stepped aside, and Crivaro hoisted Gibson to his feet.

As he put handcuffs on the doctor, Crivaro said to Riley …

"Where did you learn to fight like that?"

Riley shrugged slightly and said, "My Dad taught me."

Crivaro let out a grunt of laughter.

He said, "I should have known. He's an interesting man, that father of yours."

A little while later, Riley and Crivaro dragged the handcuffed physician into the police station, to the astonishment of everyone there.

"What the hell!" Tallhamer exclaimed.

Crivaro asked, "Have you got an interrogation room?"

His mouth gaping, Tallhamer shook his head no.

"We'll need an empty jail cell, then," Jake said.

Tallhamer followed along behind Riley and Crivaro as they escorted Gibson back into the jail. The only two cells were occupied by the Cardin brothers. At Crivaro's instruction, Tallhamer moved Harvey out of his cell and into the other with Phil. Then Crivaro shoved Gibson into the empty cell and made him sit down on the bed.

Riley joined Crivaro in the jail cell while Tallhamer remained standing in the corridor.

Crivaro said sharply to Gibson …

"You'd better start talking now. Or do you want a lawyer present?"

Gibson laughed grimly and said, "Do you mean Ozzie Hines? He's the only lawyer in town and he's worse than useless. No, I don't need legal representation. I'm ready to talk. In fact, I'm glad of this. I'm relieved."

Gibson's eyes darted back and forth between Riley and Crivaro. Again, Riley was startled by how homely the man was, especially now that his nose was bleeding.

"Tell me something," he said. "Do you have any idea what it's like being despised, even by the people you most love, even by yourself? It feels … like this."

He lifted his handcuffed hands in front of his white medical jacket and ripped it open as far as he could, partially baring his chest.

Riley almost gasped aloud as she saw that his flesh was gashed with scabbed-over wounds.

He's done this to himself, she realized.

He tortures himself.

Gibson kept talking …

"Small wonder Alice regretted marrying me. She never admitted it, she even denied it, insisted that she really loved me.

And I guess she did love me in her way. Which only made it worse as far as I was concerned."

He nodded toward the other cell, where the two Cardin brothers stood watching and listening in fascination, and said to Crivaro …

"She should have stayed married to Phil Cardin over there, loser though he might be. Instead she settled for me. In a crossroads hick town like this, she didn't exactly have the pick of men she deserved. At first I thought I was lucky to marry a woman like her. But little by little, it got clearer how she really felt about me. It got so she could barely bring herself to look at me."

Gibson shook all over, then said …

"It made me crazy. I wanted to bring her down to my level. That's why I made her play all those twisted sex games, with all those—those *toys* you saw in that room. I wanted her to feel as ugly and debased as I did. She went along with it, even pretended to enjoy it—just out of pity, I guess. That pity of hers—that's what got to be too much for me in the end. That's what drove me to kill her."

Gibson's gaze seemed to turn inward, as if he were reliving the murder.

"We'd used all kinds of instruments. Some expensive stuff bought by very discreet mail order. But it finally occurred to me that a local material was the perfect instrument of pain—barbed wire. I guess when it started, she thought it was another sick game. She soon realized the truth. The way she screamed and pleaded, the way life ebbed out of her body as she …"

His voice faded away for a moment.

"I had never imagined what it could be like, inflicting so much pain and terror. Not until I found out for myself. The thrill, the intoxicating joy. That's why I sought out those other women, killed them too, in exactly the same way. Oh, I hated myself for it. But it was like an addiction. If you hadn't caught me, I'd have kept right on doing it, again and again and again."

He fell silent again.

But Riley knew that he had said more than enough.

We've got him, she thought. *We've got him at last.*

CHAPTER THIRTY ONE

The chaos that followed was more than Riley wanted to deal with. The Hyland police station was in an uproar over Dr. Gibson's confession, and a handful of reporters had already shown up in the station foyer. Riley didn't want to have anything to do with them, and Crivaro obviously didn't either.

Fortunately, the reporters clustered around the Cardin brothers as soon as they were released. Riley and Crivaro seized their opportunity to slip out through the station's back entrance without being noticed. She was flooded with relief as she and Crivaro escaped unnoticed and headed straight to the car they had borrowed.

Crivaro climbed into the driver's seat and Riley got in on the passenger side.

Crivaro sat there for a moment, just staring into space without starting the car.

Riley wondered …

What's on his mind?

Trying to sound cheerful, she said, "We really wrapped that one up, huh?"

Crivaro tilted his head a little and said, "I guess."

Then he started the engine and pulled away from the curb.

Riley couldn't help feeling a little miffed that Crivaro wasn't showing more enthusiasm for their achievement—especially since she'd played such a big part in Dr. Gibson's apprehension.

Maybe he's just having an energy letdown, she thought.

Or maybe it was something else …

"Where to now?" she asked.

Squinting at the street in front of him, Crivaro said, "We've got to return this car to Chief Messenger in Dighton. But it's been a long day. First I want to stop somewhere to eat and clear my head. Then I'll call Lehl, have him arrange for us to go back to Quantico by chopper."

Something in Crivaro's tone bothered Riley.

What's going on with him? she wondered.

At the end of Hyland's short main street, Jake pulled into a parking lot next to Mick's Diner. Riley remembered hearing that Phil Cardin had worked there until he'd been fired. As they walked

178

into the well-lit, chrome-decorated diner, Riley was surprised to see no other customers in the place. She figured dinner rush must be over by now—and anyway, business must be pretty slow in a town as small as Hyland. Maybe a place like this picked up later at night or on the weekends.

They sat down in a corner booth and both ordered beer and burgers from a disinterested waitress. Crivaro remained quiet for a few moments as they waited for their meals.

Finally Riley dared to ask ...

"So how do you feel? About solving the case, I mean?"

Crivaro shook his head and said almost in a whisper ...

"I don't know, Riley. I'm afraid we got the wrong man."

Riley felt a tingle of confusion.

She could hardly believe her ears.

"I don't understand," she said.

"I'm not sure I do either," Crivaro said with a slight shrug. "I'm still trying to think it through. But something doesn't seem right about Dr. Gibson. For one thing, when he confessed, he was off in at least one detail. Do you remember what he said about the killing itself, about wrapping his wife up in barbed wire?"

Riley thought back until it came to her.

"He said she thought it was another sick game," she said.

"Yeah, and that doesn't fit," Crivaro said. "We know for a fact that Alice Gibson was subdued by chloroform. The medical examiner found it in her bloodstream. *That's* how the killer really managed to subdue her. But Gibson didn't mention chloroform at all. He seems to think that Alice was conscious through the whole thing."

Riley was starting to get annoyed now.

She said, "You're just nitpicking. Maybe he did make her play sick games with barbed wire before he actually killed her. Maybe he just forgot to mention the chloroform."

"Maybe, but I don't think so," Crivaro said. "I've heard my share of false confessions in my day. My gut tells me this was another one."

The waitress came to serve them their beers and hamburgers. Riley waited until the woman went away before she said ...

"Agent Crivaro, what you're saying doesn't make any sense. *My* gut has been telling me all along that the murderer is obsessed with pain. And Dr. Gibson is positively crazy about pain. You saw all the stuff he had in that room of his. You saw what he did to

179

himself, those self-inflicted wounds."

Crivaro leaned toward her and said …

"He's obsessed with his *own* pain, Riley. He's a flat-out masochist, not a sadist. He said something else I have trouble believing—that he'd forced his wife to play those games to 'bring her down to his level.' My guess is that he didn't have to *force* her to do anything. She was a dominatrix. And their kinky games were what kept their marriage together. Losing all that made him crazy. But it didn't turn him into a killer."

Riley was struggling to grasp what she was hearing.

"But what about the barbed wire?" she asked. "Isn't it kind of a coincidence that his sex games involved the same material that was used to kill his wife and the two other women?"

Shaking his head again, Crivaro said …

"Not a coincidence at all. This was something new for him. He became obsessed with barbed wire *after* his wife's death. That's when he bought it and started to use it to punish himself."

"Punish himself for what?" Riley asked.

Crivaro was starting to sound impatient now.

"Riley, how many times do I have to say it? He's a *masochist*. He feels ashamed and guilty about *everything*. And his wife's murder pushed him beyond guilt and shame, over some kind of emotional cliff into an abyss of feelings he couldn't handle. He tried self-flagellation with barbed wire. But in the end, the only way he could cope with his torment was to confess to three murders he didn't commit."

Riley didn't like what she was hearing.

It made plenty of sense, but she wished it didn't.

"That's only a theory," she said, surprised by the sullenness in her own voice.

Crivaro face twitched with anger.

"OK, don't take my word for it," he said. "I'm just a criminal profiler, not some know-it-all psychology professor. Maybe you should go back to Lanton and talk to that expert of yours. He's probably heard himself sentenced to death by now. He'd enjoy having something else to think about, something to distract him from his troubles."

Riley felt deeply stung. She could tell by Crivaro's expression that he immediately regretted his words.

"I'm sorry," Crivaro murmured. "That was really a low blow."

Riley said, "Yeah, it kind of was."

They both fell silent for a couple of minutes. Neither of them touched their beers or burgers.

Then Riley said, "If you really think Gibson is innocent, why are you letting him sit there in jail?"

"Well, he is guilty of *something,*" Crivaro said. "He assaulted you. And if he is lying about the murders, he's also guilty of obstruction. Jail is where he ought to be right now. And for his sake, it might also be the safest. He's liable to do himself serious harm if he's allowed to go home."

Another silence fell.

Finally Crivaro said, "I've got to touch base with Lehl. He's probably heard all kinds of crazy rumors about the arrest by now. I need to make sure he's got the facts."

Crivaro took out his cellphone and punched in a number.

Then he listened and grumbled …

"Damn, I can't get a connection in here. I'll go out to the car, try calling from there. I'll be right back."

Crivaro got up from the table and headed for the door.

Riley watched him through the diner windows as he headed for the parking lot at the side of the building.

Her anger and confusion were now giving way to disappointment.

We're back at square one, she thought.

We've got to start all over again.

But then she thought …

"We?"

Why did she think she'd even be part of the case anymore? Why was she even thinking of them as a team? After all, Crivaro had the ability to connect with killer's minds just as she did. He'd encouraged her developing her talent, but lately it had been off more than on. If she was wrong about everything, Crivaro would probably prefer to work without her from now on. …

And then what do I do?

She finally took a bite of her burger, but she still didn't feel like eating.

*

As the man sat alone in his parked pickup truck, his father's words echoed through his head again …

"See how it feels."

His father had said those words over and over again when he'd punished him as a child, causing him so much pain and terror …

"See how it feels."

But his pain and terror hadn't ended after that long, cruel, flesh-rending punishment on that awful pitch-dark night.

They'd continued long after Father had died.

They'd continued all these years, right down to this very day.

Even the deaths of three women had failed to release him from that pain and terror.

And now …

Everything has gone wrong.

He'd come back to Hyland because he'd heard about the two brothers being held in custody for crimes *he* had committed. He'd been hanging around town all day long, trying to decide what to do about it.

I can't let it stand, he kept on thinking.

His satisfaction from the killings had been so fleeting, so transitory. At the very least, he didn't want anyone else to get credit for what he'd done. That would add insult to injury.

But what was he going to do about it?

A short while ago, he'd been standing outside the police station when a man and a young woman dragged someone else into the jail. Soon afterwards he'd overheard the reporters as they'd clustered around the station …

"Another suspect," they'd said.

"They've got Dr. Gibson," they'd said.

The news had filled him with fury.

Dr. Gibson!

The husband of the first woman he'd killed.

I can't let it stand, he thought yet again.

And the only way to put things right was to kill again, as quickly as he possibly could—much sooner than he'd planned or expected.

He'd seen the man and the woman slip out of the back of the station, obviously trying to evade the reporters.

But they didn't evade me, he remembered.

He'd followed their car in his pickup truck. When they'd parked next to Mick's Diner, he'd parked some 50 feet away and watched the two of them as they went inside to get something to eat.

He'd stayed parked right here, hoping against hope for an

opportunity to catch the woman alone.

And now—the man was leaving the diner!

The woman must still be in there, sitting all by herself.

All he had to do was lure her outside and subdue her.

And he was sure that would be an easy task.

As he started the engine and drove up in front of the diner, he whispered aloud …

"See how it feels."

CHAPTER THIRTY TWO

Riley decided she would apologize to Agent Crivaro when he returned. She was sitting alone in the diner booth, nibbling at her burger and brooding over the argument they'd just had.

She couldn't help but admit, she shouldn't have questioned his thinking like that. And she certainly shouldn't have been so petulant about it.

I was wrong, she thought. She didn't much like the feeling those words gave her, but she knew they must be true.

After all, everything Crivaro had said made perfect sense. And she was sure he took no satisfaction in being right about Dr. Gibson not being the killer. In fact, he must have felt really frustrated about it.

She took a sip of beer and thought …

Then it will be up to him whether or not to keep me on the case.

Whether she liked it or not, she'd accept whatever decision he made with as much grace as she could muster.

As she lifted her beer again, she caught a glimpse of motion out of the corner of her eye. She turned toward the restaurant window and saw that an old pickup truck had pulled to a stop just outside.

That's odd, she thought when she heard the truck's engine stop.

She knew that there was a "no parking" sign in front of the restaurant. Why hadn't the driver continued on over to the diner's parking lot?

Then the driver's window opened. The man sitting there turned his head and peered straight at her.

Riley gasped aloud.

She felt a visceral pain at the sight of the man's face—the same kind of empathetic pain she'd experienced so strongly when she saw the body of Anna Park. But she knew that this agony did not belong to a murder victim. It was the killer's own pain.

The man's face was heavily gouged and scarred—much more so than Dr. Gibson's face.

While the she'd guessed that the doctor's face was scarred from acne or some childhood disease, the face she was looking at must have been disfigured by some terrible physical trauma …

Pain!

There wasn't a doubt in her mind …

It's him.

He's the killer.

The man stared at her for a moment, then looked away and restarted the engine, as if to drive away.

Riley felt a surge of adrenalin. She doubted she could get outside fast enough to stop him from leaving. But maybe she could jot down the number on the license plate. She pulled a notepad out of her purse, scrambled out of the booth, and headed for the front entrance.

When she stepped outside and down the front steps, she was surprised to see that the truck was still parked exactly where it had been, its engine its engine stopped again.

Now no one was at the wheel.

She looked around.

The driver was nowhere in sight.

Riley hurried to the back of the truck to write down the plate number. As she raised her pad, she heard a flurry of footsteps behind her.

Before she could even turn around, someone seized her from behind

She felt a wet cloth across her mouth.

A sharp blow to the groin, she instructed herself. *Then grab him by the hair.*

But for some reason, her arms fell limp at her side.

The rag on her face was sickeningly sweet and she felt lightheaded.

Chloroform! she realized with horror.

She was already succumbing to the effects of the drug.

Don't breathe, Riley told herself.

But she had already gasped in some of the fumes.

She made an effort to hold her breath, but the world started to go dark.

*

During Jake's phone conversation with Erik Lehl, they agreed that Jake ought to stay in Hyland. Lehl trusted Jake's hunch that Dr. Gibson was innocent, and he thought Jake needed to continue his work right here.

Lehl had left it up to Jake whether or not he would keep Riley

185

on the case.

As he sat there in the car thinking about his young protégé, he felt bad about the cutting words he'd said to Riley a few minutes ago …

"Maybe you should go back to Lanton and talk to that expert of yours."

He groaned softly and thought …

She didn't deserve that.

The girl had been disappointed by what Jake had told her because she was green and impatient. It was no wonder that she'd pushed back sullenly about it. There was no denying that she had great instincts. And her theory that Dr. Gibson was the killer was by no means a bad theory.

After all, he knew from plenty of experience that even good theories sometimes turned out to be wrong. Maybe this was a good opportunity for Riley to learn that valuable lesson.

Besides, he felt sure that he still needed her help—maybe now more than ever.

We'll talk it over in the diner, he thought, getting out of the car.

As Jake walked back toward the restaurant, a gray pickup truck roared away from the front entrance, narrowly missing him as it sped on down the street.

Jake felt rattled and irritated.

That guy needs to watch where he's going, he thought.

Jake walked on inside the diner and was mildly surprised to see that Riley wasn't sitting at their table. For a moment, he guessed that she'd probably just gone to the restroom. Her purse was still there in the booth.

But as he sat down again, he felt a tingle of worry.

He called out to the bored-looking waitress, "Did you happen to notice where the young woman who was with me went?"

The waitress squinted as she said, "Funny you should ask. She tore out of the diner in a hurry just a couple of minutes ago. I don't know what it was about."

Jake felt a rising panic.

He said, "Did you see where she went after she got outside?"

"Sorry, I didn't see anything," the waitress said. "I had to go back to the kitchen."

Jake threw enough money onto the table to more than pay for their meals, then grabbed Riley's purse and rushed outside. Now he saw something lying there on the ground. It was a notepad and pen

186

that he'd seen Riley using.

She'd gone away in that truck.

And not voluntarily.

Jake raced to the car, then sent gravel flying as he roared out of the parking lot, taking the direction he'd seen truck go.

Before long the truck came into view up ahead. Jake had a quick decision to make. The borrowed car was equipped with a siren and a flashing light he could snap onto the roof.

But did he dare use them?

Jake's imagination ran wild as he tried to guess Riley's immediate danger.

Did the driver have her unconscious or immobilized? Was he holding a weapon on her?

Giving chase might result in a hostage situation.

Or it might simply get Riley killed.

Twilight had fallen. Jake switched off his headlights and dropped a fair distance behind the truck, hoping he could follow it unnoticed. He soon realized it would be no easy task. The road wound and curved through local farmlands up into higher mountain areas.

*

Riley found herself engulfed by darkness. She realized she was bound hand and foot, and lying on a hard vibrating surface. She was lying in a tangle of something metallic and painfully sharp.

Barbed wire, she realized.

Her mental fog began to lift, and she remembered being grabbed from behind and subdued with chloroform. By controlling her breathing, she guessed that she hadn't inhaled enough to be out for very long. She was surely coming back to her senses much faster than his earlier victims.

Her assailant probably had no idea that she was regaining consciousness.

She felt a sharp bump, which sent her bouncing painfully among the spiky coils. She knew right then that she was in the shallow covered bed of the pickup truck. Her hands were bound behind her with what felt like duct tape.

She twisted her hands about and realized that she was bound loosely and carelessly. Her assailant must have been in a hurry, which was hardly any surprise, given that he'd grabbed her right

187

outside of a small town diner.

It was fairly easy to twist her hands loose from the tape, then to bend over and undo the bindings on her feet. Meanwhile, the truck was bounding and lurching over an increasingly rough road.

As the truck began to slow, Riley realized …

I've got to get out of here.

Now.

She pounded against the hard covering above her, but it didn't budge.

Then she gave a sharp kick outward and felt a metallic surface rattle and budge and give just a little. It was the tailgate, and it didn't seem to be shut quite tight. She kicked at it again and again, and the tailgate flew open just as the truck came to a complete stop. Then she rolled out of the truck bed and fell into a heap onto a hard surface.

Dazed by the fall and still dizzy from the chloroform, Riley looked around. In the deepening twilight, she saw that she was lying on unpaved ground. All she could see nearby was a thicket of trees.

Then she heard the truck door open.

Without another moment's thought, she scrambled unsteadily to her feet and began to run for her life.

*

As the sky grew darker, Jake found it harder to drive along the rough and increasingly narrow mountain road with his headlights off. But he still didn't want to give himself away to whoever was driving the truck ahead of him …

If he is still ahead of me.

Jake felt a growing worry that the driver had made some turnoff that he had missed.

He finally turned his lights on and drove faster, trying to catch up with the truck.

Soon he was sure of it …

He lost me.

Jake stopped the car and managed to turn the vehicle around in the narrow road. Still keeping his lights on, he drove back the way he'd come.

After about a quarter of a mile, he came across a turnoff he'd missed earlier—an unpaved length of road not unlike the drive that had led to the cabin where Riley's father lived. The truck must have turned in there, and he thought it couldn't be much farther ahead.

Jake turned off his car lights again and drove more slowly along the overgrown road. When the parked truck finally came into view, Jake stopped his vehicle and jumped out.

The bed of the truck was covered, but that the tailgate was hanging open. The driver's door hung open, but he saw no sign of either Riley or the driver. Off to one side was a peculiar, ramshackle farmhouse. The main part of the house was built from logs, and Jake guessed that it was maybe a century old. Other rooms seem to have been carelessly added to the place over the years. Jake wondered whether the house was abandoned. He could see no lights on inside.

He could see nothing but trees on the other side of the parking area. He still saw no sign of any person, but he knew that a killer could be watching or even aiming a gun at him from either direction.

Leaving his own gun holstered, Jake peered into the open tailgate of the truck.

He was alarmed to see coils of barbed lying in the truck bed, and a couple of patches of torn clothing clinging to the barbs.

Riley was here, Jake realized.

But where was she now?

And how could he possibly find her?

*

Riley staggered along a path through the woods, moving away from the truck as fast as she could. Branches whipped at her as she charged on, heedless of the stinging pain they caused her.

I've got to get away, she kept thinking.

But where was she going?

Where did this path lead? The light was very dim now and the area was completely unfamiliar to her.

Could she possibly make her way to a highway or a house, and safety?

She pulled up short when she nearly ran into a large object that seemed to be suspended in midair right in front of her. Whatever the bulky thing was, it was draped in thick layers of kudzu.

As she tried to make her way around it, she saw that the thing was actually hanging from a tree branch. Weathered chains showed through the twining kudzu.

This was no natural object. Somebody had put it here.

She stood very still, but couldn't hear the sound of anyone following her.

She tugged at the kudzu, peeling away wide leaves until she felt a something sharp cutting her fingertips.

Barbed wire, she realized.

Her curiosity mounting now, she pulled away another handful of kudzu.

She could see something white beneath the stubborn vegetation.

A clump of kudzu fell away into her hands.

Inches from her own face, a human skull leered mockingly at her from among the clusters of barbed wire.

Riley let out a scream of terror as she stumbled clumsily backwards.

Then she felt a hard blow behind her knees, and she collapsed onto her back on the ground.

She looked up and saw her captor's scarred face staring down at her.

His horrible grin resembled that of the skull.

"I see you've discovered Father," he said.

CHAPTER THIRTY THREE

Jake pulled out his flashlight and searched around the parked truck. He saw no clue to which direction Riley or the man who had taken her might have gone. He was on the verge of heading for the silent ramshackle farmhouse to see if anybody was inside when he heard a blood-curdling scream from some distance away.

The scream had come from the woods. He whirled and ran in that direction.

"Riley!" he yelled aloud, but there was no answer.

With his flashlight, Jake quickly found a beaten-down path. She must have gone this way. He charged down the path himself until his flashlight fell upon two struggling figures about 20 feet or so ahead.

He saw that Riley and a man were wrestling together on the ground. As Jake rushed toward them, he saw Riley pull loose from the man, draw back her fist, and strike a powerful blow to his stomach.

The man let out a sharp, groaning gasp and rolled away from her. Then he saw Jake, and scrambled to his feet. He whirled and disappeared into the pathless brush.

Then Riley was also on her feet, and seemed about to follow him.

Jake yelled, "Riley, wait!"

Riley turned and stared into the flashlight beam.

"Jake?" she asked, looking as if she didn't know whether to fight or flee.

"Yeah," he replied, reaching the spot where she stood. He thought she looked shaky on her feet, but at least she seemed to be unharmed.

Jake raised his flashlight, and the beam fell upon a grotesque shape hanging from a tree branch. In it was bundled a human skeleton, its bones long ago stripped clean of flesh, its skull staring straight at him. The ghastly specter stopped Jake in his tracks for a split second.

But he knew he didn't have time to make sense of this new horror.

He drew his weapon.

"I'm going after him," Jake cried.

Riley nodded.

Gripping his gun in one hand and his flashlight in the other, Jake rushed headlong into the brush, freshly trampled down by the man who had just fled this way.

*

Riley tore along just a few feet behind Jake until they emerged into a clearing facing a hillside. She watched as the flashlight beam searched around until it fell upon something—a wood-framed doorway cut into the side of the hill, with a rough wooden door standing wide open.

Remembering scenes from her own rural childhood, Riley realized what the place was …

A root cellar.

"He must be in there," Jake whispered, glancing back at Riley.

Riley moved up and stood beside him.

"This is probably the only entrance," she said. "We might have him trapped in there."

Jake tried to probe the interior with his flashlight beam, but at this distance, the light failed to cut through the darkness inside.

Jake called out …

"Come out of there with your hands up."

Jake's voice was answered by a bright flash and a deafening blast from inside the root cellar. Riley heard the air whistle nearby as the gunshot barely missed them. Reflexively, Jake and Riley both ducked back among some trees.

"Damn," Jake growled under his breath. "He's got us at a disadvantage."

Riley realized that Jake was right. If they came out into the open, the man would be able to see them in the rising moonlight. But he could stay invisible to them.

As she and Jake crouched in momentary decision, the sound of the gunshot echoed in Riley's mind.

She recognized the sound well from her own days hunting with her father.

It was the blast of a shotgun—possibly the same sort of stacked-barrel shotgun her father owned.

If she was right, the man had just one shot left.

She looked around until she spotted a dead, fallen tree branch.

She picked it up and threw it out into the open, where she and Jake had been standing just a moment before.

It fell to the ground with a noisy crunch, and sure enough, another shotgun blast instantly broke through the air, shattering the surface of the tree branch.

Grabbing Crivaro by the arm, Riley barked at him …

"Let's go. Now."

Crivaro nodded. Still gripping his flashlight in one hand and his gun in the other, he rushed ahead of her toward the open doorway.

Riley followed him inside, but at first the root cellar seemed dark and empty.

The jittery beam of Crivaro's flashlight searched around the small room. Then, in a sudden violent movement, the man emerged from a shadow and struck Crivaro's gun hand with a loose board.

The gun flew out of Crivaro's hand.

Riley heard a sharp, familiar, metallic click.

Crivaro's flashlight beam swung in that direction and landed on the man again. Riley realized he had reloaded and cocked his shotgun, which was now pointed directly at Crivaro.

Adrenalin rushed through Riley's body.

She remembered again her father's Krav Maga lesson …

Grab the first object in reach.

She clawed blindly at a shelf next to her and grabbed at the first thing her fingers touched—the smooth surface of a glass bottle. Without further thought she hurled it at the killer, striking him in the forehead.

The man shrieked and staggered, and the bottle shattered on the floor.

A pungently sweet odor filled the air.

Crivaro grabbed Riley by the arm and said …

"Chloroform!"

Riley understood instantly. She and Crivaro had to get out of there.

As they rushed out of the root cellar into the open air, Riley glanced back and saw their attacker collapsing.

*

The man clung to the dirt floor, which seemed to rock and tilt wildly underneath him. He remembered his experience making the chloroform, how he'd almost passed out from the fumes. And now

193

the syrupy stuff was all over his face, clinging to him, stinging his eyes, its sickeningly sweet taste and odor getting into his nose and mouth.

Despite his struggle stay conscious, he knew he was succumbing to the drug's powerful effect.

Then his surroundings became hazy and blurry and ...

He was 10 years old again, and he was struggling to free a pathetically mooing calf from the barbed wire that entangled her legs. The poor creature had stumbled into a cluster of the wire that had come loose from the fencepost.

His father was standing nearby shouting in that hard, crackling voice of his ...

"This is your damn fault, Phineas. I told you to keep that fence in better repair."

Phineas was crying now as he struggled to release one of the calf's ankles from the wire.

"Father, help me, please," he wept.

"You're on your own," his father said. "I'm going to the house to get some bandages."

Phineas got the animal free just as his father returned from the house, a first aid kit in one hand and a roll of barbed wire in the other.

Phineas wondered ...

What is he going to do with the barbed wire?

His father disinfected and bandaged the calf's legs, then took Phineas forcibly by the arm and dragged him across the meadow to the root cellar. He pushed Phineas through the door and onto the dirt floor and yelled ...

"Stay put while I teach you how it feels."

Phineas was still a skinny boy, not nearly strong enough to fight his father, who wrapped the wire around his body, twisting it in all directions, pulling it so that it tore into his flesh. Phineas tried to struggle, but had to give it up, because it only caused him more pain.

"See how it feels," his father kept saying again and again.

At last his father had him bound and unable to move, his face and arms pierced by countless agonizing barbs.

"See how it feels," his father said again.

Then he went outside and shut the door, leaving Phineas in total darkness.

194

Helpless and bleeding, Phineas murmured through his tears ...
"Someday, Father. Someday ..."

The darkness gripped him like a huge, malevolent hand, and soon he felt and thought nothing at all.

Riley and Crivaro stood a safe distance from the open door that led into the root cellar. Crivaro kept his flashlight beam on the man lying unconscious on the floor. Riley could smell the chloroform fumes even from where they stood.

"Let's stay put until the air clears in there," Crivaro said. "At least he's not going anywhere."

About ten minutes passed. The man began writhing and groaning, and the air smelled fresher.

"It must be safe now," Crivaro said. "But put a handkerchief over your nose and mouth."

Riley did as she was told and followed Crivaro into the root cellar. The man seemed to be regaining consciousness as Crivaro put him into handcuffs, and he kept murmuring ...

"Now *you'll* see how it feels, Father. Now *you'll* see how it feels ..."

Riley locked gazes with Crivaro, and she knew that they were both thinking the same thing.

That bundled-up skeleton at the end of the path was the man's father ...

His first victim.

Judging from the nakedness of those bones, it must have happened many years ago.

Crivaro had set his flashlight on the floor in order to cuff the man. Riley picked up the light and looked around at the damp, gloomy room with its cinderblock walls, wooden shelves, and heavy beams to support the wooden ceiling.

Then the flashlight beam fell on a rough-hewn wooden table, with many strands of barbed wire laying across it. Then Riley saw that the top of the table was stained with dried blood.

She shuddered deeply as she realized ...

This is where he did it.

This is where he killed them.

And she herself had narrowly escaped becoming his next victim.

CHAPTER THIRTY FOUR

Riley sat quietly and let Agent Crivaro do all the talking. They were being debriefed by Special Agent in Charge Erik Lehl about the case they'd just solved. She felt it was best to let Agent Crivaro explain what had happened. He had a much better idea of what Lehl expected to hear than she possibly could.

Besides, Lehl was directing all his questions to Crivaro, almost as if Riley weren't even in his office.

It wasn't a very pleasant feeling.

Riley still found the BAU chief to be a formidable and intimidating presence. It occurred to her that the sprawling, lanky man might have made better money as a basketball player. She certainly admired that he'd chosen instead a career in the FBI, and had risen through the ranks to take charge of the FBI's new Behavioral Analysis Unit.

As such thoughts passed through Riley's mind, she was also aware of Crivaro filling Lehl in on what they now knew about the murderer, Phineas Hutson.

People in that area of West Virginia knew that Phineas lived in a lonely, rundown subsistence farm that had been in his family since the late 1800s. But the locals never saw much of him, except during his infrequent visits to towns like Dighton, Hyland, and Wynnewood to buy farm supplies. And nobody had known much about him.

Riley felt sure that nobody had even tried to get to know the badly scarred man. But now that Phineas was in jail, he was talking freely, telling a strange and twisted story of how his father, Isaac Hutson, had once tortured him with barbed wire, disfiguring him permanently. A few years later, the larger and stronger Phineas had turned on his father, vengefully torturing the man to death with barbed wire.

Then Phineas had hung corpse from a tree branch. He'd said that the cocoon-like bundle had served as a kind of shrine for many years, a place where he found solace from the terrible pain he still carried inside him.

But as time passed, the shrine seemed to have lost its magic for him. When the psychic pain had become intolerable, he had turned to killing innocent women.

It was a horrible story, and now that Riley knew more about it, she felt more pity than outrage against Phineas Hutson. The man had never really had a fair chance in life. Not that his early trauma excused his monstrous actions.

But Riley asked herself …

What does it take to push a man like that over the edge?

She wondered if she'd ever know.

When Crivaro finished the debriefing, Lehl heartily congratulated him on solving the case. He also congratulated Crivaro on the guilty verdict the jury had just reached in the Brant Hayman trial.

Then, at last, he turned his gaze on Riley and said in a daunting tone …

"And now, young lady, what are we to do with you?"

Riley suppressed a shudder of dread.

What does he mean? she wondered.

The last time she'd met with the man, he hadn't been the least bit happy with her.

And he didn't seem to be all that happy with her right now.

She stammered, "I—I'm not sure what you mean, sir."

"No?" he said, glaring at her.

Then Lehl turned toward Crivaro and asked …

"How would you evaluate Ms. Sweeney's work with you in West Virginia?"

Crivaro shrugged slightly and said …

"It was excellent—and essential. If it weren't for her, I suspect that the case would still be unsolved."

With a slight growl, Lehl said, "I thought as much."

He looked at Riley again and asked, "Do you wish you could go back to the Academy?"

Riley felt a tingle of expectation.

"Yes, sir," she said. "Very much so, sir."

With just the faintest hint of a smile, Lehl said, "I'm rather glad to hear that. Because I've already spoken to the Academy director, and I persuaded him to readmit you. It would be a shame if you were no longer interested."

Riley felt her face flush and her breath quicken.

It was all she could do to keep from jumping out of her chair and letting out a whoop joy.

"Thank you, sir," she said, trying to keep her voice from

shaking. "Thank you very much."

The chief let out another slight growl and said to Riley …

"We've got one more thing to discuss. This ugly business about Senator Gardner—well, the truth is coming out about his predatory behavior, and there's no putting the genie back in the bottle. He'll be thoroughly investigated, and hopefully he'll be brought to justice. But you've got to remember, Gardner is a powerful, spiteful man. And he knows that you're to blame for his downfall. I doubt that you've heard the last of him. He's likely to seek out some kind of revenge."

Riley shuddered at the thought.

"I understand, sir," she said.

"Good," Lehl said. "I want you to contact me directly and immediately if he makes any sort of contact with you."

"I'll do that," Riley said.

Lehl nodded and said, "That will be all. You both may go."

As they walked through the building toward the front entrance, Crivaro said to Riley …

"I meant what I said back there. You did a fine job."

Riley thanked him, and her heart swelled with pride. She knew that Crivaro had been one of the first profilers in the recently founded BAU. Praise from him was high praise indeed.

Then Jake said, "Don't let it go to your head, though. You've still got to survive at the Academy. That means you'll have to do better there than you did before. But I've got a feeling you'll make it. And when you do …"

He fell silent as they kept walking.

Finally he added, "Well, it's like Lehl tells me … it's about time for me to learn to play nice with others."

It took Riley a moment to register just what Crivaro meant.

Then she realized … he was suggesting that they might be partners someday.

Riley felt a lump in her throat, but she told herself sternly …

Don't cry, damn it!

Sounding a little emotional himself, Jake said, "Riley, I may not have said this before, but you remind me a lot of myself when I was your age. In fact, you kind of remind me of myself right now. We've really got a lot in common."

Then with a chuckle, he added, "Mind you, that's not necessarily a good thing."

Riley laughed and said, "That's OK. I can live with that."

As they walked on in silence, Riley basked in her happiness at knowing she was going back to the Academy. It would be great to share a room with Francine again. And maybe she could manage to see more of John Welch, even though he was in a different group from hers.

When she and Jake stepped out of the building, Riley was startled to see who was standing nearby, looking anxious and obviously waiting for her.

"Ryan!" she exclaimed.

Then she said to Crivaro …

"That's my fiancé."

Crivaro chuckled and said, "Yeah, I get that. I'm out of here. I'll see you later."

Riley felt grateful that Crivaro was getting out of the way so she and Ryan could talk alone. But what did they have to say to each other?

And why is he here?

She was even more surprised when Ryan ran up to her and hugged her.

He said, "Riley, I've been looking all over for you. I checked at the Academy, of course. But they said you weren't an agent in training there anymore. It sounded like you'd gotten kicked out."

Riley smiled at him and said, "Well, they told you wrong. I just got reinstated."

Ryan said, "I'm glad to hear that."

Riley looked into his eyes and wondered …

Does he really mean that?

She couldn't tell just yet.

They sat down together on a nearby bench, and Ryan took her by the hand.

Ryan said, "Riley, I'll cut to the chase. I've been acting like an asshole lately."

Riley grinned and said, "I won't argue with you about that."

Then her smile faded and she said, "But I don't suppose I've been at my best either."

"You've been just fine," Ryan said.

Ryan squeezed both of her hands and added …

"I've realized lately, I'd be an idiot to let you go."

Riley shrugged shyly and said, "Well, I won't argue with that either. But …"

"But what?"

"What about that woman? Her name is Brigitte, right?"

Ryan blushed a little and said, "Look, when I said nothing was going on between us, I meant it. Brigitte and I are just friends and colleagues. Not that I didn't really enjoy seeing you go all postal with jealousy."

"I'm glad you found it so entertaining," Riley said lightheartedly.

They fell silent for a moment.

Then Riley shook her head and said, "I don't know, Ryan. Our lives are so separate. At least they will be for as long as I'll be in in the Academy."

"That won't be forever," Ryan said. "Meanwhile, what do you think we should do?"

Riley looked at her left hand, feeling suddenly glad she hadn't removed her engagement ring.

She said, "I think we should get married, Ryan Paige."

Ryan smiled in a goofy way that she'd always loved.

He said, "What a great idea, Riley Sweeney."

They shared a long kiss.

Then Ryan said, "So, what have you been doing lately?"

Riley's mind boggled at the thought of trying to tell him everything, including how she'd pretty much single-handedly ruined Senator Warren Gardner's political career, and how her former college professor was now on death row, and …

Everything else.

"Um … I've been having a bit of an adventure," Riley said.

"Tell me about it," Ryan said.

Riley hesitated. How would Ryan react to hearing about her involvement in such a weird and dangerous case?

Then she decided …

Well, he'll just have to deal with it.

After all, it looked like she had a future with the BAU.

She started to tell him all about it.

TAKING
(The Making of Riley Paige—Book 4)

"A masterpiece of thriller and mystery! The author did a magnificent job developing characters with a psychological side that is so well described that we feel inside their minds, follow their fears and cheer for their success. The plot is very intelligent and will keep you entertained throughout the book. Full of twists, this book will keep you awake until the turn of the last page."
--Books and Movie Reviews, Roberto Mattos (re Once Gone)

TAKING (The Making of Riley Paige—Book Three) is book #4 in a new psychological thriller series by #1 bestselling author Blake Pierce, whose free bestseller Once Gone (Book #1) has received over 1,000 five star reviews.

A serial killer, suspected to be using an RV camper, lures and kills women across the country—and the FBI turns to its youngest and most brilliant agent: 22 year old Riley Paige.

Riley has managed to graduate the FBI academy, determined to make it as an FBI agent. But when she is assigned her first official case with her new partner—Jake—she wonders if she is cut out for the task.

Riley and Jake, immersed in the RV subculture—and into the depths of the killer's mind—soon realize that nothing is what it seems. There is a psychopath at large, stumping them at every turn, and willing to stop at nothing until he has killed as many victims as he can find.

With her own future on the line, Riley has no choice but to find out: is her brilliant mind any match for the killer's?

An action-packed thriller with heart-pounding suspense, TAKING is book #4 in a riveting new series that will leave you turning pages late into the night. It takes readers back 20 plus years—to how Riley's career began—and is the perfect complement to the ONCE

GONE series (A Riley Paige Mystery), which includes 14 books and counting.

Book #5 in THE MAKING OF RILEY PAIGE series will be available soon.

Blake Pierce

Blake Pierce is author of the bestselling RILEY PAGE mystery series, which includes fourteen books (and counting). Blake Pierce is also the author of the MACKENZIE WHITE mystery series, comprising eleven books (and counting); of the AVERY BLACK mystery series, comprising six books; of the KERI LOCKE mystery series, comprising five books; of the MAKING OF RILEY PAIGE mystery series, comprising four books (and counting); of the KATE WISE mystery series, comprising five books (and counting); of the CHLOE FINE psychological suspense mystery, comprising four books (and counting); and of the JESSE HUNT psychological suspense thriller series, comprising four books (and counting).

An avid reader and lifelong fan of the mystery and thriller genres, Blake loves to hear from you, so please feel free to visit www.blakepierceauthor.com to learn more and stay in touch.

BOOKS BY BLAKE PIERCE

A JESSIE HUNT PSYCHOLOGICAL SUSPENSE SERIES
THE PERFECT WIFE (Book #1)
THE PERFECT BLOCK (Book #2)
THE PERFECT HOUSE (Book #3)
THE PERFECT SMILE (Book #4)

CHLOE FINE PSYCHOLOGICAL SUSPENSE SERIES
NEXT DOOR (Book #1)
A NEIGHBOR'S LIE (Book #2)
CUL DE SAC (Book #3)
SILENT NEIGHBOR (Book #4)

KATE WISE MYSTERY SERIES
IF SHE KNEW (Book #1)
IF SHE SAW (Book #2)
IF SHE RAN (Book #3)
IF SHE HID (Book #4)
IF SHE FLED (Book #5)

THE MAKING OF RILEY PAIGE SERIES
WATCHING (Book #1)
WAITING (Book #2)
LURING (Book #3)
TAKING (Book #4)

RILEY PAIGE MYSTERY SERIES
ONCE GONE (Book #1)
ONCE TAKEN (Book #2)
ONCE CRAVED (Book #3)
ONCE LURED (Book #4)
ONCE HUNTED (Book #5)
ONCE PINED (Book #6)
ONCE FORSAKEN (Book #7)
ONCE COLD (Book #8)
ONCE STALKED (Book #9)
ONCE LOST (Book #10)
ONCE BURIED (Book #11)
ONCE BOUND (Book #12)
ONCE TRAPPED (Book #13)

ONCE DORMANT (Book #14)
ONCE SHUNNED (Book #15)

MACKENZIE WHITE MYSTERY SERIES
BEFORE HE KILLS (Book #1)
BEFORE HE SEES (Book #2)
BEFORE HE COVETS (Book #3)
BEFORE HE TAKES (Book #4)
BEFORE HE NEEDS (Book #5)
BEFORE HE FEELS (Book #6)
BEFORE HE SINS (Book #7)
BEFORE HE HUNTS (Book #8)
BEFORE HE PREYS (Book #9)
BEFORE HE LONGS (Book #10)
BEFORE HE LAPSES (Book #11)
BEFORE HE ENVIES (Book #12)

AVERY BLACK MYSTERY SERIES
CAUSE TO KILL (Book #1)
CAUSE TO RUN (Book #2)
CAUSE TO HIDE (Book #3)
CAUSE TO FEAR (Book #4)
CAUSE TO SAVE (Book #5)
CAUSE TO DREAD (Book #6)

KERI LOCKE MYSTERY SERIES
A TRACE OF DEATH (Book #1)
A TRACE OF MUDER (Book #2)
A TRACE OF VICE (Book #3)
A TRACE OF CRIME (Book #4)
A TRACE OF HOPE (Book #5)

CPSIA information can be obtained
at www.ICGtesting.com
Printed in the USA
LVHW031614060919
630200LV00010B/657/P